FALL FROM GRACE

FORGE BOOKS BY WAYNE ARTHURSON

Fall from Grace

A Killing Winter (forthcoming)

FALL FROM GRACE

WAYNE ARTHURSON

A TOM DOHERTY ASSOCIATES BOOK

NEW YORK

FALL FROM GRACE

Copyright © 2011 by Wayne Arthurson

Edited by James Frenkel

A Forge Book
Published by Tom Doherty Associates, LLC
175 Fifth Avenue
New York, NY 10010

www.tor-forge.com

Forge® is a registered trademark of Tom Doherty Associates, LLC.

ISBN 978-0-7653-2417-7

First Edition: April 2011

Printed in the United States of America

0 9 8 7 6 5 4 3 2 1

I'm completely indebted to my wonderful daughter, Vianne, who keeps me honest and makes me laugh. And to my brilliant and beautiful wife, Auni, because I couldn't do any of this without her.

ACKNOWLEDGMENTS

Thanks to the Canada Council of the Arts and the Alberta Foundation of the Arts for their support in the writing of this project. Also thanks to my agent, Linn Prentis, who took me on saying it would be difficult to sell a book written by an unknown Canadian; my editor, Jim Frenkel, who bought the book written by an unknown Canadian and made it better; the late Neal Leatherdale, who gave me my first job in journalism; novelist Minister Faust for letting me use the term *Kush*; Geoff, Howie, and John, the boys in the band (The Ways); and those police service members and journalists who offered insight and knowledge. Also great thanks to my mom, my dad, my sisters, and all my family members who supported my writing career, and everyone else who helped in any way.

FALL FROM GRACE

1

"Do you want to see the body?"

It was not an unusual question; I've been asked it before, and I will probably be asked it again. But the key question at the moment was whether to accept the offer this time or to turn around and just walk away.

We stood at the edge of a farmer's field, squinting even though it was overcast. That's part of life on the Prairies. When the sky is more than two-thirds of your existence, there's no choice but to squint, even on an overcast day. At this time of year, the whole world was gray. The leaves had turned and fallen to the ground long ago and the golden stalks of grain had been harvested weeks before, leaving behind stubby shoots. The cleansing white of the first snow could come sometime tonight or around Christmas, who knew? If you're betting your life savings on the issue, save your cash and buy a lottery ticket. The odds are better, although Halloween is sometimes a safe choice for the first day of winter. Nothing like little kids walking the streets in search of candy to bring out Old Man Winter and all his accoutrements.

The only bit of color in our vicinity was the bright orange crime scene tent. Underneath that lay the body in question. The cop who had asked the question gestured toward the tent with his chin, keeping his hands in his pockets because like most of us this time of year, he didn't think it was cold enough for gloves. But when he stepped outside he realized his mistake. Of course, he could have gone back into the house to get them, but that would have entailed several minutes of searching through a drawer or box or cupboard of winter clothing that had been forgotten since sometime last spring.

And admitting that this collection of clothing still exists is a major psychological step in the annual life of a Western Canadian, at least for those of us who live on the Prairies. Denial plays a major role in this particular change of seasons. And for the cop to go back into his house to retrieve a pair of gloves and accept that winter was on its way was tantamount to admitting that he was an alcoholic or that his marriage was finally over and it was time to move on. Even so, if you were looking for something to bet your life's savings on, then bet that this cop would have his gloves tomorrow and would keep them with him till some time around April, maybe even May, depending on what kind of winter was awaiting us this year.

"Come on," he said with a grin. "You got a few minutes before the rest of your gang shows up, so I'm offering you an exclusive."

I looked at him and sighed. "The last time you let me look at a body, Detective Whitford, I . . . Well, let's just say it's something I really don't want to remember, but am unable to forget."

"This one's different," he said with a shrug. I shot him a quick look of disbelief.

"I mean it," he quickly added. "Honestly. Last time you were a suspect of sorts, and in order to confirm or deny your involvement I had to forgo giving you any warning of the condition of the body. Your reaction showed that you were not involved and in the end it all worked out, did it not?"

"Maybe for you, but not for me. It's a visual image I could have done without."

"Okay, although I won't apologize for what I did, I am sorry that you had to go through it," he said, pulling a hand out of his jacket pocket and placing it on my shoulder. "Consider this offer as my way to make it up to you."

"You've got to be kidding," I said with a cruel laugh. "You want to make up for showing me a dead body by offering to show me another dead body? I thought I was the one with mental problems but you are something else."

"Listen, Leo," he said, enunciating his words to make a point. "This one is different, I promise you. And this time, you are not a suspect; you're only a journalist out here on a story. And at the moment, you're the only journalist. But there will be others, and the offer I'm making now will expire the instant I see one of their vehicles come over the horizon. You can't tell me that it won't make your story better if you got a quick look at the body."

I sighed. He was right. The other lemmings were no doubt only a few minutes behind me and we would all have the same story of an unknown dead body in a field, with the photos all showing the same orange crime scene tent in the distance. The only way to make my story stand out, even from the moving pictures and early-supper deadlines of the TV stations, would be to accept Whitford's offer, step into that tent, and get an up-close and personal view of the body. I looked back at Whitford. He was sporting a smile that intimated he had read every thought that had run through my head.

"Okay, you got me," I said, shaking my head.

"Good." He nodded, turned, and walked toward the tent. I followed, looking away from the orange tent, trying to brace myself for what was inside. I took in the open barrenness of the landscape and wondered what compelled people, any kind of people, to settle in a place where the prominent colors were brown, gray, and white; where the growing season was barely one quarter of the year; and the length and breadth of the land was dwarfed by the immensity of the sky. The eternally optimistic, that's who, because only people with a totally optimistic worldview would look at this seemingly dead countryside and figure that it would be a great place to build a life, start a family, and/or create a civilization.

Then again, maybe they were seduced by the seemingly constant sunlight. This day may have been overcast, but that was an anomaly. For the most part, sunshine was the norm, even during those bitterly cold days when the light lasted less than the average workday and the cold could kill you if you weren't prepared. But maybe they knew that; maybe they understood that even in the dead of winter, there would be light, yes, diffused to a constant orange glow because of the sharp angle of the sun, but light nevertheless. And that was enough to stay.

Since I was a descendant of those people, including those original settlers, those first idealists who crossed the Bering Strait more than twenty thousand years ago in search of a better world and food, I couldn't just turn off those optimistic genes. I wouldn't enjoy looking at the body in the tent, but at the very least I'd probably be the only journalist who would get a confirmation of race and gender. Not much of a scoop, but a scoop all the same. And back at the paper, that would earn me the grudging respect of my fellow reporters and editors. But only till the deadline passed. Then we would be all back on the same page.

2

❋

Inside the tent the world acquired an orange tint, and even though I had been invited inside, strangely happy to be out of the brisk wind, I waited by the opening. A crime scene is a crime scene, I've learned, and there was really no reason for me to get any closer. What I needed to see was square in the middle of the tent, and even though a couple of forensic cops were hovering around the body, I could see her clearly.

I knew that it was going to be Whitford's responsibility to break the news to her family, if she had any, and though I knew cops like him would always lie by saying she looked peaceful, he wouldn't be lying in this case. She was on her back, eyes closed, arm tucked behind her head with the right leg bent slightly at the knee. It was as if she was resting on the floor of a tent after a long hike in the mountains and any minute she might sigh and roll over.

To distract myself from the fact that there was a dead human being just a few feet away from me, I constructed a preliminary lead in my head: *Police are treating the discovery of an unidentified female body in a farmer's field east of Edmonton as a "suspicious death."* Of course, neither Whitford nor anyone else had used the words *suspicious death* since I arrived, but in theory, the discovery of a dead body is always considered suspicious by police until such time it's considered not. Still, the presence of the bright orange tent, the forensic team, and a detective from Homicide—Whitford—added a bit more credibility to my lead, and I was completely confident that no one would have a problem with my using the term in the story.

A second later, after I took in the features of her face, the darker tone of her skin, visible even in the orange tent, and her straight black hair, I added the word *native* to my lead. Of course, I was making an assumption based on visual clues, because there are many nonnative people who have native traits and vice versa, especially in this part of the world.

Myself, I fell in the vice versa category, expressing the physical traits of my French-Canadian father. Despite my mother's recently acquired treaty status and her native features, if my body was found in a field, *Caucasian* would be the word used for my racial category. But again, I was pretty confident that my choice of words was correct. With natives, Aboriginals, First Nations peoples, or whatever you called them/us, being the largest minority population in the city and with the same group also leading the way in being victims of crime, my lead felt accurate. Maybe not completely true until the identity of the victim was confirmed, but accurate. And that was all that was needed at this moment in the story.

People always assume that newspapers are keen to print the truth, but that's wrong. The first goal of a news story is to be accurate. There's a big difference between accuracy and the truth. There was no need to make any corrections now unless Whitford or one of the other police in the tent said something before I left.

With my lead written and a couple of follow-up sentences instinctively falling in behind, I realized that as I was looking at the body, I had been holding my breath. A common affliction, I had learned over time, that strikes everyone when they come upon a dead body, whether they've seen several or it's their first experience. Since they aren't breathing, you don't either for several seconds. So when I finally exhaled a large gust, the two forensic cops stopped and looked at me. Both of their faces showed the same questioning expression, nothing harmful, just wondering if I was a piece of evidence important to their case.

There was nothing to do except shrug, because since I was a guest, a civilian one at that, in this tent, it wouldn't be proper for me to speak. In fact, because I had seen enough, I would have much preferred to leave. But I was unable to because there were now questions in the air about me. It was Whitford's responsibility to answer them, and he did.

"Don't worry about it, he's a media contact and I thought it wouldn't be a problem if he came into the tent for a few seconds. Anybody got an issue with that?" He phrased it as a question, but the slowness of the question and flatness of his tone was in fact telling everyone that they really shouldn't have an issue with it. And since he was the homicide detective on site, he was the ranking police officer, so allowed to make such a comment.

One of the forensic cops replied by turning back to his work while the other frowned and squinted to look me over more closely. He took a deep breath. "He's not a shooter, is he?"

Whitford shook his head. "Nope. Just a print journalist, nothing more."

The frown didn't leave the forensic cop's face—I could tell he didn't like having me there—but he finally nodded. "Okay, as long as he stays where he is now, keeps his hands in his pockets, and leaves within the next thirty seconds."

Whitford nodded, not being the type of cop to shove his weight around. He, like me, knew that although he was the ranking cop in the tent, Forensics also had the right to overrule anyone and anything they thought was contaminating the scene. "And if anything comes up because of this," the Forensic said, jerking his chin in my direction, "you deal with it. Understand?"

Whitford nodded again. "Actually, he's just leaving," he said, placing a hand on my forearm, the classic "Is there a problem?/ Come with me" move that they teach all police as their initial tactic when someone needs to be removed from a location. I had about three seconds before the grip strength would increase and about six before my arm would be twisted behind my back. I didn't need any encouragement; I had seen enough and was keen to leave the tent.

I nodded at Whitford to signal that I understood. Simply pulling out of his grip and turning away would have been not just impolite, it might also have triggered Whitford's policing instincts, and I would have found myself face-first on the ground with a knee in my back. When he let go of my arm, I turned and left the tent with Whitford directly behind me.

We walked back to the fence, back to the spot where I had parked the car from the paper. Before I turned away and we went back to our respective jobs, I asked him the question that had been in the back of my mind for the last few minutes. "Why did you let me into the tent? And don't give me that crap about helping me with my story or making amends for what happened last year."

He looked around me, taking his time before answering. I wondered what he thought about in that time, wondered if he was thinking about the eternal optimists that settled this land, whether this event would get him into trouble in the end, or maybe he was just reminding himself to wear gloves tomorrow. "I know we're both experienced enough to realize what I'm going to say will not be part of any story or anything. But it's just something that has to be said, you got it?"

I gave him the confirmation he asked for. "Most of my story's already written in my head so there's no need to add anything else,"

I told him. "I'm just personally curious to know why you let me in the tent, that's all."

"I let you in because I wanted you to get a true look at the body. And when I mean you, I don't mean you personally, just someone like you. If someone else from another media outlet had arrived first, someone that I knew would do a good story, not just anyone, mind you, but someone similar to you, then I would have let them in, you understand?"

"Yeah, but why? What you did goes against every single media relations procedure the Police Service has. I'll do my best not to make it look like you did anything wrong, but people are going to talk, most likely one of those forensic cops in there."

"Don't worry about those guys. I can handle those guys. They won't turn in another member, no matter what he does."

"Yeah, but that still doesn't explain it."

"Let's just say I have my reasons. Some I won't share with you because I can't and I won't. But the real reason is that I wanted to give her a face, to make you and maybe the people who read your story understand that there was a real person there. Everywhere we go, every newspaper we read, every TV show or movie we watch, there's a victim, usually a female, and it's all part of the scene, to be expected in many ways. By letting you into the tent, and seeing what you do with that experience, I'm reminding everyone that these people are human beings just like the rest of us, and to file them under the heading of victim so we don't have to deal with them on a more real basis isn't the right thing to do."

I could only shake my head. It was such a naïve attitude for these times, especially coming from an experienced homicide detective. And I told him so.

"Maybe so," he said with a shrug. "But as a homicide detective with experience, maybe I've earned the right to be naïve in such matters. Maybe it's a good thing."

"Like I said before, people say that I'm the one with mental problems, but you, my friend, should get yourself looked at."

Whitford kept his hands in his pockets and offered a sad smile. "See you around, Leo," he said, and then turned to head back to the tent. I watched him for a few seconds and walked toward my car. I was parked behind a series of police vehicles, a couple of cruisers, Whitford's unmarked car, and the Forensics van. The buffalo emblem on the first cruiser showed me it was from the RCMP, not the local Edmonton Police Service. In it sat a lone Mountie, sipping from a Timmie's cup and writing in his notebook. I walked over to him—slowly, so he would see me coming. He set down his pen and notebook when he noticed me and rolled down his window.

"May I help you?" he asked, in that polite and efficient police voice that they probably teach all police at the academy.

I first introduced myself, name and media affiliation, and then asked if he was the first on the scene. He nodded.

"Did you find the body?" I asked, quietly noting his name on the badge above his right pocket.

He shook his head. "Farmer did. He made the mistake of calling us."

"Mistake?"

"Yeah. You see that range road back there?" He gestured with his paper cup to the gravel road behind us. "That is the proverbial county line. City's on this side, county of Strathcona's on the other."

"Right," I said, drawing out the word. "Out of your jurisdiction."

"You bet. As soon as I saw that, I called the EPS boys, so they could handle it."

"So you didn't see the body or touch it."

"Didn't even step into the field once I realized where it was, thank God."

"Why *thank God*?"

He paused, his face showing concern. "You're not going to quote me, are ya? I mean, if you want to know something about the case, you should talk to your friends in the tent." This was his way of saying he had seen everything that had transpired.

"Naw, the EPS guys gave me all the information. I'm just naturally curious. Can't help it, comes with the job description. If you don't want to tell me, that's okay." I let the sentence fall but didn't move. I waited to see if he would answer. He might have, but since he was a cop, he would realize what I was doing and wish me a good morning, in that nice polite and efficient way the Mounties have of saying, 'It's time for you to get the fuck out of here now.' All other cops try to emulate that tone, and while a few can do it pretty well, only a Mountie can pull it off with such ease.

But it didn't come. "*Thank God* means I get to go home and watch the hockey game after my shift is done today instead of filing the paperwork on another one of these."

"You mean there have been others?" I said, smelling a bigger story than just a body in a field.

"Only a few in the last bunch of years since I've been stationed here. Three, four tops."

Three or four could be a lot or not much, depending on how long this Mountie had been stationed in Strathcona. If it had been just a couple of years, it was a lot; if it was five to ten, it was pretty average. "So you've been here long?"

He shrugged. "Five years, I guess. But this is my second time. My first happened right out of the Depot and that was, what, fifteen years ago, so I'm including that in there as well."

I deflated, realizing that three to four dead bodies in a field over a twenty-year period was nothing; there was no larger story, just the one I had written in my head.

"Oh, well, thanks for your time. I better head back to the city and file my story."

"You have yourself a nice morning," the Mountie said, without any hidden meaning.

3

❀

I was expected back at the paper, but instead of heading into downtown, I took a left on Fiftieth Street and followed it until the industrial zone faded into residential. I trolled through the neighborhood until I found a 1960s-style strip mall that housed your typical neighborhood shops such as a place that sold knitting supplies, a butcher shop, a bank, one of those payday loan spots, a pizza delivery spot called Double AA Pizza, plus an independent convenience store, originally run by a family of Chinese immigrants in the sixties, then passed on to the Lebanese for the seventies and eighties, and was probably now in the hands of some family from the Indian subcontinent. There was also a possibility that the Punjabis had moved on and immigrants from the Sudan or Eritrea had taken over.

Also in the mall was the ubiquitous liquor store, one that no doubt popped up during the Klein revolution of the nineties in which the selling of liquor was taken out of the hands of the provincial government and given over to the private sector.

Probably the only good decision ever made during King Ralph's fourteen-year reign over the province, because instead of being able to buy liquor at one of only twelve Alberta Liquor Control Board (ALCB) stores, with hours limited from noon to 10 P.M. and no sales on Sundays, you could now buy it from one of countless small corner liquor stores that popped into existence the instant the legislation was signed. Nothing like an ex-journalist in power to make booze more readily available. Don't even ask me about the legal gambling options, because I could go on.

But of all the stores in the strip, it was the bank I was looking for. I was still feeling a bit jittery from seeing the body in the tent so I felt the need to take care of a bit of business to get myself back into the world before filing my story. Even though the actual news deadline was midnight, I knew I would have to write a few paragraphs for the online edition of the paper.

I had a couple of hours before that deadline, and in the paper business, two hours before deadline is an eternity. I could write and file the full story about the body in the field, highly readable and factual, in twenty minutes, even less if I was pushed. So writing a few paragraphs for the online edition was peanuts. I had plenty of time. Still, one of the city editors would be on my butt the instant I walked in the door, so I knew I had to be quick.

There were plenty of empty parking spots right outside the front doors of the bank but I parked a ways away, snuggled in between a large, burgundy pickup and a late-model domestic sedan, an old-man car 'cause the only ones who seemed to drive those things were men sixty years old and over.

After stepping out of my car, I waited a bit by the car, letting my glasses darken to the outside light. One good thing about having a regular job again was the availability of benefits. As part of the strike settlement, the paper gave each staffer five hundred bucks a year as a benefit top-up, for items not covered under the basic plan. Even though I had been a scab, I got the same deal, pretty much covering the cost of my new glasses.

It had been almost three years since I had had new glasses and the world looked pretty wonky the first time I put on my new lenses. Everything was beautifully clear, in perfect focus, but it was a little disconcerting. It took me only a week or so to get used to the new glasses, but it had been only about six months since I had become a solid citizen, with a real job and a real place to live, and I still was not used to it. Every time I took a walk downtown, I had to consciously remind myself not to ask people for spare change. I would adjust, I knew that, but it was a gradual process.

My piece of banking business was short and quick. If luck was on my side, I could get it done in less than a couple minutes and then I'd be back to work before anyone realized I was out longer than expected. Or I wouldn't. The odds were about evenly balanced, which to a gambler like me are probably the best I could get anywhere.

When my glasses reached the desired darkness, I adjusted my ball cap so that the brim hung a little lower over my face, and walked up to the bank and stepped through the doors. I grabbed a form from the dispenser, scribbled on it, and since there was nobody waiting, stepped to the front of the line. Three of the four tellers were helping other customers; the one without a customer was sorting bills into a pile and writing a few figures on a sheet of paper.

My heart rate increased slightly and I started to breathe through my mouth, as my mind gave birth to a pang of worry. I felt an urge to look up at the cameras and around for any other staff or recently arrived customers, but that would only draw attention to myself. The goal was to make myself as inconspicuous and undistinguishable as possible. No doubt there would be photos, maybe even video footage, of my presence, but I knew they would mostly show a white guy with a ball cap and sunglasses, as normal as you could find in this city. I could be anyone.

I took a slow, deep breath, and allowed everything to slow down for me. In a few seconds, I was back to my normal self, a bit nervous but outwardly calm and collected.

The teller made eye contact with me and, with a smile, invited me to step forward. I did, without returning the smile, and slid the deposit sheet forward, holding it tight to the counter with three fingers.

The teller glanced down at the deposit slip and his smile faded. The hand reaching for the slip jerked back as if it was escaping from a mousetrap. His eyes widened as, for another second or two, he looked back at what I had written on the deposit slip:

"Please give me all your money. Sorry and Thank you."

He looked up, insulted, but worried. I knew that he was searching in my eyes for the joke, but I shook my head. "Quickly please," I said, glancing down at the slip to remind him why I was there. "And thank you very much," I added. Nothing like a few *thank yous*, and *pleases* in the right places, even when it's a command for *no dye packs, please*, to give them efficiency in their manner.

The teller gave me another look, but this time it was a deeper one. I gave him nothing in response; no emotion, no blinks, no smiles, just a blank face. I had no gun, no knife, no weapon of any kind, and there wasn't even a threat in my note, but the instant the teller looked back in my eyes, I knew I would successfully rob this bank.

South of the border, with their armed security guards, even in the smallest bank in the smallest town, this would be just another form of suicide. But up here in the Great White North, with our slightly tougher gun laws, our overriding sense of the rule of the law (thanks to the Mounties for that), and a nationwide system of banks with centralized training and procedures, things were a bit easier. Robbing a bank like this wasn't that difficult, even without threats or a weapon.

It's a lot like gambling. When you step up to the teller and hand over the note, you've got to have a certain recklessness, a "who gives a shit because it's only money/life/jail/death" attitude. You've got to show the teller that you mean business. They may think that you don't have a gun or any sort of weapon but you can't let them trust that feeling. They have to believe that you are serious about what you are doing and that they had better do what you've asked or there'll be trouble.

Maybe it's my outward appearance of calm and my polite attitude that pushes these tellers to realize that I'm not someone to be trifled with, I don't know. I guess that's why the poker-playing reporters at the paper are reluctant to invite me to their games. When there's a hand with big money at stake, the only thing I worry about is the basic poker stuff, whether the odds of my hand winning are good and/or if I'm being bluffed. Nothing else. I don't worry about whether I can afford to lose that money, whether I'll lose that month's rent or grocery money or car payment with my bet. I've already lost everything in my life due to gambling, so a few hundred or even a few thousand bucks makes no difference to me. You can't truly gamble if you focus on that kind of stuff, and it's a weird sort of freedom. So when there's a big pot at stake, I'm not calculating the cost of the bet on my life, job, and family because I've made and lost that bet already. More than once.

Then again, the reaction of tellers probably has nothing to do with me, and more to do with their training that tells them to give the money without a fuss. Even with the dramatic nature of robbing a bank, everything always seemed to go so smoothly that the other tellers and customers usually couldn't tell the bank was being robbed. It was almost as if it was starting to lose its appeal. But I had to watch out for that because that kind of attitude would only drive me to the casinos, and once I walked though those doors, there was no coming out. This kind of gambling seemed a lot safer. Strange, but that's just the way it was for me.

Outside the bank, barely five minutes after I strolled in, I walked toward the parking lot. Running would attract attention. I weaved in and out of the parked cars, even stepping into the convenience store to buy a couple of lottery tickets before heading back into the parking lot. By then, I already had removed my cap and opened my jacket to make a slight change in my appearance.

Sirens wailed in the distance but again I walked through the lot, this time directly to my car, the same way a convenience store customer would. The burgundy pickup was still there but the old-man sedan had been replaced by a dark green SUV. I climbed into the car, started it up, and pulled out. I was about a hundred meters away from the strip mall heading north toward the River Valley when I saw in the rearview mirror a couple of cruisers zip across the intersection toward the bank.

I cruised through the neighborhood, acting like someone looking for an address by leaning forward to look out my side windows every couple of seconds. I did this for another five minutes or so and then turned back onto Fiftieth Street heading north until 101th Avenue. Then I made a right toward downtown and my awaiting deadline.

4

The newsroom was what one imagined a major metro newsroom would look like: a large open room filled with clusters of desks, computers, and people typing on keyboards. Since it was about twenty minutes before the online deadline, the place was crowded with reporters of all types and beats pounding out miniature versions of their stories that could be included on the online edition of the paper.

This was a new thing to me, having two daily deadlines for two different editions of the same paper. But since readership of the actual printed version of the paper had been steadily dropping, there was more and more emphasis on creating an online presence. And with every media outlet and bloggers doing the same thing, the speed at which news had to be processed and delivered had increased exponentially since the last time I had worked. Now, instead of writing one story about the body in the field, I was required to write two: a short one for this online deadline and then a longer, more standard news story for tomorrow's print issue. Once the print issue was delivered, my longer story would replace the shorter one in the online edition and the cycle would start again.

During my first couple of weeks back at work, it was a bit of an adjustment to adapt to this new way of delivering news, but the required skills were the same and a deadline was still a deadline.

In my two decades of journalism, I had never missed one. Even during the tough times when my life was falling apart. The power of information, the rush of having news that no one else had, and the desire to be the first to break that news or impart that information, was a powerful addiction, sometimes even more powerful than gambling.

Entering a busy newsroom, with its high ceilings and clattering noise, each individual in a world of his own but everyone joined together in the same united purpose, always reminded me of walking into a casino. The jolt of adrenaline, the quickened heartbeat, and the hope of coming through with a win was almost the same. But unlike a casino, there was always some sort of success in a newsroom, some sort of achievement once the story was written. And with the deadline, there was always an end to your time there. While you could always leave a casino—they did kick you out after a certain time—I could never really come to a conclusion. I always seemed to need something more; even if I was winning, it was never enough.

I wove my way through the huddles of desks, heading toward the city section, which sat near the northeast corner of the room, roughly sandwiched between the sports and business sections. I was barely fifteen feet away when I was accosted by one of the assistant city editors. Mandy Whittaker was her name; she was a gangly woman in her mid-thirties, her long hair pulled back into a ponytail so that she looked much older than she was, more like an old hippie than an up-and-coming news editor. She was a pretty good assistant CE, smart, competent, and a little hard-nosed, but that was part of the territory.

When you're responsible for making sure that twenty reporters get their stories filed on time, and then need to edit those stories and decide which ones go where in the four pages of the city section, you have every right to be a little hard-nosed. Of course, she was a little tougher on me because unlike all the other reporters in the city section, I had not been walking a picket line a couple months ago.

I had been a scab, was still a scab to many here, someone who had seen the strike as a way of getting a job, even temporarily, at the paper, which before the strike had a reputation as one of the best in the country. I wasn't completely proud of what I had done, but it did get me off the street and into a better situation, and there were a few other things in my background that would be considered worse than being a scab, so I was able to sleep at night.

That said, the situation at the paper was a little confused because of the strike. Editorial staff and other unionized workers like printers, et cetera, battled management for five long months only to see their union crumble at the hands of Jacob Whyte. The Eastern-based press baron, contrary to union predictions in the early days of the strike, managed to put out a paper every day for those five months, thus keeping the advertising monies rolling while the union coffers were depleted. Of course, Whyte had had the help of a number of scabs, insiders like reporters who had defied the union and stayed at their jobs and outsiders like me. Except for three of us, none of the outsider scabs were given permanent positions; they had neither the talent nor the skill to last long when the real reporters came back. Even though I was a scab, at least I wasn't one of those insiders who didn't walk the picket line.

The animosity between the strikers and the insiders, many of whom had been friends, was deep and infected the newsroom like a nasty boil on the ass. So while Mandy had some trouble cracking the whip on some of her union fellows, she had no trouble using it on me when it was called for. "You're late, Desroches," she shouted at me without getting up from her desk.

"Sorry, boss," I said with sincerity. "Something came up and it couldn't be helped."

"Just so you know, this isn't a small-town weekly where you have all week to file your story. Every day's a deadline here." It was an obvious crack at me being a scab, because most of the scabs hired during the strike were small-town reporters from weeklies, looking to try work at a daily. Many of the editorial staff thought all of my previous newspaper experience had been at weeklies, but they were wrong. They were also wrong in their contention that working at a weekly was easier; it was only different and, in many ways, tougher.

At a daily, you usually only wrote one story a day, about five a week, and once you wrote it, you went home. At a weekly, especially if you were the only reporter/photographer on staff, you not only wrote the stories, you edited them, took and developed the photos, laid everything out, and if the paper printed its own issues, you also helped fold and inserted flyers. Also, five stories a week wouldn't cut it at any weekly, even if there was another reporter on staff. My record for most stories in one issue at a weekly was thirty-eight, not one shorter than 250 words. If Mandy or anyone else at this paper that slagged weeklies as the minor league of newspapering ever attempted such a task, they would quickly change their attitude.

"According to my clock, Mandy, the city section's deadline's not for eight more hours so I got plenty of time." By now, a number of reporters had looked up from their work to watch us.

"Yeah, but if you also check that clock of yours, you'll realize that we now live in the twenty-first century and in this century there are these machines called computers, which allow us to access something called the Internet. And on the Internet, we have an online edition of the paper which has a deadline of twenty minutes from now."

A number of retorts popped into my head, but I kept them to my-self, partly because I had walked into that comment and deserved the dressing-down, but also the guilt over being late because of my trip to the bank was starting to creep in. "Okay, okay, boss. I'm rightly chas-tised and will have the story for the online edition."

"I need 150 words from you and they better be good."

I nodded and sat down at my computer and started typing with-out taking my jacket off. A good reporter, especially a good police beat reporter, never turns off his computer because all that booting up takes too much time. There was a bit of a lag due to the machine jumping out of its sleep mode and the first words of my lead ap-peared on the screen a few seconds later, but they quickly caught up with me. And since I had been composing, editing, and recom-posing the story in my head throughout my drive from the bank to the paper, I was done in five minutes, plenty of time for Mandy to read it, put in her edits, and then send it off to the online editors who would do a quick proofing before popping it online for the whole world to see.

With the online deadline met, it now was the perfect time to take off my jacket and take a break; grab a bite to eat or something. Seeing the body in the tent and then paying another visit to a bank was starting to take its toll. My mind was whirling with various thoughts, with the worry over how good the video surveillance sys-tem was at the bank, whether the teller got a good look at my face, if someone in the parking lot tied in the departure of the paper's car with the bank robbery and noted its license number, and then wouldn't someone from the police ask the paper who had signed out Car 14 and then take my name, run it through their system, and then come to escort me out of the newsroom in handcuffs? All those thoughts and the fact that I had another dead body in my file of seen images did not put me in the good place.

I could feel sweat starting to bead on my forehead and my eyes beginning to water, sure signs that I'd better take a break before things got worse. A trip to the bathroom and a nice fifteen-minute panic attack in one of the stalls would have been just fine. Nobody would question it because panic attacks were part and parcel of the newspaper business and the fact that I had seen a dead body this morning would be the considered reason for my short meltdown.

But I wasn't given time for that break; Mandy's voice called out to me. "Desroches? What's this?" I turned and saw her heading in my direction. Instead of simply editing and filing my story for the online edition, Mandy had printed off a hard copy and was brandishing it like some sort of weapon.

I did my best to gather myself together. "What's up, boss? Did I miss some new development in the CP style book?"

She ignored my joke. "How come you identified the gender and race of the victim when the sites for other local media don't? Everybody has an unidentified body while you have her being female and native. Tell me why."

"It's called a scoop, Mandy. Didn't they teach you that when you got your degree in English lit?" It was a nasty crack but it was justified. If any other reporter in the room had written the story, she would have come over and given them a nice pat on the shoulder for a job well done. Since it was me, I must have done something wrong. She didn't trust my journalism, and for a reporter to have an editor not trusting him was a major insult.

"Just tell me how you know the body is a native female and nobody else does."

"I know it's a native female because I'm a better fucking journalist than the rest of those losers who have the story. Like I said, it's called a scoop, and instead of coming over and giving me shit about it, you should be saying, Nice job, Leo."

Again she ignored me. "Just tell me how your story has this info and the others don't."

Her attitude was making me angrier, but instead of grabbing her by the throat and giving her the basic lecture on why scoops were good, I took a mental step back. "I know the body was native and female because I saw the body." I paused, and watched the effect it had on Mandy. Her face dropped and she could no longer stare at me. And then I added the kicker. "And I saw the body because they let me into the tent."

Those words caused Mandy to step back and lean against the desk behind me. The hand that was holding the hard copy of the story dropped to her side.

"They let you into the tent?" a voice demanded. It wasn't Mandy; she was shocked into silence for the moment. The question came from Brent Anderson, another police-beat reporter who had the desk next to mine. He had been a reporter at the paper for about seven years, a solid reporter who wrote good copy. He probably wouldn't win any awards for his work, but it was readable, didn't need much editing, and always arrived hours before deadline. In many ways, Brent was just like me except when his day ended, he went home to his wife and family, and I went to a small room under the stairs in the basement of a rooming house.

"Who let you into the tent?" he demanded.

"Are you talking about the crime scene tent?" Mandy said, finally getting over the initial shock. "They let you into the crime scene tent?"

I nodded.

"Who let you in the tent?" Brent demanded again. "They never let anyone in the tent."

"Whitford," I said over my shoulder.

"Whitford?" Anderson asked. His voice was a shocked whisper.

"Al Whitford let you into the tent? You've got to be shitting me!" He wasn't being insulting; he was just incredulous that someone like Whitford would let a reporter into the crime scene tent. And despite Whitford's earlier explanation, I, too, was still surprised and confused about it.

"Who's Whitford?" Mandy asked.

"Homicide detective," Anderson and I both said at the same time. And Anderson added, "Whitford let you into the tent? Why would he do that?"

I shrugged. "I don't know. It was the craziest thing." And then I turned to the assistant city editor. "So that's how I know the body was female and native. You can believe it or not but let me tell you this, I'm no Jayson Blair, so this is how it's going to work." I waited for a second to see if Whittaker knew the name Jayson Blair, the *New York Times* reporter who got caught faking a bunch of his news stories. She blinked a couple of times and that told me she knew the name. Most good reporters did.

"First, you believe me, run the fucking story as is, and say something like, Good job, Leo. 'Cause if you don't, then I'm fucking out of here." And I wasn't kidding. I had an editor who didn't trust my judgment, and when that happens the only thing you can do is leave. I wasn't in a great place personally, financially, and emotionally to leave the paper but if my story didn't run the way I wrote it, I had no choice.

"Nice work, Leo," said a voice to the left.

Everyone turned and Whittaker couldn't help but gasp. It was Larry Maurizo, the managing editor of the paper and the guy who had hired me months ago. I had just spent almost two years living on the street, but a crazy situation at a local reserve had convinced me it was time to get my shit in gear again, and he was the first person I called. I knew that he was managing editor of a paper in the middle of a strike, and might be looking for staffers. I was right, although he did take some convincing, especially since I was not in the best condition, both physically and mentally.

Fortunately, Maurizo had remembered that time I had given him his first newspaper job. And with Jacob Whyte constantly breathing down his neck to put the paper out every day during the strike, he was also desperate for anyone who could put together stories that were slightly readable. In his first job working for me as a reporter/photographer at a weekly, Larry was a decent writer armed with the basic knowledge of how to write a story using the inverted-pyramid technique, but with little real experience.

We only worked together for about fifteen months, but in that time he showed a willingness to learn, and although I never expected him to reach the position of managing editor of a major metro daily, I knew he would at least be able to forge a good career as a journalist. The younger Maurizo had been a bit shy, but as an ME who not just ran the paper but defeated the union in a strike, he had showed a tough-as-nails attitude and didn't suffer fools gladly. He was, like most good editors, fair. If you did a good job, he let you know or left you alone. But if you screwed up or attracted his attention for negative reasons, he could be ruthless, almost like a Roman emperor. So his appearance at the edge of our little drama was a newsworthy event. Brent quickly divested his role in the production and turned to his keyboard even though he had long since written and submitted his story.

Since I had known Larry as a wet-behind-the-ears journalist, I wasn't scared by his arrival. I knew he could fire me as easily as he had hired me, but I had been fired before and probably would be fired again. If not here and now, then sometime and somewhere else. Larry was completely aware of that, but as long as I didn't undermine his authority and did my job, I was fine.

"Larry? What are you doing here?" Whittaker stammered.

"I'm here because I can hear you guys across the room, and despite what people might think, chaos doesn't work in a newsroom."

"That's okay, it's only a little matter of editorial concern and we've got it under control here, don't we, Desroches?" Whittaker looked at me and raised her eyebrows to ask for my support. I gave her nothing because that's what she deserved.

"That's total bullshit and you know it, Whittaker," Maurizo snapped. "What I've gathered by watching this for the past few minutes is that because of your failure to trust one of our reporters, a reporter that I hired, we're in a situation where that reporter is threatening to quit. Am I right?"

"Well, it's not as simple as that. I was just trying to confirm an anomaly in Leo's story. He has information that the other outlets don't, and I was—"

"Since when do we give a shit about what the other news outlets are running?" Larry interrupted. "We are the most credible news outfit in this city. Have been for almost a hundred years. We do not check what the other outlets are running to confirm our stories; they check us, you got that?"

Whittaker nodded, but couldn't stop herself from talking. Despite the situation she was in, I had to give her some credit for standing up for herself. "I just wanted to confirm the details in Leo's story."

"Then next time you want to confirm something in one of our reporter's stories, don't accuse them of fabricating something. I'm sure Leo has the answers you wanted, and if you had asked him nicely, he would gladly have given those answers. It looks to me like you just let some past baggage get in the way of your normally good judgment. If we're going to remake this paper into what it was, then everyone has to put that baggage behind him and work together."

Whittaker nodded. "Yes, you're right. You're right." Even though Whittaker agreed in public, I knew that she didn't completely agree in private. In fact, I knew there were a lot of staffers who weren't interested in working together and were just biding their time, waiting for Maurizo to be fired or, most likely, promoted, or for better options, like a new job, to come their way. None of this was likely to come anytime soon so this kind of dysfunction was here to stay. I couldn't help but smile at the silliness of the situation, and unfortunately, Maurizo noticed it and thought I was smiling at Whittaker getting the shit kicked out of her.

"And you got nothing to smile at, Desroches," he said, turning on me. "You arrived twenty minutes before deadline and when your editor calls you on it and asks about an anomalous fact in your story, you get *All the President's Men* on her. Next time get back on time and don't be such a jerk, okay?"

I nodded, realizing that there was no point in pursuing the matter further. Maurizo was quite aware of my history and no doubt my late arrival was twigging some alarm he had set when he first hired me. I would have to be more careful from now on.

"Okay, here's what's going to happen," Maurizo said to both of us. "We're going to run Leo's online story as is and Whittaker, you're going to tell Leo he did a nice job for getting a scoop."

"Nice job, Leo." Whittaker nodded. "It's a good scoop."

"And you, Leo," Maurizo continued, "you're going to apologize to Whittaker for being a jerk and for being late and then fill us in on what happened out there."

I fulfilled all requests and when I was finished, Maurizo stepped in. "Okay, what do we know about this Whitford character? Anderson, you were in on this, so help us out."

Anderson tried to look surprised that Maurizo had noticed him, but when he realized he wasn't in trouble, he offered to help. "He's a homicide detective, good guy, good cop, helpful if he can be. But this seems to be totally out of character. I have never heard of any reporter being allowed into a crime scene tent."

Maurizo nodded. "Right. Leo, how do you know Whitford so that he would let you into the tent?"

"To be honest, this is the first time I've had any dealings with him while I've been at the paper. He just knows." I paused, not sure how to explain how Whitford and I met. "I guess you could just say, he knows me from before."

Maurizo nodded again. "Right," he said, and nothing else. Of all the staffers at the paper, he was the only one who knew what the term *from before* meant to me. It had come up a couple of other times in my half year at the paper and I knew that it was a topic of much gossip and speculation. A few thought it meant that Maurizo and I had simply worked together on another newspaper in another time and place and left it at that. That was something that we had never denied; in fact, a couple of times, over drinks after a deadline, I had admitted that I had given the ME his first newspaper job.

But there were other theories ranging from stories that I was an alcoholic or a drug addict and had lived on the streets to stories that I had done time, or had even been a cop, worked undercover, and because of a difficult case which threw off my mental equilibrium, had disappeared for a while. The fact that a homicide detective for the Edmonton Police Service was part of *from before* would add more ammunition to these stories.

"Okay, then, did Whitford give you any indication about why he let you into the tent?" Maurizo asked after a couple of seconds.

"He only said he wanted to give a face to this victim, to remind people that victims of crime are human beings, not just dead bodies without personality."

"That's it?"

"That's it," I said, although I didn't say that Whitford had said any media outlet would have done, and that I was just lucky to have been the first on the scene. I wanted to give my scoop more journalistic credibility than the fact I was lucky enough to arrive before everyone else did.

"Okay, let me run this by you guys and see what you think," Larry said, which meant, *This is what is going to happen, I'm just being polite asking for your opinions.*

"Leo, you'll write the main story about the body in the field, expanding on your online piece. And we'll run that A-1, above the fold, unless a plane crashes or the Oilers make a trade." Which was unlikely because the hockey season was just starting and it was too early for the finger-pointing to begin. A-1 above the fold meant front page at the top, which made it the top story of tomorrow's paper. Everyone around was shocked, even me.

"A-1? You sure, Larry?" Whittaker asked. "No disrespect, but found bodies rarely make the front page of the city section, and the fact that Leo found out she was female and native when everyone else didn't, doesn't rate front-page coverage."

Everyone nodded, even Larry did, because it was true. Just because someone was dead and found in a field didn't mean it was big news. Sure, death was a bigger story than life, which was why I was sent to cover this story and why it would run in tomorrow's paper, but it didn't rate being the top story of the day.

Then Larry spoke. "That's true, but what makes this story different is Leo going into the tent. And since nobody ever gets into a crime scene tent unless they're police, Leo here is also going to write a sidebar about what it's like in a crime scene tent, who was there, what it looked and felt like, and why he was invited. We'll call it a rare, exclusive story to show those other news bastards that we're still ten times better than them at covering the news of this city. In fact, the first words of your lead will be *In a rare, exclusive blah blah blah.* You can do that, Leo, give me that lead and about four hundred words on that, writing it as a major exclusive?"

"Yeah, I can do that, but—" I didn't get the chance to finish because Larry interrupted.

"And if you use the word *I* or the expression *this reporter* I will personally fire you and kick your ass out the door, but before that I will take you down to the pressroom and stick your right hand into the press so you'll never write again, you understand?"

I should have been insulted by that comment, but I couldn't help but smile. "You forget who you're talking to, Larry. Those are the exact words Neil told you during your first month of work in Olds."

Larry paused for a second, recalling the memory, and he, too, couldn't resist smiling. I knew this exchange would be repeated throughout the newsroom and my mystique quotient would rise within the editorial staff. "And do you remember what I told him in response?"

"Yeah, and I see that despite your rise in power, you haven't changed that obnoxious part of your nature," I told him. Whittaker and Anderson visibly cringed when they heard that, and it would also be repeated often.

"I'll be even more obnoxious if you say you can't write this sidebar for me."

"No worries about that, Larry. I can pull this off."

"Knew you could but I just wanted to check," he said with a nod. "And quote Whitford on why he invited you into the tent, that's important."

"He's going to be pissed off about that," I said.

"And he'll probably get in deep shit because of it," Anderson added.

"Tough. He's the one who let a member of the media into the

tent so he'll have to deal with whatever comes of it. Since he's a homicide detective, I'm assuming he's a big boy who can handle himself. Actually, I'm pretty sure he was aware that something like this would occur and is ready for whatever happens.

"And since he wanted a face on this victim, we're going to do our best to give her a face. Once we learn who this person is, we're going to find out as much as we can about her and keep writing about it. You think you can handle it, Leo? 'Cause I'm giving it to you. It's a big job, but at least you won't be chasing sirens for the next little while."

It had been a long time since I had been given a continuing assignment such as this. I knew that I could handle it, but deep down there were always those words of discouragement and worry. I sometimes had the tendency to get obsessed about a story or events and get lost in them, similar to the way I could get lost in gambling, but what could I say to Larry? Sorry, buddy, can't handle this story, give it to someone else?

Whittaker had the same view as I did although she knew little about my background. "You sure you want to keep this with Leo? I mean, writing the stuff about today, that's okay, but the long-term, lengthy investigations we usually hand over to Murray. That's his job, basically, and he does have seniority over Leo here."

Whittaker was talking about Tom Murray, the paper's resident *auteur,* or feature writer, who usually did the really long pieces like profiles of murderers, their victims, and other stories that not only took more time to investigate and write but required a bit more creativity than the average newspaper article. It was a strange suggestion coming from Whittaker, because one of the dividing issues about the strike had to do with seniority.

Many reporters didn't like it when their colleagues who had been at the paper for a long time got their pick of stories and/or were handed stories that other reporters had dug up. And many of these senior reporters thought that their experience and length of service should have meant something and merited some rewards. It was in fact one of the reasons the union imploded, because in typical union fashion, it favored those with seniority and alienated a lot of young reporters who had originally supported the strike.

Maurizo thought about the suggestion for a few seconds, and I knew he was weighing the pros and cons of using me to do this. He knew that going with Murray would have been the typical decision and that no one would hold it against him, seeing as Murray was a better writer than me. And since Murray had been one of those who had crossed the picket line, it would be seen as a reward for his loyalty to the company and a continuation of the seniority status quo.

"That's a good suggestion, and the way things used to operate," Larry said firmly, "but I think it's time the paper rewarded its reporters for their hard work and initiative. Leo's on the story."

5

❈

Writing the second story took longer than usual. While the first one was a simple 250-word crime story, the sidebar was different. I could have pounded it out as fast as the main story, but since Larry had personally stepped in, defended me, and given me the opportunity to write it, I felt I had to put a better-than-average effort into it. I opened with a description of the victim, how peaceful she looked lying on the ground in the orange glow of a tent, and then expanded the scene to reveal that she was actually dead and this was a crime scene.

I described how the Forensics were professional in their duties, like it was just another day at the office for them, but at the same time, they were respectful of the body and determined to find all the details they needed. I made note of how exclusive this situation had been, how members of the media were never invited into a crime scene tent, but answered the reader's logical next question by using Whitford's comments about how he wanted the victim to have a face, not just to be dismissed by the general public as another dead body.

There were a number of things I didn't include, like Whitford's name—I called him "an EPS member who wished not to be identified"—my personal feelings about seeing another dead body, information about the weather, and any of the comments from the Mountie. That was nothing new, just normal journalistic operating procedure. It's not necessary to tell the whole story; some details can be and are left out. It's mostly due to time and space issues, but also it's not necessary to provide all the details or to give the whole story because in truth doing that may detract from the tone one wants the story to have. And with any story, there's always the possibility that it may develop legs, and those other details may fit better in follow-up articles.

Before I put the story through, I asked Anderson for his input. A rare request but I wanted the opinion of a writer that I respected. He agreed, but on one condition. "Tell me about Larry when he said he would put your right hand into the press so you could never write again," he asked.

"Why?"

"He uses that line all the time and I was hoping to respond with his own words the next time he uses it on me. Make him think, you know?"

Anderson was taking a chance considering such a move, but since he was a solid performer in the newsroom, he might get away with it, although probably only once.

"Okay, let me set up the story a bit before I tell you. First off, the paper in Olds was a really good paper, been around since 1899 or something like that, with its own press in the back that was constantly printing papers for the rest of the weeklies in the area. That fucker was huge, loud, and it would shake the entire building when it was running. And on Mondays, Tuesdays, and Wednesdays it ran nonstop, and there was no wall separating it from the front room where the reporters, typesetters, and ad sales folks worked, so I had to write my stories with this monster constantly roaring in my ears. And I never could do a phoner interview because there was no way you could hear anyone, so it forced you to go out and actually interview people in person, which was good.

"The people who were publishing the paper when I was there, were the grandkids of the guy who founded it in the first place, before the town was actually a town. The publisher at the time was this old dude named Neil, who had married into the family. He looked like a big, old farmer, kind of like Jed Clampett's bigger brother. He always had this roll of bills in his pocket, mostly fifties and hundreds. Once I had to go to some event and there was a five-dollar admission charge, even for the media, so I asked Neil if the paper could pay. It took him almost twenty minutes to flip through all those bills to find something as small as a five.

"And every time you said something to him, he grunted 'Huh,' so if you didn't know him, you thought he couldn't hear you, but it was just a fixed-action pattern, a tic that he had. He had heard you, and if you tried to repeat what you said, he would bark at you.

"So this was an old-timey weekly, the kind you really don't see anymore, and it was here that I hired our fearless leader Larry Maurizo."

"You gave Larry his first job in the business?" he asked incredulously. "Don't let that get around much because there are a lot of people here who would kill you for it."

"Yeah, yeah, whatever," I said, waving his comment away because a lot of people already knew that and were actually afraid of me because of it. "Except for Larry and a few reporters like yourself, most of the staff here wouldn't last a week at a weekly so there's no way I'm afraid of them. But Larry, when he was a kid, I thought he would be one of those guys who wouldn't last, who would call it quits after a month or so."

"Obviously, he didn't."

"No, he didn't and that's good because he's one of the best in the business. I know he's a bit of an asshole and that most people here hate him because of the strike, but the one thing about Larry is that he loves newspapers, he loves the business and he loves this newspaper. That asshole attitude is just that he's passionate about putting out a really great paper and he doesn't like it when people don't share that passion.

"Believe it or not, if I know Larry, he was pretty proud that you guys went on strike. He would never admit it, but the fact that you stood up for something you believed in and it had to do with the paper, earned a lot of respect from him. He had to do what he had to do, but he knew that when the strike and all its fallout was over, this paper would become stronger, that all that passion you guys had during the strike would come back to your work at the paper. I bet that before the strike, a lot of people were just marking time, going through the motions. Now I think more people are personally invested in the paper and are going to show those corporate bastards why you matter."

He nodded but the look on his face told me that he wasn't convinced by my argument. "That's partly true, but there is still a good-sized group that doesn't care anymore and is hoping that the newspaper fails."

"Yeah, but in time those guys will be weeded out and either be let go with some type of package or they'll quit and finally write the book they've always wanted to write. And that will bring in new blood that, with direction and mentorship from folks like you and Larry, will create new passion for the paper."

"Yeah, yeah, that all sounds nice but I'm sorry if I don't believe it. I don't really want to talk about the strike now because it only depresses me. So tell me about Larry and his first job."

"Right. So it's an old-timey paper, with what looks like an old-timey publisher and a complacent editor. Or at least that's what bright-eyed, journalism-degree-holding Larry Maurizo thinks when he gets there. Sure, he's willing to learn, but to him, we're a bit backward with our cut-and-paste layout and our weekly broadsheet. 'Everybody knows,' he says in the first week, 'that tabloid is the way to go.' And I have to admit that Larry was partly right, we still hadn't gone over to computers yet, and yeah, that broadsheet was wide but that's what the people in town were used to. Many of them didn't like the tabloid style; it reminded them too much of the new city paper. They liked a paper that you had to stretch your arms to read.

"But he was respectful, Larry. He listened to the advice I gave him and he wrote good copy. There was a time when I took him to his first town council meeting. I was introducing him around, informally, mind you, because being on the town council in a small town, even being mayor, isn't a full-time job like it is in the city. It's almost a volunteer thing and they all have their real jobs in the daytime so I introduce him to the mayor, and while I'm doing so, another councilor comes into the room. And the mayor sees him and makes some sort of crack about this guy's attitude at the last meeting, you know, innocent banter about how he hopes that so-and-so doesn't get all annoyed about something like at the last meeting because he made it last too long.

"And even though we sit through the meeting and get the typical small-town council stories, little Larry is all excited about what the mayor said. He thinks he's got a great story, a bit of political intrigue that he can use and then reuse once all the reaction comes in from the previous crack. Larry thinks he has a scoop, and if he was covering council here in Edmonton, he would. But in Olds, he doesn't."

"Why the hell not? That makes sense if someone makes a comment like that. He's the mayor talking to a reporter so he's got to watch himself."

"Obviously, you've never worked at a weekly, either," I said with a shake of my head. "In a small town, when the mayor makes a joke about someone else, even another councilor, it's not a news story, it's only the mayor making a joke. If you turn it into a story, and then another story when you get a rebuttal comment, and keep the controversy going, you might as well close up shop right then because no one is going to trust you or your paper, so people will not only stop talking to you, they'll stop advertising with you, stop taking their printing to you, and so on.

"And I told Larry that and he didn't believe me, he really thought he had a story. He just thought I was a complacent editor who wasn't really interested in real news. But in a small town this wasn't real news, wasn't even close. But Larry kept at it, he wrote a story, and instead of giving it to me, he handed it over to Neil, the publisher, thinking that he could convince this small-town rube that he knew how to bring real news to the paper."

"So what did the old guy do?"

"Despite his look, Neil was not someone to mess with. He may have looked like an old farmer, but this guy flew a fighter plane in the Battle of Britain, got shot down but managed to crash-land his plane with only a broken leg. And when they sent him back to Canada, he ended up in Alberta training new air force recruits to fly planes. He was also a strong supporter of the Liberal Party, which in small-town Alberta is about like supporting the Antichrist. But Neil wasn't afraid to make his views known, and although people disagreed with him, they respected him for standing up for himself and what he believed.

"So when Larry finishes his spiel about the newsworthiness of the story, Neil nods and asks him for the copy. Larry hands it over and smiles at me while Neil reads it. But after giving it a good read, Neil rips it to pieces and tosses the pieces into Larry's face. And he stands up, his full six-three height towering over Larry, and growls, 'If you ever write or do anything like that again, I'll not only fire you, I'll drag your ass to the press, and stick your right hand in so you'll never write again.'"

"Yeah, so what did Larry say to that?"

"For a while, Larry says nothing. In fact, nobody says anything because, of course, we're all watching. The smart move for Larry would be to mumble, Sorry, and walk away. But Larry doesn't walk away. All he does is look like a hurt puppy because his scoop is now in pieces at his feet. And then, I don't what he was thinking but he blinks a couple of times, stands up straight, and says, 'I can always write one-handed with my left.' And he turns and walks past the press and out the back door.

"Neil shakes his head and walks over to me. I ask him if Larry is fired but Neil shakes his head. 'Nah. He's a got a lot to learn but he's an obnoxious prick so I'm guessing he has a bright future in this business.'"

Anderson laughed, thanked me for the line, and took the hard copy of my sidebar. He made a few marks with his pen and then handed it back, calling it a masterpiece.

I typed in his changes and then sent the story directly to Larry's computer, also cc'ing the piece to Whittaker. A few minutes later, Larry came out of his office. Whittaker saw him and followed behind. Larry's face was blank but I knew I had written a good story so had no reason to worry.

"Go home, Leo," he said as he arrived at my desk. "There are a few minor things but I think Whittaker can handle it from here on, right, Whitaker?"

"No problem," she said. "One of our shooters even got a nice shot of the tent in the field so we can package that up with the story."

"Excellent," Larry said. "Excellent work, everyone. Paper's going to look nice tomorrow. But Leo, you go home and get some rest. You, too, Anderson. No reason for you to hang around here, either."

Everyone grunted in acknowledgment. I entertained the idea of inviting Brent out for a beer but realized he had family at home and probably wanted to go see them. I pulled on my jacket, muttered thanks and good night, and left the building.

6

It was six o'clock by the time I was outside, but it was already dark. Typical for late fall. The days were getting shorter and shorter, the arc of the sun getting lower in the south sky and the shadows longer. In a few more weeks it would be dark by four and by the time Christmas rolled around, we'd be only getting seven hours of daylight, not a lot for the most part, but at least the sun would be shining. People new to the city always commented on that. Even though winter was cold and the days were short, the sun shone most of the time. And the sharper angle changed the wavelength of its light to the warmer reds and oranges, so even the color of the air would change.

Since I didn't have a car, but still lived relatively near downtown, I was a walker. My trip home took me north along 101st Street up to 104th Avenue where I cut through a large open lot where the old railway used to run toward my neighborhood. From there, I headed west along 105th, behind Grant MacEwan College and its concrete towers, until I got to my house, which was located in a neighborhood officially called Central McDougall.

However, over a number of years, it had been given a series of informal names based on the immigrants who lived there at the time. It had been called Little Saigon in the seventies and eighties because of the Southeast Asian boat people fleeing the Vietnam War and its aftermath. Those folks had moved, and in the past ten years or so they had been replaced by refugees fleeing African wars in Ethiopia, the Sudan, Somalia, and the like. The new name was now Little Mogadishu or, more informally, Kush.

It was a decent neighborhood, full of old houses, three- and four-story walk-ups, and mom-and-pop restaurants and stores. Newer developments such as the college, condos, and a plethora of franchises were starting to gentrify the place, but that pace was still slow north of the old railway line. Despite these changes and the emergence of a vibrant African spirit to Kush with restaurants and stores offering food and goods from East Africa, it was still considered a rough part of town with johns trolling for streetwalkers along 107th Avenue, homeless folks pushing shopping carts filled with empties, and the odd gang-related shooting.

For someone like me, it was perfect: close enough to walk downtown and to other amenities, but still dangerous enough to keep the rents low. Unfortunately, there was one area of my walk home that always gave me pause. On the corner of 101st Street and 104th Avenue, just at the edge of downtown, there was a casino, an industrial warehouse of a building dressed up with neon and three-tone paint to give it a garish look.

Casinos were nothing new for Edmonton. Outside of Nevada, this city had more gambling space per capita than any other city in North America, a fact that some people in the chamber of commerce liked to celebrate, while others didn't. The proliferation of casinos and video lottery terminals, those electronic gambling machines throughout the province, was another legacy of the Klein era, those fourteen years when a beer-drinking, cigarette-smoking, gambling politician ran the province. It was nice getting private liquor stores but having more casinos than anyone else and VLTs in almost every single bar in the province made things a little difficult for someone like me.

The proceeds of gambling were a cash cow, bringing over a billion dollars into the province's coffers and also helping many charities. Albertans assuaged their guilt over using gambling to raise government money by allowing nonprofit groups to "volunteer" to work at casinos for a few days every two years. In return they would get a portion of the proceeds of the take during those days.

It was hard for any group to say no to an average of fifty thousand to eighty thousand dollars every two years in return for a few hours of volunteer work. Still, with Klein and his cronies gone, things were changing. Many school boards, churches, and other nonprofits had passed directives disallowing their members or any group connected with them to accept any money from gambling sources.

Of course, I could have taken a different route home to bypass the casino. There was no need for me to tempt myself every day after work. But the selection of my route home was a test. I was like the alcoholic who pours himself a drink he hopes he won't drink or the sex addict who flips through the escort ads on the back pages of one of the alternative weeklies. There was that thrill of temptation, the imagining of what we could be doing, of returning to the comfort of our addiction. It is a comfortable place to be, in our addiction, because we know exactly how we're supposed to act, what we're supposed to do, and how we're supposed to feel. And even though we may be destroying ourselves, it's at least someplace where life is easier. Living in the real world, with real people, is much harder. So much harder.

Because of the image of the dead body in the field, today was a more difficult day than normal, a day I knew I could easily say "fuck it" to it all and step through those doors into the beautiful oxygenated air. But today was also a day of honest victory, where the simple act of arriving at a place before anyone else brought a type of success I hadn't experienced in a long time. When one lives in and for a casino and gambling, luck is a major force in your life and this time luck was not in the cards or the numbers or the order of finish of a horse; it was in the real world. And in that, I took strength and walked past the casino toward my home.

I followed the path I had taken for these past months in the real world and arrived at my place, my little suite in the basement of a dilapidated house in the Kush. My room was in a postwar bungalow sitting in a nicely sized corner lot, the siding bleached pale, with flakes of paint hanging off the window frames. Twenty or thirty years ago, when some family lived and grew in the house, it might have been one of the nicer houses on the street, but now it stood as one of the few houses left. Three- and four-story walk-ups surrounded it, and directly across the street was an industrial park that had also seen better days. There was a small, unattached garage in the backyard but it leaned to the north like a slouching teenager.

The back door gave direct access to the basement without having to enter the main floor. The original owners of the house were long gone; the upstairs residents were now a bunch of students attending the nearby Grant MacEwan College. I climbed down the stairs, an invisible presence to the preoccupied upstairs residents.

The basement was a dark, damp place, the concrete walls of the foundation crumbling and dripping with condensation. Cardboard boxes of various sizes were stacked throughout the basement along with old toys, bikes, and the other refuse created by an annual revolving door of students. There was an old gas furnace pumping away somewhere behind all the boxes, a washer and dryer set from the sixties, and a single shower stall next to the washer and dryer.

My room was a small rectangle, slightly larger than my bank-machine bedroom from the previous night. Outside light streamed in from a tiny window near the ceiling. The room was neat and clean, the air smelling slightly of humidity mixed with a lingering scent of pine cleaner. A twin mattress and box spring were pressed into the corner of the two inside walls, away from the cold, wet concrete. My bed had comforter and sheets tucked in between the mattress and box spring, and a thin crease between the pillow and the comforter.

A frayed carpet spread out from underneath the bed, covering most of the floor. There was a small end table with a shadeless lamp directly beside the bed. A matching wardrobe/dresser set were shoved together against the outside wall with an eight-inch-screen TV on top of the dresser.

Right next to the dresser and filling up the rest of the wall was a Formica-top kitchen table with a matching chair. A single-burner hot plate and small microwave sat at the back of the table against the wall, a jar of change on top of the microware. The microwave was also doing double duty as a bookend for a line of about twenty books.

As I lay on my bed, my only piece of furniture that could be sat or lain upon, I decompressed, congratulating myself for my day and my victories. But when I pulled the wad of bills out of my pocket, I remembered the bank and fell back onto my bed, shivering. I lay there forever, waiting for the heavy footsteps of police-issue boots as they came down the stairs to take me in for bank robbery.

Two steps forward, and two steps back. It was always that way.

7

❄

I robbed my first bank by mistake. It was two weeks after getting a job at a new paper, some months after living NFA (no fixed address). Despite my disheveled appearance, the managing editor and I had worked together at another paper and he was desperate for a night copy editor, another pig on the rim. It was a dull and sometimes depressing job, so to have someone also desperate for work made me the perfect choice.

After two weeks editing night copy, I was presented with my first real paycheck in a long time. The ME gave me that first check himself, coming out of his office and handing me the white envelope, surprising the hell out of the other pigs on the editing rim. "Considering your circumstances, I'm bringing your check to you," he said, trying to punch some authority into his voice. He may have scared the others on the rim, but I had seen him as a small-town reporter fresh out of journalism school so I wasn't impressed by his appearance. "But this is the only time, Leo, because once you take it in your hands, I'm ordering you to head to the closest bank right now and open yourself an account so we can do a direct deposit. Do I make myself clear?"

I almost smiled at his order, but I knew it would unwise to undermine his authority. Despite our past relationship, a managing editor has got to look like he's in power. So I just grabbed the envelope. "Yes, boss," I said, tempted to flash him a salute but knowing that that would have also undermined his authority.

Then I headed out of the building, looking for the nearest bank. It was cold so I had my gloves on and my hood pulled over my toque to cut down on the biting wind. Unfortunately, the nearest bank was the same location where I had ended up sleeping in the ATM foyer during a cold snap several months ago, so I went on by. I was trying to put that past behind me, to forget my lost years, and coming to that bank over and over again, as I rebuilt my life, wouldn't do.

Instead, I walked a few blocks to the north, where there were plenty of banking options. I chose one named after an eastern Canadian city and stepped in. The shock of the lights confused me for a second. It was like stepping into a casino, but instead of putting money in it to lose, I was putting money in it to save.

For a few seconds, I had no idea what to do; I had no recollection of how to fill out a deposit form or to open a bank account. I was like a prisoner being left on his own, to make his own decisions after years of being locked up. Instead of filling in the required boxes on the form, I flipped it over and wrote: "Please give me all your money." The stupidity of the words made me chuckle, and allowed me to get back into myself. For another laugh I wrote "Thank you" and then flipped the form over and filled in the spots, save for my name and account because that would come later when I opened the account. And with my first paycheck in years and the hope for a new life, I stepped up to the next open teller.

"May I help you?" she asked. I handed over the slip. A second later, her eyes widened with a look of total fear, her expression reminding me of those times when I would walk up to strangers, begging them for spare change. But this time, it was confusing because I was a citizen with a real job and real money. All I needed was a real bank account and I'd be set.

"Is there a problem?" I said in a soothing voice, but it only exacerbated the situation.

Her face had turned white and her breath was caught in her throat. "P-p-please don't hurt me," she whispered.

"Why would I do . . ." I started to say, but stopped when I looked down and saw that I had handed her the deposit slip the wrong way. My joke was facing up and was no longer funny. I tried to explain the situation but she was no longer listening to me. She had opened her cash drawer and, with shaking hands, started to stack bills on the counter in order of denomination, the blue fives, the purple tens, the green twenties—probably the biggest stack of them all—a bunch of red fifties and about four or five of the brown hundreds. When she finished she backed a step away, her eyes filled with terror.

I looked about but everyone else was busy with their own work. I looked back at the teller and she had started to shake, her gaze moving back and forth from the stack of bills to me.

She was deathly quiet but her expression screamed, Take it! Take the money! Take the money and go! There was nothing I could do. I had robbed a bank, and considering my history, no amount of explanation or pleading would help me. A tear started to run down one side of the teller's face and I knew that any second she would fall apart and my life, the one that I had worked so hard to get back together, would follow along with her.

I swept my hand across the counter, grabbed all the money and my note, and shoved them into my pocket. I turned and quickly walked out of the bank, jaywalked across the street, and pushed through the revolving doors of a downtown shopping center.

I walked in and out of shops, doing my best to look like an average shopper but I had no idea what the hell I looked like. When a clerk approached me to see if I needed help, I stammered, "I'm looking for a gift for my wife." That statement made my shaken appearance okay; I was only a harried husband trying at the last minute to find a gift for his long-suffering wife.

I went through this charade a number of times, using some of the bills from the bank to pay for these goods. I was in the world but away from it, in that time of emptiness that I always fell into when I gambled, that time that has no meaning, no sense, just a debasing comfort that all addicts dream to return to, so they don't have to face the harshness of their terrible reality.

Until that time, I had had no idea that another such place existed outside of gambling, and in a strange sort of way, it brought me a piece of freedom. From then on, when the pressure to gamble became too much for me to bear, I would visit a bank.

8

✳

There was nothing new in the story the next day. It didn't normally take too long for police to identify a dead body. Most people, even street people, prostitutes, drug dealers, and formerly homeless journalists, usually carried some type of ID, even if it was a driver's license that was long since expired. What took time was finding a next of kin, a distant relative or close friend to confirm the identity of the deceased.

And Canadian law also stipulated that police could not release the identity of a person killed as a result of criminal activity or a car accident or any similar event to the media until the family (or some family surrogate such as a guardian and so forth) was officially told of the death. That was to prevent somebody from reading in the paper that one of their immediate family members was dead. And even if a media outlet discovered or knew the name of the victim, it was also unethical and illegal for them to print or mention the name until they got official ID confirmation from the police.

So, based on the location of the victim's body, her race, and the way she was dressed, I assumed that she was a street prostitute and it would take at least a couple of days until I received any ID information so that I could investigate her life.. The question was then what to do with my time until such information was made public.

I could have sat back and taken it easy for a day or so, but there was something about a busy newsroom that discouraged this kind of behavior. I could have asked for another assignment, a one-off quickie for the next issue, and I would have received one. But if the identity of the girl in the field came through much sooner than expected, I would have to drop that story into the hands of another busy reporter to focus on my more important assignment.

I decided to forgo another assignment, but in order to keep myself somewhat busy I ran a morgue check using the paper's Infomart archive system. Infomart allowed any reporter to read any story in the paper's morgue, the archive of past issues. It worked like any search engine. All you had to do was type a name, a phrase, whatever, and it would give you a listing.

Like with most search engines, you could get a lot of irrelevant responses if you weren't specific enough or if you typed in a popular name, like Wayne Gretzky. It also went back only as far as 1985, but it was way better than searching through back issues yourself, or asking some overworked and overprotective librarian to do the search for you.

Of course, most of the librarians had been laid off in a cost-cutting measure a couple of years ago, and though one of the "concessions" the paper made in order to end the strike was to look into the possibility of hiring back a librarian or two, no move had been made in that direction. And probably never would.

I typed in *"dead body in field,"* making sure to use the quotation marks because I didn't want to include all stories with the words *dead, body,* and *field.* Enough people had died in this city over the past twenty years, and since two of the major economic engines in and around Edmonton were agriculture and petroleum products, I shuddered to think how many times the word *field* was used, not just in a single issue, but in the past couple of decades.

Even so, I got a large number of hits, sixty-seven of them, to be exact. Apparently there were a lot of dead bodies found in the fields around the city in the past. But in reality most of them weren't as serious as expected. The biggest listing had nothing to do with dead bodies but with a local play from a decade ago called *Over My Dead Body* produced by a group called Out of Left Field Players.

The rest were all true dead bodies although most turned out to be suicides—nowadays most newspapers don't run stories on suicides unless it was someone famous or an extremely public suicide—or stories about farmers or oilfield workers being killed in industrial accidents.

In fact, there were only six stories about female bodies being found in a field, and when I delved deeper into them, looking for follow-up articles relating the identity of the person or the circumstances of the death, only three were similar to the story I was working on. So only four such deaths in Edmonton for the past twenty years wasn't that big a deal. If you looked at any other Canadian city, you'd probably find the same number.

I was about to get the system to print all the articles relating to these three when Larry came by my desk.

"Can I talk to you for a sec, Leo?"

I set aside my work and turned to face him. "Sure, Larry. What's up?"

"How's the story going?"

I shrugged. "Not much happening. Police haven't released the ID yet so there's really nothing to be done. So in the meantime, I decided to check the morgue for any similar stories from the past. Don't want to repeat ourselves too much."

"You did?" he asked, his eyebrows rising in surprise. "That's some good reporting. Find anything?"

"Only a few articles on similar deaths. Nothing like the type of story you're looking for." I wasn't sure if I should be insulted by his reaction, because it could have meant he didn't think much of my work ethic. I decided to let it go because the other day he did stand up for me and gave me a chance when he didn't have to. He was also the only one at the paper who knew about my background so maybe he was justified in his reaction.

"Is that why you came over to talk?" I asked him.

"Actually, I had another thing in mind," he said, perching at the edge of the desk behind him. There was another reporter working there—another crime reporter named Edgar Franke, decent writer but more interested in joining the sports section—and for a second, he looked like he was going to say something about Larry sitting on his desk. But he changed his mind and went back to writing his story.

"I seem to recall that sometime during our past conversations, you told me one of your parents was Cree. Your dad, right?" Larry continued.

"Actually, it's my mom."

"And what does that make you?"

"I don't know, her son, I guess?"

"Don't be obtuse. I'm asking if that makes you an Indian."

"They're no longer Indians, but natives, First Nations, Aboriginal." I guess I should have said *we* but getting used to the fact that I'm an Indian was a constant process. Sure, growing up, I knew where my parents came from and it was kind of cool letting friends know that I was half Cree or one quarter Cree or one sixteenth Cree, depending on what story about her bloodline Mom was talking about.

Back then, it was neat to pretend I could smell things in the air other people couldn't or hear the sound of something approaching from a distance, or track the trail of another kid when playing hide-and-seek. It was all bullshit, no doubt about that, but it was no different than Mike Hamilton saying he was a better basketball player because he was black or Randy Brignell saying he knew kung fu because his mom was Korean. Those kinds of differences were okay growing up on the army base. They were fun differences, differences that made playing war or hide-and-seek or James Bond or whatever more fun.

They were safe differences while behind them we were pretty much all the same, just a bunch of army brats trying to make friends as fast as possible and have as much fun as you could until you or someone else was posted to another base, best friends lost forever in the administration of the Department of National Defense.

Of course, Mike Hamilton may have been black, but his family didn't celebrate Black History Month or Martin Luther King's birthday. And Randy Brignell's mother may have been Korean, but the only time they ate Korean food was never, because there wasn't a Korean restaurant near the PMQs. And though my mom was Indian, or native, First Nations, or Aboriginal, nobody spoke a word of Cree in the house. Nobody spoke a lick of French, either, but that was Dad's side of the family.

"Yeah, right. Whatever the word is these days," Larry said off-handedly.

"Aren't you the sensitive type? Maybe I should file a grievance if you're going to talk that way," I said sarcastically.

He was about to respond to that but I cut him off. "But if you're asking if I got a treaty card, the answer would be, No, I don't, although my mom does now. Don't ask why, 'cause she never really expressed any interest in getting one until after Dad died. But if you're also asking if people would think of me as native, then I have no idea. It's a huge gray area, especially considering that I look like my dad. Most people look at me and the words *Aboriginal* or *First Nations,* or even *Indian,* aren't the first things that pop into their head. Why you asking anyway?"

He rubbed the hair on the top of his head. "Well, the city is launching its new Aboriginal Outreach Program. They're trying to improve relations with the Aboriginal communities in the city and they're asking for a number of key businesses, the paper included, to appoint someone to be an ambassador of sorts to this program. And the publisher asked if I could find someone in the editorial department who could not only take up that role but also become an ad hoc Aboriginal issues reporter. Someone whose job it is to report and cover, only on a casual basis, mind you, Aboriginal events and stories. And I thought of you because I remembered that you told me one of your parents was native."

"Isn't there anybody else? I mean, you got me on this 'giving a face to the dead body' story and now you want me to take on another role? Jeez, Larry, make up your mind, willya?"

"It's only a casual thing. I still want you on this other story. In fact, this will be your first story as the Aboriginal issues reporter, bringing to life the story of this poor girl. Nice work on the sidebar, by the way. You did a hell of a job capturing the scene."

"Yeah, thanks, Larry. But about this Aboriginal relations ambassador?"

"Aboriginal issues reporter."

"Yeah, that. Isn't there anybody else more suitable for this? Surely there must be someone else on staff with more . . . more native connections than me. How about Les Ghostkeeper? He'd be perfect. He's got the Aboriginal name and, more importantly, he's got the look, the braids and all that."

"Les is a shooter. If we need shots of a powwow or something else, we'll send him. But we need someone who can write on this. And based on my research, you're it."

"There's nobody else in editorial that is a bit more native than me? Or at least looks more native than me?"

Larry shook his head. "Nope. You're our only native son." He chuckled.

"That's not funny, Larry. And neither is the fact that I'm the most Aboriginal person on the editorial staff. I think the paper should rethink its hiring policy as it relates to minorities."

"Well, if more natives become journalists then we'll think about it. But as of today, you're it and you better get your coat."

"What the hell for?"

"As I said, the city is launching its Aboriginal Outreach Program today," he said, looking at his watch. "And it starts in about an hour. At the Native Friendship Centre on 101st. We want you to be there, make a short speech like the rest of the ambassadors about the importance of Aboriginal relations, and then write up a short piece. Lester will be there to get some shots."

"You want me to make a speech?"

"Not a long one. And don't worry, all the other ambassadors will be doing the same thing, so it's no biggie. The important thing is that you're there and that when it's done you write a story."

There was only thing for me to do. "How many words?" I asked.

9

The Native Friendship Centre was a concrete block of a building just north of downtown in what many people still called the inner city. The area had many features of what the term implies: decrepit houses, strolling prostitutes, stumbling drunks, discarded crack vials and used syringes. But it also had wide streets with large trees stretching over the road, old houses, families, single-parent and otherwise, eking out a living, and their kids hanging from swings and monkey bars while johns in cars picked up hookers.

Artistic types had also looked to the neighborhood as a place to buy (and then renovate) a cheap house without selling out or working a day job to pay for a huge mortgage. A good idea because, though the houses were old, they were also big and sturdy, with deep yards and paved alleys in the back.

I parked the car in the lot, taking note of the mayor's SUV parked in the handicapped spot by the front door. In my head, I wrote a few sentences of a story describing this infraction but pushed the idea aside. No doubt the mayor would be embarrassed by such a story, but was it an actual story? The mayor did this all the time, everyone knew about it, but it was one of those things the city decided to let go. Instead, I probably did what everyone else did when they saw his shiny SUV, I kicked up gravel as I walked by.

The main hall was filled with various members of the city's Aboriginal community, people in suits looking like Joe Businessman with Aboriginal faces, folks in leather fringed jackets, and others in various types of casual dress—T-shirts, leather jackets, jeans. It could have been any gathering at any community hall in the city, but for the few white faces, the mayor and his entourage near the stage, and me.

Glances were sent my way as I entered and then, once I was filed away in the "another white man" category, I was put aside. I wasn't ignored; a white man couldn't be ignored when he walked into a room full of natives, the same way a native person wasn't ignored when he walked into any restaurant, club, or public space in the city. The difference was that when a white man walked into a room full of natives, he wasn't automatically assumed to be drunk and looking for a handout.

The mayor stood on the stage as he gave a speech. His Worship Robert Johnson was the kind of mayor you'd expect for our fine city at this point in time: white, nearing middle age, an ex-CFL place kicker who turned to selling cars after winning his fourth Grey Cup. Stocky without being fat, he was friendly, with a big wide smile that made him look like he was honestly happy to see you and wanted to help. He wasn't known for his brightness; he had the tendency to think that the best idea in the world came from his most recent conversation. But then again, he wasn't stupid; he was quick with a joke and had an almost savant ability to remember the faces of people he'd met only once.

But there was always something about Mayor Johnson that bugged me. Maybe it was the fact that no matter how nice his suits looked or how many times people called him Your Worship, et cetera, he couldn't seem to shake that car salesman look. Although I could hear the mayor speaking, I didn't really listen to what he was saying. It was something about building bridges between the city and community, as if the Aboriginal community was separate from the rest of the city like some kind of mysterious island. I clicked on my recorder. I knew I should also have taken notes, but I figured one of the communications flunkies would have a transcript of his speech in case I missed something.

There were a bunch of other suits lined up on stage, various government and business types who were all part of this new Aboriginal liaison initiative, and it seemed that everyone was supposed to say something. Larry had also said I was expected to say a few words on behalf of the paper, introduce myself, and pass my card around. So I moved to the front, waiting for my name to be called so I could shake hands with the mayor and the elders on stage and say something really intelligent to convince the crowd (and myself) that I could do this job without offending them.

I reached the stairs to the left of the stage and felt a hand on my shoulder. I looked back and saw Lester Ghostkeeper, the shooter from the paper. Like all shooters, he was wearing a camera around his neck along with a brown vest covered with pockets. Despite this uniform, with his coloring and long black hair pulled into two braids, Lester fit in with the crowd.

"Been here long?" I asked him.

"Yeah, got a bunch of shots of the mayor and some elders shaking hands, a short smudge ceremony, stuff like that. Nothing earth-shattering but it should work. How about you? Any suggestions that might tie in with the story?"

"At the moment the story is the farthest thing from my mind. I'm still thinking about what I'm going to say."

"Yeah, I heard about that. Didn't peg you as native but then again there you go. Guess I should say congrats on your promotion."

"A promotion usually comes with more money and some benefits but I think this one is just going to create more work for me."

"That's the way it usually works," he said, looking past me at the stage. "Looks like you're up. I'll get a nice shot for your own files if you want."

Someone called my name and I stepped onto the stage, still unsure of what to say, but I figured I could make something up on the fly. I had done this before, mostly at the small-town newspapers where I used to work, and I knew that before I spoke, I was supposed to shake hands with everyone onstage. But my outstretched hand was ignored by the mayor. Instead of looking at me, he was looking at Lester. "Come on. Don't be shy, Mr. Desroches," he said, waving at Lester to come forward and mispronouncing my name, adding a third syllable instead of just having two. "Come introduce yourself to your people."

Lester looked extremely uncomfortable, and the mayor, although still smiling and waving, had a bit of an angry look in his eyes because Lester wasn't responding to him. Since many in the crowd knew that Lester wasn't Leo Desroches, they were silent, embarrassed and disappointed by the gaffe and unsure of what to do. That silence, and the fact that one or two of the elders onstage were shaking their heads and rolling their eyes, tipped off the mayor and his entourage that something had gone wrong. I pushed aside my annoyance at being ignored and stepped in front of the mayor and grabbed his hand. There was a confused look on his face and he seemed to want to say something, but I gave him a friendly slap on the shoulder, like he had just told a funny joke, and then stepped up to the mic. The crowd stared at me, unsure of how to respond.

I didn't think about what I was going to say, I just let the words flow naturally. "I know what you're thinking, 'cause I've been thinking about it ever since I got this job: 'Who the hell is this white man and what is he doing in a place like this?'" Someone from the mayor's entourage gasped but there were a few giggles coming from the crowd and from the line of elders onstage. "And I'll be honest,

I have no idea how to answer that, except to say something that my Cree mother always used to tell me: 'Just because you look like your dad, don't forget that it takes two people to make a person and there's plenty of my blood inside of you.'"

Okay, Mom never said that, but these people didn't need to know that. I continued. "And while I'm being honest, despite what Mom says, I still feel like a white man because that's how I grew up. As a kid I knew little about my native culture, about our past, the good and the bad, and while that's meant I've never been subjected to the racism, institutional and personal, that plagues natives in this country, it also meant I was saddled with a stigma of shame, that maybe I should hide the Aboriginal side of me because, for whatever reason, many people in this city and country felt it wasn't a good thing.

"Still, I've also had the feeling that I missed out by not being able to celebrate that side of myself, so hopefully my position as the Aboriginal issues reporter will help me touch that side of my being. I'd like, at the very least, to help the native community in this city and maybe in some way become a member of that community. Thanks for your time, and if you need to contact me for whatever reason, I'll be leaving a bunch of cards at the back and by the front door and those numbers are my direct line and cell phone.

"Thanks again for this opportunity and I, uh . . ." A lump in my throat and heaviness in the pit of my stomach stopped me. I stood there, looking at the crowd of unfamiliar yet familiar faces, some of them smiling, some of them nodding, some just staring, my eyes misting. I couldn't think of anything more to say; my mind was filled with a deep sense of sorrow, the same feeling that would always hit me after the first moment in a casino after months or years of being good.

I stepped back from the mic, and instead of turning toward the mayor and the rest of the people onstage, I went in the opposite direction, quickly walking down the stairs and moving through the crowd. I needed to clear my head and I wasn't going to be able to do that here. I had to leave the room. The crowd allowed me to pass, and there wasn't any uneasiness about it.

Somewhere in my addled brain I think I heard some applause, but my emotions were lost to me. I hoped to make it to my car, but as soon as I got out the front door and felt the blast of cool air on my face, tears were streaming down my cheeks. I quickly turned the corner so as not to be seen and fell back against the wall, and dropped my butt to the ground, breathing deep in order to stay centered. But I couldn't; I hit something that I always knew was there but also thought was under my control. Guess I was wrong, which had happened before.

10

❀

"Smoke?"

I looked up, and one of the elders from the stage was staring down at me, a lone cigarette extending from a pack held in his out-stretched hand. His face was blank, but it still made me feel calm.

I lifted my hand to wave it away and opened my mouth to say, No, thanks, but I froze. Even though I didn't smoke and would normally refuse any offer of a cigarette from anyone, I realized that in many native cultures, the Cree included, an offer of tobacco, no matter how minor, could be an offering of peace and friendship, a sacred thing. To refuse, even if you don't smoke, created an insult on par with spitting in a priest's face when he offers the host or slugging a Buddhist monk 'cause he smiles at you.

So I sat there, wondering if I should take the smoke as a gesture and just pocket it. But would that further insult him? Was the offer of the tobacco just the first step in a ritual I couldn't comprehend? Was I expected to light up and share in the smoke as a bond of friendship? I shut my eyes, knowing that this was just another re-minder that I shouldn't have agreed to Larry's proposal. What the hell did I know about being Indian if I couldn't even figure out how to accept or refuse the simple offer of a cigarette?

The old man seemed to understand what I was thinking because his blank expression morphed into a smile so slowly that I barely saw it happening. "You know," he said with a soft Cree accent, the slur of the English barely noticeable, "I think it was Freud who said 'sometimes a cigar is a just a cigar.' So if you need or want a smoke, take the cigarette; if not, don't. We're just hanging out, not negotiating a new treaty."

I finally let out the "No, thanks" I had been holding in, shaking my head at my own stupidity. The elder nodded and then slid the smoke back into the pack and tucked that into his storm rider pocket.

I pulled myself to my feet, shaking the cold out of my legs, and for about a minute we leaned against the west wall of the Friendship Centre watching the scattering of cars roll back and forth along Ninety-seventh Avenue. I wondered how to break the silence, how to engage the elder in conversation, but since I was still feeling the lingering effects of my emotional outburst, I was a little embarrassed. I should have said something besides, "Think it will snow soon?" Something deeper, more significant, something less banal, but that's all I could come up with without sounding like a moron.

The elder took a deep puff of his cigarette and gave me a thoughtful look, as if I'd asked him, Why is there air? or, Do you know the meaning of life? After several seconds he nodded and shrugged at the same time. "Maybe, but you never know this time of year, you know?"

"Yeah, guess you're right."

We fell silent for another minute or two. Traffic was starting to pick up a bit, rush hour about thirty minutes away from its peak. The wind started to make me shiver so I wondered if I should go back into the building for my coat or just cut my losses and head back to the office and write my story.

"So," the elder said out of the blue, making me jump and pulling me out of my thoughts. "Where do your people come from?"

The elder's question was similar to those I got asked whenever I said that there was native blood flowing in my veins, but it had never been expressed in that way. Everyone always asked where my mom came from or how native I was, in blood fractions. Nobody had used the words *your people* in that way, not even Mom. Her side of the family was just those Indians, sometimes Uncle So-and-So or Auntie Such-and-Such, but never *her people*.

Unlike Dad, who could and would trace his family lineage back to Champlain, reminding us over and over that even though we didn't speak a bit of French save for *"Voilà Monsieur Thibeau, voici Madame Thibeau"* and *"Où est l'autobus?"*, if Quebec ever separated from Canada, we would have no trouble getting dual citizenship, probably even before all those Algerians and other Africans who now lived there.

But every so often I would hear the odd story from Mom, or from a visiting relative or during one of my rare visits to Mom's hometown, so later on in life I was able to piece together some type of history of my mother's side of the family.

The elder was patient and quietly waited for me to figure out my answer. Maybe he was aware of the significance of his question and was allowing me the time to figure things out. Or maybe he was just being polite.

"Mom was born in Norway House. That's in northern Manitoba, just north of Lake Winnipeg," I said, pointing to the east. "So I guess that's where my people are from."

The old man nodded and, after a pause and a puff, said, "Swampy Cree, right? Did a lot of fishing?"

"Yeah," I say, remembering my massive Uncle Walter who just happened to be in Winnipeg as we were driving on a family trip to Quebec. I recalled meeting him for breakfast at some diner, and the sight of him measuring the distance between the seat and the table in a booth to see if he could fit his gut in. I also remembered

Dad saying Uncle Walter was a fisherman, but couldn't figure out where he would fish in the Prairies. It only made sense when I saw Lake Winnipeg a couple years later during the one and only trip we ever took to Mom's hometown. "They also did a bunch of trapping and building of York boats when the Europeans dropped in. Mostly Scots and Scandinavians from the Shetland Islands, just north of Scotland," I said, with a nod.

"Ahh, so that's where the red hair comes from," he said, pointing at my head.

I smiled, but shook my head. "Actually that's from my dad's side. French Canadian."

He started to speak fluent French, with a touch of Québécois in the accent. Before he got too far and expected me to answer, I held up my hand.

"Sorry, don't speak French except for what I learned in high school, and that was pretty useless."

"*Pas de français?* Not even your dad at home?"

I shook my head. "Nope."

"Then probably no Cree, either."

I nodded. "Right. No Cree. Just basic English, and considering all the accents flying around my house, it's a wonder I learned how to speak that."

"Oh, I think you speak English quite well. That was a heck of speech you made up there. Short, but you sure made a hell of an impression. Nobody's going to forget who Leo Desroches is, or what he thinks. By the way, I'm Francis. Francis Alexandra."

He held out a hand and I shook it. I felt the temperature rise as my face turned red. "Yeah, well. I probably should have worked something out in advance instead of just blurting out a bunch of crazy stuff."

"Nah, you only said what most of us were thinking. You were honest and that's all that counts. Just too bad you don't speak Cree. A lot of our people, like you, have lost touch with the language. Still, we have classes every Wednesday night; you should drop in."

"Yeah, sounds like a good time but I don't think so. To be honest, with this new job, I don't really have the time."

"No doubt, but you should really think about it. Sure, it's mostly kids and you'll probably be the oldest student, but it'll be a good way to connect with the community."

"Learn Cree from scratch? I doubt I'd be any good at that. I think learning a new language at my age would be tough."

"You never know till you try, right?"

"What? You the teacher, or do you get a commission for every student you bring in?"

"Ha, they would never let someone like me teach impressionable kids like you a new language. I just liked what you said and I think one way of getting to know your native culture is to learn the language."

"Then maybe I should learn French."

The old man smiled, showing his mouth of decayed dental work. "Why the fuck not? But Cree first."

"Why Cree first?"

"Just makes sense since you're not the Franco issues reporter, right?" He slapped me on the shoulder and then tossed his cigarette onto the road. The wheels of various cars extinguished the butt. "But think about it, Wednesday at seven. Just drop in and check it out. Liked the speech and I hope to see you again."

11

Her name was Grace Cardinal. That's what it said in the police press release that appeared in my e-mail in-box the next morning. Any concern I had about whether she was native or not disappeared at the sight of her last name. Cardinal was a very popular surname for many northern Alberta Cree. Contrary to popular belief, it had nothing to do with religion, nothing to do with Roman Catholic missionaries stealing native children, forcing them to attend their schools, denying them their native heritage and language, and saddling them with a good and proper European surname that reflected the Church. In actuality, the name Cardinal came from a Montreal-based fur trading family whose sons and nephews and cousins were some of the first fur traders in northern Alberta. And these men did marry Cree women, producing many children, all named Cardinal.

However, this family alone was not enough to spawn the thousands of Alberta natives with the same last name. Cardinal just happened to be one of the first European surnames in the native communities, and when various Cree started dealing with new European legalities such as birth certificates, contracts, and the census, they weren't allowed to use their Cree names, so many just used the name of a neighbor or some other member of their band who did have a European last name. It was no different from the English taking the name of their family's trade and then shortening it to Smith or African-American slaves being given the names of their owners.

It was good to give the body in the field a name, to take another step in giving her more status as a person, rather than just a victim. The release also gave me two more facts about her: she was nineteen and she was "known to police due to her high-risk lifestyle." The second comment was policespeak for "she was a prostitute and, therefore, partly to blame for ending up dead in a field." Of course, nobody in the police would ever come right out and blame a victim for being murdered, but by using the term *high-risk lifestyle* they covertly held her partly responsible for her own death.

At the same time, they were also telling the regular folks in the city that they had nothing to worry about; that this body found in the field wasn't one of their neighbors, a member of their family or somebody they worked with. They were saying that people like them, who didn't live high-risk lifestyles, didn't have to worry about high-risk trials and tribulations like being murdered and left in a farmer's field.

The release also noted that an autopsy was pending and that no cause of death had yet been determined. I wrote all these facts into a little story as an update for tomorrow's paper, but I knew I needed more. Larry had assigned me to give Grace a face and a life, but at the moment I only had the same facts that every single media outlet in the city had. Despite my scoop a couple days ago, we were once again all on the same level and no doubt there were one or two other journalists who were looking for more on Grace. I had to get more, and after sending the story through the system, I called Detective Whitford to see if he was still in a giving mood.

He wasn't. "All I got to say to you, Leo, is 'Fuck you. Fuck. You.'"

"Oh, come on, Detective Whitford. I'm not asking for much, just a last known or maybe a family contact."

"After what you did to me? Do you have any idea of the shitstorm your 'exclusive article' caused? Do you know that I was not only personally reamed out by our media relations department and my immediate superior but the chief himself gave me a courtesy call, telling me I personally had to contact every single news director and editor in the city and apologize to them and to reiterate that it's not police policy to let members of the media into a crime scene tent?"

"What did you expect to happen when you let a member of the media into the tent? Did you expect me to let it slide and do nothing about it?"

"Yes, I did, especially when you told me that you had already written the story in your head, and getting into the tent wouldn't change that."

"That was my original plan, but when my editors demanded to know how I knew the victim was female and native, I had to tell them. And once I told them, it was a choice between keeping my job or doing what I told you I was going to do. I'm sorry you got shit for it, but you had to know something like that might happen when you let me in. I mean, you're not new to this game, Detective."

On the other end he sighed, and I knew I'd scored an important point. "At least you could have given me a heads-up."

"Sorry, Detective. Things are pretty busy at the paper prior to deadline and I had two stories to write. And to be really honest, I never have the time to warn people about the fallout my stories may cause. It's not in my job description. Besides, you're the one who said you wanted to give this victim a face so she's not just another dead body in the field. That was your quote directly to me. I'm only asking you to help me continue what you started."

"Then again, fuck you, Leo. Fuck. You." Despite his words, the tone of his voice was less harsh this time, meaning that things were okay between us again.

"So can you offer me any further information about the victim such as a last known or a family contact? I'm sure you'll offer that information if any other media outlets call you."

"Sorry, Leo. If you want anything more than what's in the release you'll have to look elsewhere because you're blacklisted at the moment. One of the more consistent messages I've been getting from those people reaming me out is that Leo Desroches gets only the basic media information from us. And nothing else. If he wants anything else from the Edmonton Police Service, then the answer is supposed to be 'Fuck you.'"

"You get that from the chief?"

"Yeah, pretty much."

"But they were only specific about me?" I asked. "Nobody said anything about the paper, did they?"

There was a pause as Whitford realized what I was talking about and must have wondered how to react to it. He finally said, "No," and it was as ambiguous a *no* as anybody could have said. It could have meant, Don't ask me to do this, or it could have meant, They didn't mention the paper and I get what you're saying. The way he said it also told me that people were eavesdropping on his call, not listening directly to our conversation but listening to his side.

"Do you know Brent Anderson?" Brent, who was working on a story and listening to my side of the conversation at the same time, stopped writing and looked up with an inquisitive expression on his face. I waved a hand to stop him from asking any questions.

There was another pause, and then, "Yes." Again, as ambiguous as his previous statement.

"Well, Brent has a desk right next to mine and he says hi." Brent looked even more confused but I just smiled as if nothing was wrong.

Again, another pause, this one longer than all the rest. I figured he was smart enough to know what I was asking him and to weigh the options of what would happen if he did it. Finally, he sighed. "Third time, Leo. Fuck you." And then he hung up.

I wasn't concerned with how he had ended the call. There was a bit of lightness in his voice, a lilt that told me he understood but that even so, I was being a dick to ask him. Or he might just be telling me to fuck off and I would never hear from him again. I stood up, went around my desk toward Brent's side. "What the hell was that about?" he asked, turning his chair around to face me. "Why are you bandying my name around without my permission?"

"It's just a little favor, Brent, and I'll owe you one," I said, slowly turning his chair back so he could face his computer. "I just want you to check your e-mail for me, if you could."

"Jesus, Leo. What the hell are you doing?" he said. He tried to turn back toward me, but I held his chair in place.

"Just check the goddamn e-mail, Brent. You're not in any trouble, okay?"

He clicked on his mouse a few times and his e-mail in-box came up. Like those of most reporters for a major metro daily, it was covered in red letters indicating more than a hundred unopened e-mail messages. Ever since the paper started putting each reporter's e-mail address at the end of a story, we were deluged with messages ranging from comments about our stories to spam to messages from crazies who knew in their hearts that the way we wrote made us the perfect vehicle to tell their truths, to everything else in between. He clicked on his "get new messages" link, and while a bunch more red lines appeared, there was nothing with an EPS prefix. We tried again and again over the next few minutes, but nothing came up. Whitford hadn't understood, or if he did, he wasn't interested. I would have to find Grace another way and it would be much more difficult, maybe even impossible.

"Thanks, Brent," I said dejectedly. I was about to head back to my desk when he tried once more. "Hold on, Leo. I think we may have something," he said. "I take it you're waiting for something from Detective Whitford, am I right?" His mouse-free hand was pointing at one of the red lines.

"Yeah," I said, leaning over his shoulder to see the screen better. There was a message from someone named Whitey.

"Didn't know he had a nickname," he said, clicking to open the message.

"Please don't use it next time to see him, because then someone might know that he uses his personal e-mail to talk to the media." It had taken Whitford so long to respond to my request because he had gone off-site. Because he had committed some infraction by letting me into the tent, someone was probably watching his e-mail use at the EPS, to ensure he wasn't sharing information he shouldn't be sharing. The message was simple. No greetings, just the letters *DL,* which was Whitford's way of saying they had found her driver's license, and an address. It was exactly what I was looking for.

12

※

The foster mother remembered Grace, and obviously, her defenses were down because it only took a little bit of convincing to get her to let me in. She was a chunky woman in her early forties and she wore a loose sweater and sweatpants, probably in an effort to hide her weight. The house itself wasn't dirty but it wasn't clean. It was quite obvious that kids lived here and ruled the place. Toys were scattered across the floor, along with crayons and torn pieces of paper with half-finished drawings. There were a few plates with half-eaten pieces of food, and half-filled glasses with various drinks placed haphazardly on various coffee and end tables.

The furniture was old and out of style, but in decent shape, no holes or rips. The TV was blaring, competing with various types of music and squeals of laughter and children's yelling coming from somewhere down the hall. The walls were covered with photographs, tons of them, with different kids at various ages, many them generic school photos. But there were others of people on vacations gathered in a group for the family picture at whatever place they had stopped. Interspersed with these photos were certificates, the kind you get just for participating in some sport or event or class. There was even the odd child's drawing of high quality, jammed into a plain black frame and given a place of honor on a wall.

The smell of fresh cooking, some type of stew with a touch of sage and basil, lingered in the air. And even though I noted the lack of any Aboriginal features in Mrs. Lewis's face, I noticed a slew of dreamcatchers hanging from the ceiling, slowly spinning as the breeze from the forced-air furnace kicked in. The place had a sense of chaos, but it seemed under control. *Lived-in* was the proper term. Still, because of my upbringing I had to fight the urge to clean up the place.

Even though we had lived in a small three-bedroom "personnel married quarters" house, a PMQ, most of the house was off-limits to us. Our living room was used only when guests were over. The rest of the time it was blocked by baby gates, the furniture covered with tight plastic sheeting. We weren't allowed to touch anything in the kitchen, never allowed in our parents' room, and barely allowed to play even in our own rooms.

Our only place of refuge in any of the PMQ houses I lived in was the basement. Mom and Dad gave us a tattered couch and armchair, a rectangle of used carpet, an old black-and-white TV (no cable), and free rein to do what we wanted, as long as we kept quiet. Growing up, I had to keep most of my toys not in my room but in the basement. So it should come as no surprise that even now, I spent most of my time at home in the basement. The former foster home of Grace Cardinal looked like the kind of home I wished I'd grown up in.

The look on Janet Lewis's face was friendly, yet worried. She had already received the bad news about her former foster child, so there was also a touch of grief. I had to be very careful because while tears made for a good story, I didn't want her to become a mess of weepiness. I turned down her offer of milk and cookies but she insisted and disappeared into the kitchen.

There was nervous energy in her walk, but it was nothing unexpected. She had nothing to hide, no skeletons in the closet, no abused children chained to a post in the basement, but she probably had had too many visits by police and social workers in the past few days because of Grace. No doubt this was the nightmare that all parents, even foster parents, worried about.

While she was gone, I wondered if my parents ever had the same nightmare. Not that I would ask them. Mom would dismiss my queries with a wave of her hand and change the subject to talk of the weather. Dad would grunt and tell me not to be stupid.

I took in the place, looking for any photos of Grace or any clues about whether she had been still living here. There were too many photos for me to determine whether Grace was in any of them, but I knew I would have to ask; couldn't have this kind of story without one or two of those. There was also a black address book in the middle of the table. I was about to pick it up and start flipping through when Mrs. Lewis came back into the room.

She was carrying a tray of cookies and started saying, "I'm sorry, my husband is at work," but a couple of kids, seven or eight years old, came barreling into the room, screaming up a storm. One of them clutched a toy, holding it in the air while the other chased him, grabbing for it. "Gimme, gimme," the kid shouted while the other laughed manically. They did a couple of circuits of the room, ignorant of our presence, until Mrs. Lewis reached out to stop the one with the toy. The other kid banged into his back and took the opportunity to grab the toy. They tugged back and forth for a few seconds until Mrs. Lewis grabbed the toy herself. "Jason, Vincent. Please be quiet. We have a guest."

The kids froze as soon as they realized I was there. Even at this young age, these products of the Children Services system knew that I could be a person of authority, possibly someone who had the power to change their lives in the blink of an eye. I didn't, but the way they shrank back reminded me of how I used to act when Dad came home after a long assignment. They clung to Mrs. Lewis, looking to her for protection and at the same time also offering her some.

The one who'd first had the toy, Jason, I guessed, was brave enough to speak. "Are we in trouble?" He didn't look to be native, although I could have been wrong. The look on Janet Lewis's face was loving yet heartbreaking. While she was trying to reassure the children, she knew how the system worked. While I wasn't here to take these children away, one day someone could. "No. No," she said. "Everything's all right."

"It's Jennifer, right, she's in trouble again," whispered the other kid. This was probably Vincent, who with his dark skin, wide nose, and straight black hair was obviously native. Odds were that more than half of the kids who had come through this home were native.

"Shut up," hissed Jason.

Vincent reddened but his foster mother gave him a squeeze. "Nobody in this house is in trouble and nobody is going anywhere," she said. The firm tone of her voice seemed to help the kids relax. She took two cookies from our plate and gave each kid one. "But this gentleman is here about an important matter, so please go back to your room and play there. And be a little quiet."

Vincent and Jason grabbed the cookies but left the room reluctantly. They walked out slowly, looking at the floor, but still stole a few looks at me. Once they reached the threshold of the hallway, they gave me one last look and dashed away, screaming the way kids do when they're having fun.

Mrs. Lewis offered me an apologetic smile and the plate of cookies. I refused with a polite wave of my hands. "I'm sorry to do this at such a difficult time but I'm hoping to get as much information about Grace as I can. At the paper, we're trying to move past her being a victim and to show she was a human being who had a life prior . . ."

Mrs. Lewis, who had been holding in her grief ever since I walked through the door, started to cry. Her sobs were deep and soul crushing. Vincent and Jason, and another foster child, a teen-age girl about fourteen, must have heard the noise and appeared in the doorway. After a second, the girl stepped in and placed an arm around Janet but the two boys stayed back, shocked into immobility by the unexpected collapse of their foster mother. Vincent, the native boy, gave me a look of hatred and fear because he knew that I was the one who had caused this pain.

One of the more interesting features I had written in the past was a story about the employees of funeral homes, and how they dealt with death on a daily basis. Sure, I had seen death more often than the average person but it wasn't a daily occurrence. In that short day or so I spent at the funeral home interviewing the workers as they prepared bodies and worked with their grieving clients, I learned that while it was human nature to try to make those suffering feel better, it was not the best thing to do. Grief was a natural process, not something you have to fix. So those funeral home employees taught me that it was best to be professional, but compassionate. Compassionate, but not cold. And silence, I learned, was the key. In times like this, it was best not to speak until spoken to. In order to get the full story on Grace's life, I would have to wait.

13

Once Mrs. Lewis got herself together and again sent all the kids out of the room, she started to tell me Grace's story. It was good for Grace in the beginning. Although her mother was a teenaged native girl, Grace was adopted by a loving couple. They raised her for several years, giving her the home that normal kids like me got. However, the relationship soured, and the couple split up. Instead of one of them taking custody of their little girl or at least sharing it, they sent her back into the system.

It was hard to imagine, being four years old and having the people you call Mom and Dad tell you that you are no longer important enough for them to take care of you, and you are now going to live with strangers.

For a few years, until she was about ten, it was a lot of strangers. Grace, not surprisingly, wasn't the perfect child after this, and since there was a strong likelihood that her birth mother drank and took drugs during the pregnancy, it was also likely that Grace suffered from fetal alcohol syndrome, which meant she couldn't really think about the consequences of her actions.

While most foster parents were decent enough folks who did their best for the kids they were given care of, it was a tough job, and some foster homes don't always provide the best environment for these kids. There were the odd assholes who were only in it for the money or for the chance to exercise some weird psycho power over a bunch of vulnerable kids. Still, despite the problems, the system worked as well as it could and it was better than sticking kids in a bunch of run-down orphanages like they used to do in the old days.

Grace came into the Lewis home just before her eleventh birthday. "She was a tough kid to get to know, she had a skin thicker than concrete, but she was still a sweetie. So lost, so lonely," said Lewis. "All she needed was a lot of love and bit of structure and that's what we tried to give her."

"How was she in school?"

"The first few months were tough but the important thing with FAS kids is to give them structure. You've got to get them up at the same time, give them a schedule of their day, which class is where, what time is lunch, all that. And it took Grace time to get used to that, but once she did, she flourished. The teachers who first thought she was just another foster kid on the way to being a dropout were shocked at her transformation. She wasn't the brightest student in the bunch, she was never on the honor roll, but she got her work done on time, never skipped class."

"Pretty much a normal kid, you're saying?"

"You could say that. I mean, once she settled in, knew where she stood, and realized that she was going to be here for a while, she was great. It took longer to break through her thick skin, but these kids, you can't blame them for being who they are. Especially her." Tears came to Lewis's eyes. "I can't understand why her adoptive parents could have given her up so easily, she was just a sweetheart."

I shook my head to show sympathy, but I personally knew it was actually very simple to leave your kids behind. You just had to walk out the door, completely convinced that their life would be better without you in it. Sure, there were piercing and intense stabs of pain when I thought about my own, but at least they (and I) were lucky enough to have my ex-wife, who loved and took care of them. I shuddered to think what would have happened to Eileen and Peter if Joan was not there and they were put into the hands of the Children Services branch of the government. Would Eileen have ended up dead in a farmer's field and would Peter be found languishing in some drug den, his body shut down by an overdose? But then again, I was lucky I didn't have to worry about that because Joan would never fail them, never let them fall. In her hands they were safe and didn't miss me at all. At least that's what I kept telling myself.

To keep my emotions in check, I focused on the interview and continued to ask Mrs. Lewis questions to get the rest of Grace's story. She was in many ways a typical teenager. She listened to loud, oppressive music, experimented with various hair and clothing styles, even smoked pot and got drunk a few times, but nothing that couldn't be fixed. In the end, she graduated high school, an incredible feat for someone who came through the foster-kid system the way she did, and she was considering a career in social work or something with kids. She even applied to attend one of the community colleges to upgrade some of her high school classes so she could get into a program.

"Did she attend?"

Lewis said nothing. Only shook her head.

"Why not? What happened?"

"She turned eighteen," she said with a shrug. And that pretty much said it all. One day she was a child, someone the province was required by strong legislation to protect and support, and then the next day, she wasn't. There were a few programs to help such kids with the transition, but since the province wasn't required to support those young "adults," they weren't given a high priority with funding.

"My husband and I talked about letting her live here after she turned eighteen," Lewis said, answering what would have been my

next question, "and we figured we could do it. It would be a bit difficult, we would have to cut something somewhere, but in the end,
missing a few luxuries is nothing compared to helping someone you
love as if she was your own. But Children Services was so desperate
for us to take in another couple of kids or so. They kept hounding
us, 'you got to take so-and-so, he's got no place to go, you have to
take this other little guy because his mother can't take care of him,'
and what do you say to something like that? You can't say no."

Many people did say no, I thought. In fact, most of us say no
most of the time because there are thousands of these kids everywhere, and the number of foster parents willing to take in at least
one kid is tiny compared to the number of kids out there. You
couldn't blame Children Services for pressuring the Lewises and
you couldn't blame the Lewises for letting Grace go. Without people
like Janet Lewis, the lives of kids like Grace, Jennifer, Jason, and
Vincent would be too horrible to imagine.

Of course, a good number of kids like them don't make it and
end up in difficult circumstances like drug addiction, prostitution,
or violent crime, and are dead by the time they turn thirty. But at
least sometime somewhere in their lives, they were lucky enough to
have someone like Mrs. Lewis to love and take care of them. In the
end, it may not seem like anything was done, especially since Grace
was now dead, but there was a time when she got to be a kid without worrying about where her next meal was coming from or where
she would sleep at night. And there was someone who not only remembered her but also would always love her. Not much, one might
say, but it was something.

I didn't want to ask the next question, but I had to. "When did
she start working the streets?"

Lewis looked up at me as if had slapped her in the face. And in
a way, I had. In the space of one question, I had told her she was a

terrible parent and failed Grace. "Grace was a good girl," she hissed at me. "She was."

"I know that, Mrs. Lewis, and you did the best you could. No one could ask for better, but sometimes even the best isn't enough for some kids. And according to the police she was working the streets. They have evidence to that effect."

In truth, I had no idea if Whitford had any such evidence, but her body having been found in a farmer's field outside of the city was enough for me. In this city, the only women found in such circumstances were murdered prostitutes. Facts didn't lie. "Whatever you can tell me won't get her in trouble because it's too late for that. The only way you can help her now is to tell her story, and maybe some of the information you give me, the same information you probably gave the police, will help find her killer. To tell me the truth, that's the only thing you can do for Grace now, except for loving her and remembering her."

I knew I was full of shit, but I felt a need to know more about Grace, to get more of her story. I wanted to find out how she went from a loving home to end up in a field, and I needed to do this to Mrs. Lewis so she would show me and those who read my story the deep pain she was feeling.

Despite what people continually proclaim, they aren't looking for good and happy events in the news. Sure, everyone likes the bit about the kid being saved after falling in a well, or the dog rescued after being trapped on the spring ice of the North Saskatchewan River. But if a newspaper had only those kinds of stories, people would stop reading it.

People want to read about other people's pain and suffering, and they also like to talk about these stories to their friends, family, and coworkers. Many, many years ago, I wrote a story about a horrific murder/suicide in which a father and husband slaughtered his family, also killing the girl who rented the basement suite downstairs before cutting his own throat. Because of the number of people killed and the horror of the story, it ran on the front page.

I did my best to forget it, but when I visited my parents that week, one of the first things my mother asked me was if I had heard about this story, describing the details of the crime and the speculations about who he'd killed first, and so on. I told her that of course I heard about the story because I wrote the damn thing myself, didn't she see my byline on the front page. But she kept going, kept talking about how sad it was, and how this family died and wasn't it horrible and so on. The only way to get her to stop talking about it was to threaten to leave. Even then she managed to slip it into the conversation while we were eating.

So it's true that newspapers cover the "bad" stories in order to sell newspapers because they *do* sell newspapers. It's the kind of thing people read and talk about. But that never made it easier to cover these stories. Lewis had fallen into a fit of weepiness and I just sat there watching her, hating myself for creating such pain and hoping that whatever information she had would help me.

"She would call every month or so and I would try to get her to come home and stop doing all that stupidity and get a real job," she said, blubbering through the words.

"But she said I didn't understand, that I didn't understand who she was, what she needed. The money was too easy and it was kind of fun, which I didn't understand. How could that be fun? But she was FAS, and with no more structure in her life, she had no conception of the consequences of her actions. I tried to tell her that, tell she should come home or at least get help, but she would always laugh at me, like I was some sort of old lady who didn't know what life was about. Jesus, I raised over a hundred kids, I know what life is like, I know what it can do, but she was a kid, they always think they know better. Always. And she was no different. So the last time I talked to her was a month ago, and even though we argued as per usual I told I loved her and to be careful."

"What did she say to that?"

She shrugged, defeated, but strong again. Strong enough to go on because there were other kids in the house who needed her. "She said she loved me and told me not to worry because the girls had it all worked out, they protected each other and they knew to stay away from the yellow pickup."

I sat up with a start. "Yellow pickup? What's that mean? Did she say?"

"I don't know. From what I got from her, it was just an expression her roommate used when she used to go out to work. I don't know what it means."

"This roommate, she have a name?"

"Jackie."

"You have a last name?"

"All I got was Jackie."

"Address?"

She looked at her address book, hesitated for a second, but then decided to give it to me. I wrote it down in my notebook, and after a pause it hit me. "That's only a couple blocks . . ." was all I got to say before Lewis started crying again.

"You don't think I don't know that?" she said through her sobs. "You think I don't know that I could have just walked over and helped her out but I didn't? You don't think I didn't think about doing that but kept making excuses and now she's dead?"

"It wasn't your fault she died. There's wasn't anything you could have done," I said, trying to make her feel better. But she wasn't buying it. Why should she? Like the rest of us, she had forgotten about Grace, maybe not forgotten about her but was too busy with her own life to find the time to help. And now Grace was dead, there was nothing more to be done. She would just become another one added to a long list that nobody was compiling.

Mrs. Lewis waved me away. "I'm sorry, but will you please leave? You got what you need so why don't you just get the hell out of here?" There was nothing mean-spirited in her voice, just a desire for me to leave.

I would have left her right then, but in fact I wasn't finished. "You don't have a photo of her, do you? We need it for the story. We'll give it back, of course, but it won't be right without . . ."

I would have babbled on, explaining why I needed the photo, but didn't. Lewis left the room and a few minutes later returned with what looked like a high school graduation photo. She said nothing when she handed it to me. Instead, she gave me the saddest look in the world, a look that showed she felt more pity for me than I did for her.

14

There was a bit of a line at the bank and for a second I thought about leaving but couldn't. It would be like a heroin addict not shooting up after making a buy or an alcoholic not downing the drink after it's been poured. Every fiber of my being was telling me that what I was doing was wrong, stupid. Pick any word that means that same thing and it had crossed my mind. I couldn't count the number of times I told myself to leave, to give up this stupidity, or how many times I ran through the scenarios in which things went wrong. But all of that was just posturing, just a means to fool myself into thinking that I was under the control of some unseen force and not responsible for my actions.

I was definitely responsible, because I had made the decision to stop at this strip mall, thought about where I should park, determined where I should run if things got out of hand, and worked out all the little details that were necessary when one robbed a bank.

It's something addicts do all the time. The rest of their lives may be messy and chaotic, but there is always a ritual involved in every addiction, a set of steps that an addict takes in order to feed his addiction. Often it's a set of physical tasks, like the heating up of the heroin, the filling of the syringe, and the tying of the band around the bicep, but many times it's mental, and if you were watching from the outside, you wouldn't see it. All you would see is stupidity and self-destruction. But the ritual is always there.

For many addicts like myself, the ritual is also a major part of the rush. The details of seeing where the bank was situated in the strip mall and whether or not there was a back alley nearby to run into if someone gave chase were all part of it. It was a lot like fore-play, getting the juices flowing prior to the climactic event. If I just walked into the bank without thinking about those details and without admonishing myself for being so stupid, then the act itself would feel empty.

The first time I robbed a bank was like that, and while the rush I felt while it was happening and the jolt of adrenaline and endor-phins into my system set me off for days on end, I knew that I had to add more to the experience to create something even more in-credible. I also knew that I was robbing banks partly because I wanted to get caught and be punished for the crimes of my past, while another part of me didn't want to get caught too easily.

So I was ready when someone shouted at me as I made my way across the parking lot after robbing the bank. I knew there was a back alley to the west of the strip mall and I knew that that was the place to go. Trying to escape using the car would have been stupid because while I wouldn't be immediately captured, someone would get my plate and the police would show up at the paper or grab me at home, the sound of their police-issue boots stomping down the stairs to announce their arrival.

So I took off down the alley, jamming the money into the front pocket of my pants. I didn't look back as I ran, to see how close he was to me or if he was gaining because that would only make it easier for him to catch up and also give him a better chance to see my face.

"Hey," he shouted again, and that told me he hadn't started run-ning after me yet and that I probably had a five-second start on him. I rounded the corner of the strip mall, down the short breeze-way, and turned to head down the back alley behind the mall.

There were a number of Dumpsters behind the mall and across from them were a series of fenced backyards. The alley headed in two directions, north and south, and a couple houses down, there was a sidewalk that headed west, away from the mall into the neighborhood.

I quickly assessed the situation, and in less than a second, I made my decision. I pulled off my hoodie, tossed that into a Dumpster, and then my cap went over one of the fences into someone's backyard. I dashed down to the sidewalk, went around the corner a couple of steps, and stopped.

I untucked my shirt, slipped off my glasses, putting them into the pocket where the money was, and mussed up my hair. I pulled my cell phone out of my pocket, held it to my ear, and waited until I heard the footsteps of my pursuer crunching on the gravel of the back alley. I then threw myself back against one of the fences, hard enough that one of the boards cracked but not hard enough that I hit the back of my head. I fell to the ground, my cell phone flying through the air, and shouted, "Hey. Watch it!"

My pursuer appeared around the corner a couple seconds later, his face completely out of focus because I was not wearing my glasses. "You okay?" he asked, bending down slighty to check.

I slapped his hand away. "Fuck you," I bellowed. "You guys are crazy running around like that. You're going to hurt someone, you assholes."

He jerked back as I slapped him, looking west down the sidewalk along the neighborhood street. "Sorry, man. Some guy just robbed the bank and I was just chasing . . . Did you see where he went?"

I rolled over on my hands and knees, searching for my cell. "Who the fuck cares where he went?" I shouted. "As long as he doesn't come back." I found it, shoved it into my pocket, and slowly got to my feet.

The guy reached out again to help but I slapped his hand away again. "And you're fucking crazy, chasing a guy who robbed a bank. You're going to get yourself killed."

I turned and walked away, heading in the direction I had just come from, toward the strip mall. I limped a bit and grumbled to myself to keep up the charade. And I didn't look back to see if he was following me. The whole world was a blur but I still managed to find the convenience store and buy a pack of smokes, using a bill from the robbery to pay for them. Only then did I feel comfortable putting on my glasses.

By this time, there were two cop cars parked in angles in front of the bank. Two cops were inside the bank talking to the staff, while another was heading toward the back alley, guided by my pursuer.

I kept my head down and slowly walked into the parking lot, cutting between various cars until I found mine. I climbed in, gently shutting the door behind me. My hands were shaking so hard that it took me several tries to get the key into ignition. I knew that driving away would be one of the hardest things I would do in my life, but I told myself that if I didn't, it would be over right there.

I took several deep breaths and told myself to break it all down into steps, just do them one at a time, without thinking what would happen next. The first step was to get the car out of the spot. I managed to do that and next I would have to drive the car out of the parking lot without doing something that would attract anybody's attention. I drove the whole way to the paper one step at a time, and while it probably took only fifteen to twenty minutes, it seemed like an all-day trip.

By the time I parked the car in its designated spot, my hands had stopped shaking. So when I signed the car back in, my hands were steady enough to fudge the time on the sheet so it looked like I had arrived a half hour earlier.

15

✱

The next day I went to talk to Grace's friend Jackie. The basement apartment in which they lived was located in a run-down, three-story walk-up. Paint peeled from the walls, the carpets were dotted with cigarette burns and broken glass, and the smell of urine permeated the air. As I stood by the door, the scent of marijuana drifted from apartment 102, and after I knocked, there was the hurried sound of someone scuffling. I saw a shadow drift across the peephole and it became quiet. I knocked again and a bird squawked a couple of times but no one answered. I knocked once more, harder this time, almost hammering against the door.

A tattooed dude in shorts and a wifebeater opened the door down the hall, an angry look on his face. "Shut the fuck up or I'll fucking kick your ass," he shouted, starting to come out of his apartment. I'm not a little guy but neither am I big enough to be intimidating just by my physical presence. This guy certainly was. He was the same size as me but was covered with tattoos, and spewing anger. When he saw me, he moved down the hall.

I could have run, and should have run because he didn't have any shoes and probably would not have followed me out of the building, but I didn't. I was already prepared to bluff my way into Jackie's apartment, to pass myself off as some sort of cop, and since I was already in the zone, I kept it going. I had nothing in the way of a good hand, a low pair at best, but you can never win at gambling if you don't take big chances once in a while. So I put my big bet into play.

I stepped away from Jackie's door, spread my feet apart as if I was standing at ease, slapped my right hand against my right hip and held up the left, pointing the index finger to the sky and my thumb toward the wall, making an L or gun shape.

I had seen enough takedowns, either in person or on TV, to know that cops only use the open-hand *Halt!* signal when directing traffic. Whenever they're directing an actual individual to stop, the hand signal is shaped like an upturned gun, which gives a subliminal signal to the suspect that deadly force is a possibility if things continue down this path.

I also shouted, "Back off!" with that firm and authoritative voice that I'd inherited from my dad, the ex-MP who had been buried with full military honors years before.

With a recent murder victim having lived here, the number of police visiting the building must have increased in the past few days. Not only that, Jackie's neighbor probably had plenty of experience with police himself, because he stopped so quickly that he almost fell over. He caught himself, raised his hands, and backed up a step.

"Whoa, whoa," he said, a look of fear and surprise bringing total destruction to the anger in his face and body. "Take it easy, buddy. I had no idea you were a cop."

"That gives you no excuse to threaten to assault a private citizen," I said, flicking at my belt to give the impression that I was opening the snap of my nonexistent holster. "So I would suggest that you get back into your apartment and hope that I don't call in a cruiser to book you on a six four nine."

I had no idea what a 649 was, but then again, neither did the tattooed neighbor. As far as he knew, he had almost assaulted a cop and was only seconds from being arrested for another crime. He may have started with the higher cards in this deal but he did not end up with the winning hand.

He backed up all the way into his apartment, hands held high, eyes continually staring at my hand against my hip; he slipped back into his apartment, slammed the door, the dead bolt locking and the security chain clicking into place.

I remained in my position all through this and for a few seconds afterward to continue the show for all of the neighbors who were no doubt watching through their peepholes.

I turned back to Jackie's door and figured that I might as well continue in character. "Jackie. I know you're in there," I said, banging with my fist and keeping that authority in my voice. "So you can either open it up and we can talk nicely. Or I can bust it in and we can go downtown. It's your choice."

After a pause, I heard a sigh on the other side of the door. The dead bolt unlocked and the door opened just wide enough to show her face.

She was shorter than I expected, about a head or two smaller than me, and behind the smell of the marijuana was the smell of something that my dad used to call the scent of an old person. Something stale and decaying. Her face was spotted with acne and still carried a lot of baby fat, which was kind of cute now but in a couple of years could easily become a double chin.

"What do you want, cop?" she said with defiance, but I knew it was only an act. Despite being a prostitute she was basically a scared teenager without anything or anyone to support her.

"May I come in?" I asked with my polite voice.

She laughed. "No fucking way, cop. I let you in and that gives you the right to search anything you want. I'm not stupid, you know."

"I'm not a vampire, you know, I don't really need your permission," I said, still with my polite voice. "There's enough of a stink of grass for me to walk past you, but since I don't really care about that, I'm being polite and all. So you gonna let me in?"

She seemed to think about it but I knew she was only stalling. Finally, when she realized that I wasn't going to go away and there was nothing she could do to get rid of me, she stepped back and opened the door. She wore a loose sweatshirt with matching pants. "All right, come in if you have to. I don't really care."

I stepped in but only as far as the entryway. I decided to wait until she invited me in farther. The smell of pot and staleness was even stronger inside. From where I was standing, I could see into the kitchen and the stacks of dirty plates, pots, and discarded junk-food bags on every inch of the counter, the sink, and the stove. The cupboard under the sink was open and the garbage was overflowing, mostly with ashes and cigarette butts.

I took in the scene and filed it in my brain for use in my story, to give a sense of where Grace had lived. I could have pulled out my notebook, but the ones the paper gave us were white with the words REPORTER'S NOTEBOOK on the front. The notebook of a cop was usually small and black, so if I brought out my book, she would realize that I wasn't a cop. And I had no idea what would happen then. Kicking me out was possible, but then again, maybe the guy across the hall was a friend or a client and she would call him over once she realized I was bluffing. I wasn't keen on dealing with that.

"Haven't been out in a while?" I asked.

She shrugged, but said nothing.

"Guess not. Probably not since Grace died. Am I right?"

For a brief second, the look of a scared teenager crossed her face, but she quickly recovered and offered me one of resignation, as if she knew she'd been caught but didn't really care. But she did care, I could feel it. "Yeah, I'm really sorry about that, I know she was your friend. I know it's hard when you lose a friend."

"She wasn't my friend, she just lived here," she said, again speaking with defiance, although she couldn't hide the hurt on her face or the fear in her eyes.

"Okay, whatever you say. No matter. I'm just following up the investigation into her death and I was wondering if you can tell me the last time you saw her."

"Can't remember," she said quickly. "Okay, you done now?"

I ignored her last comment. "You sure? It's really important."

She lit up a cigarette, and though she tried to look tough and cool as she did it, there was a tremor in her hand. "What the fuck do you care?"

"I'm here, aren't I?"

"Big fucking deal. You cops don't care. We know that."

"Who's we, Jackie?"

She looked lost for a second, but recovered. "I was talking about us, you know, me and Grace, that's who I was talking about."

"No you weren't. You were talking about someone else. Who's we?"

"It's the royal *we,* you know, like the fucking queen."

"Nice try," I said with a smile, but also a questioning look.

She puffed a few times and then shook her head. "Okay, you probably know what I do sometimes to make a few bucks, right?" I nodded, knowing that *sometimes* was probably an understatement. "I'm talking about me and the girls. We know you cops don't care. Girls getting killed all over the place and nobody does anything."

In my head, I repeated what she said a couple of times so I could get the quote. I probably wouldn't get it exactly right in the story but it was important to get the gist of it. According to all the information I had, there had been only a few similar killings like Grace's; nothing to get worried about. Were we missing something? But I couldn't let Jackie see my confusion, I had to keep up the charade of being a cop and figured a pithy statement like "We do the best we can" would work. It did.

She laughed; it was a cruel sound. "Yeah, right. That's funny. The best you can. Which is fucking nothing, if you ask me. Grace has been dead for more than a week and you cops keep coming in and asking the same goddamn questions. If that's your best then I hate to see your worst. Don't you guys fucking talk to each other once in a while?"

"So you do remember when you saw her last?" I said, ignoring the comment. "A week ago?"

She let out a disappointed sigh. "Yeah, okay, I remember when I saw her last. She was heading out to work and—"

"By work, you mean out to the streets?"

"Man, you cops are fucking morons. Where the hell do you think she was going? To her corner office to hang with the gang by the water cooler? Of course she was heading out to the streets, to make a few bucks because we were a day late on the rent."

"You didn't go with her?"

That question caused Jackie to lose all of her street toughness and she became a little girl, a girl about the same age as my daughter. I tried to imagine how she'd arrived at this point in her life, what had happened to her to cause her to end up selling her body on the street and living in a dump like this.

The desire to sit her down and spend hours asking questions about her life to get her story was almost overwhelming, but there was no way I could do that because I was here for Grace's story, not hers. Although Jackie's life story was probably just as heartbreaking and sad, she was doomed only to be a character in Grace's story.

Maybe if she died, I could delve a bit deeper, but probably not. The paper had only room for one story of this kind, despite the fact that I could fill issue after issue for years with only the life stories of women and girls like Grace and Jackie.

She looked down at her feet and I barely heard her say, "I was sick. I had the flu."

"So you stayed home, while she went to work?"

"Yeah, she wanted to stay home, feed me soup and shit like that. She was always doing shit like that, but like I said, rent was due so I told her she had to go to fucking work 'cause I couldn't."

"So she left and that was the last time you saw her. Did she say anything?"

She nodded, but said nothing at first. Tears finally appeared and her eyes turned misty. She choked back a sob or two. "She said she'd be back in a couple of hours."

"But she didn't come back, right?" It was an obvious question, but I was looking for a reaction.

"Nope," she whispered, the tears now flowing down her face.

"Did you report her missing?"

Despite her tears, she laughed. "Yeah, right. What good would that do? Nobody gives a shit about a missing hooker." She looked at me for a second and then nodded her head. "Especially you cops, because it makes things easier for you. Just one less street worker you have to worry about, right?"

And she was right. Every year, hundreds of women like Grace were reported missing and nothing happened. If she was white and not a sex trade worker, not someone with a "high-risk lifestyle," there would be a major search, front-page coverage, television vans stationed outside her home, helicopters provided by the army to aid in the search, and pleas from police for tips. And if she was found dead, no effort would be spared, no stone left unturned, to find her killer.

But for Grace and the others like her, nothing happened when they were reported missing, because prostitutes went missing for a number of reasons and not all of them grim. And if a missing prostitute was found murdered, the investigation was usually perfunctory when compared to one involving a "regular" citizen. Once it was declared unsolved, it was filed on another list that no one really looked at because we are probably all scared by the number of woman on that list. Or we don't really care because it was just another dead Indian hooker that got what she deserved because of her choice of career.

In order to not feel overwhelmed by the hopelessness of it all, I returned to my line of questioning. "So she said nothing else when she left?"

"Nope, nothing else."

"Did you say anything?"

"I told her what I always told her when she left," she said, choking back sobs. "I . . . I told her to be careful. To stay away from the yellow pickup."

My heart jumped at the sound of the words. *Yellow pickup.* That was the second time I'd heard that. "What does that mean?"

"Yellow pickup?"

"Yeah, stay away from the yellow pickup. I've heard that before. What does that mean?"

Jackie shrugged "It's just something we tell each other, like don't eat yellow snow, stay away from the yellow pickup."

"Yeah, but why? Why should you stay away from the yellow pickup?"

Jackie said nothing but she bent over, rolled up her right pant leg, and showed me a mass of scar tissue on her knee. "About a year or so ago, I get into a yellow pickup, seemed like a decent guy, nice smile and friendly. Old guy, you know, a bit of gray hair, older than you but okay looking. I don't know why he's picking me up, but I figure, what the hell, a john's a john, don't question, just do the fucking job.

"So we get a few blocks away and he grabs my arm, not in a nice, 'hey, let's fuck' kind of way, but in a 'you're not getting out of this truck and there's nothing you can do about it' kind of way. So I jabbed him in the eye with my fucking finger, and when he lets go, even though the truck's still doing about fifty, I opened the door and jumped out, fucking up my knee.

"Grace wanted me to go to the hospital but I said, 'No fucking way,' they'd just want to know why and call the cops. It bled for a day or so but then it stopped and I kept a bandage on it for weeks and it fixed itself up all right after a while. It looks bad but it's okay. But that's when we came up with, Stay away from the yellow pickup. It means just that, but it also became our way of saying, Be careful."

"So you think she got into a yellow pickup?"

"Yeah, maybe, but what difference does it make? She's still dead, right?"

I nodded and decided that I could no longer keep track of her comments, and slowly pulled out my notebook. But she didn't really see me. She was probably realizing that she was lucky not to have ended up in a farmer's field and then starting to feel bad that her friend did.

"So can you describe what this guy looked like, the one driving the yellow pickup?"

It took her a few seconds to come back and then she shrugged. "Yeah, sure, but will it make any difference?"

"It might," I say. "It might, but to be honest I really don't know."

She nodded, agreeing, but before she did, she saw the notebook. "Hey, you're not a fucking cop, are you?" Jackie said. I looked up from my notebook and saw her staring at me, her face impassive, despite the tears.

"No. I'm not," I said. And then I told her who I was and what I was doing.

"Jesus fuck piece of shit." I was unsure whether she was describing me, herself, or the situation. I started to apologize but she didn't hear me. She stubbed out her cigarette on the wall, not caring about the mark it left. "You know, because I haven't been out working, I'm a bit short on the rent and fifty bucks would really help. I mean, I did help out with your story so there should be something in return."

"I'm sorry, I don't have fifty bucks."

"Twenty, then. Even twenty would help out." She leaned closer to me, the scared teenager completely gone. "I'll give you a blow job. You're not a cop so it would be okay."

I sighed, pulled out my wallet, and gave her the twenty. I passed on her offer of a blow job.

16

✺

I was walking back to the car, furiously writing notes about my interview with Jackie, when a voice said, "I knew you weren't a cop," and I was shoved forward and slammed to the ground. My knees connected with the concrete with a bash of pain to my legs and a shudder so hard that blood spurted out of my mouth as a few of my molars bit into my tongue. I was hit again on the back, this time with something harder, the heel of a boot or a rock that cracked my shoulder, knocked the wind out of my lungs, and drove my head forward to bash into the side panel of my car. There was a blast of light from the collision and then I fell into a well of darkness.

Sometime later, a year, a week, a second, I awoke into the light, a hazy and painful light that jabbed at my head and felt as if it had scraped the top layer of skin from my body. I had a few friends who suffered from migraines and they had told about the agony that light could cause; I now understood them. I couldn't breathe and first thought it had to do with my injuries and that over time the ability would come back.

There was also something heavy on my chest, and as my vision slowly began to refocus on the real world, I realized that the weight came from a knee pressing against my chest. Jackie's neighbor was putting his entire weight on that knee as he leaned forward, his face just inches from mine. Even then I had trouble making him out through the pounding in my head and the haze in my eyes.

Something flashed in front of my eyes, a mirror, a piece of glass, I wasn't sure. But it was sharp, I was sure of that because I felt the point of it pressed against my face, like a sting from a wasp.

"Bet you thought that was funny, didn't you?" Jackie's neighbor growled at me, the bitter smell of cheap booze and cigarettes blowing into my face. "Bet you had a big laugh over the crazy neighbor who thought you were a cop, who thought he was about to get arrested or shot for being stupid. Bet you thought that was pretty funny. But nobody's laughing now, are we, John?" He called me John because that's what he thought I was, a john doing an in-call visit with Jackie.

The wasp sting moved away from my face and a second later I felt it against my ribs. "Having trouble breathing?" he hissed. "That's okay because where you're going, you won't have to worry about breathing. The knife will just slide in nicely and you'll bleed out like a fucking pig. I know you'd like me to say that it won't hurt but it will. Bad."

I felt the pressure of the knife pressing against my ribs, and even though he had broken the skin, he hadn't gone deep enough to cause serious injury. Despite the state of my vision and the pain coursing through my body, I knew he was partly bluffing.

He might have assaulted people, beat them up either in fights or just for fun, but he had not killed anyone. That was a big step that many didn't take, despite the anger, pain, and horror of their lives. It was a big line to cross, even for those who had a history of violence.

But this guy was close, he was near the edge, and it wouldn't take much for him to step over and take me with him. I had to find some way to stop him, and the only thing I could think of in my terrified state was my pants pocket, something that I hadn't taken out the night before and how that might appease his anger.

I was still unable to breathe and that worked in my favor because it made me move my hand slowly toward my pocket. He didn't even notice until my hand was all the way in. And when he did, he pressed more of his weight against my chest, something cracked, and a flare of pain burst through me. He added more by twisting the knife. But he didn't push the blade in deeper, he only made the wound slightly bigger.

"What the fuck is wrong with you?" he screamed. "Are you stupid enough that you want to die now?" He grabbed my wrist with his other hand and yanked it out.

The bills fluttered in the air and it took a second for my assailant to realize what they were and why I had put my hand in my pocket. Then the weight slowly eased off my chest and the knife pulled away from my body. In that second, I gulped several swallows of air and managed to squeeze enough strength in my body to push and roll away.

I half expected another attack, this one with the knife stabbing in deeper and my life thumping away as my heart pumped the blood out through the wound, but for a few seconds there was nothing. Only the sound of feet scuttling around me as Jackie's neighbor scurried to gather up the bills from my recent banking escapade.

I had no idea how much money I had gathered—I never counted—and I wondered if it was enough. Enough that he would leave me alone and let me live, I hoped.

I crawled toward my car, the vehicle now a sanctuary instead of just a means of transportation. And every inch I crawled brought an anthology of agony—my head hammered with every double beat of my heart, every breath brought a gasp of agony and spit of blood, every scrape across the concrete brought a sandpapering across my skin and a torment of bones and joints bruised and cracked by the attack. But still I moved on because I had no choice.

Even with my offhanded bribe, every second I spent near Jackie's neighbor would make it more difficult to escape. I had almost made it to the car, when I felt a knee slam against my back. My head snapped forward but I was lucky; it didn't hit the sidewalk. With my hands pulling me forward, my head connected with my right forearm and it provided a cushion from the cement. It wasn't much of a cushion—there was still a blast of light and pain as I connected—but it was much better than the skull making direct contact with the ground. I figured I had, at the very least, a concussion, but there was a good chance that I didn't have a permanent, or fatal, head injury.

The knee in the back hurt like hell, but the fact that I was still able to breathe told me that Jackie's neighbor had accepted my offer. He wouldn't kill me, but that didn't mean I would be let off easy. "You're lucky I need the money, asshole," he whispered in my ear. "But if I see your ugly face around this neighborhood again, John, I will fucking kill you. Make no mistake about that. I will kill you."

The knee left and I was able to take deeper breaths again, although each one was punctuated with a sharp pain. I made no move to crawl away, because I knew it was over. He had to get his final shots in. A few seconds later, a boot connected with my right thigh and then another shot between the legs. Pain detonated in my groin, and surged and shuddered through my body like the eruption of a volcano against a peaceful and unsuspecting countryside. I retched several times before my stomach emptied itself of its contents. I faded in and out of the dark and light.

17

✳

There was tapping, like a bird on a window. And there was a voice, distant, as if someone was talking to himself in the apartment next door. I first thought I was back at my place, sleeping in my bed. It was spring, the birds picking at the anthill that encircled the house and the students upstairs worried about upcoming exams. But then the sounds rose in volume until the tapping became a slap of a hand on glass and the voice was a polite demand.

"Are you okay, sir? Are you okay?"

The vision of my tiny yet warm place disappeared and as I woke, the memories of the attack flew back, along with reminders of pain in all the parts of my body. My head spun and my stomach protested, retching, but with nothing there, it became just a series of painful spasms. It lasted either a week or only a few seconds, and in that time, I realized that I was no longer on hard cold concrete but on something softer.

Like a drunk coming off a bender, I opened and closed my eyes several times, shaking my head to clear the haze that had settled over me. The tactic worked a little bit, and in the clouded clarity of the moment, I realized that somehow, after the light and dark after the attack, I had managed to get into my car. Or maybe some kind Samaritan had helped me up off the ground and deposited me in it.

I liked the idea of that; the concept of a kind passerby, maybe a witness to the attack, coming to my aid and giving refuge out of the cold air. But then I quickly dismissed the vision. I wasn't in the best of neighborhoods, and though the people who lived here were no more good or evil than those who lived in other places, there was more of a sense of desperation here. No one would probably do me more harm but if anybody did anything to help, they would make a call instead of actually coming over.

I had somehow managed to climb into my car on my own, my body instinctively knowing that an unconscious person in a car garners more respect that an unconscious person lying on the sidewalk.

It took barely a second for me to go through all those thoughts in my head, and a second later, I turned to see who was calling me. The act of just turning my head made the world spin again but I shut my eyes for a second, held the stomach under control, and then took another look. It was a cop, a young cop by the looks of it because his uniform didn't seem to fit right. And now that I was moving, albeit slowly, the sense of urgency had faded from his voice.

"Sir? Are you okay, sir? Do you need any assistance? Would you like me to call you an ambulance?"

I must have looked pretty bad if an ambulance was being offered, but that was the last thing I wanted. Calling an ambulance would force me to make a trip to a hospital to get my injuries assessed, and I didn't want to delay getting back to the office.

With Jackie's comments, I had all that I needed to write the story about Grace, her life and what people thought about her, and I wanted to get that into the paper as soon as possible.

I also wanted to check into the information about a yellow pickup and about more prostitutes being murdered. I probably had nothing but I needed to keep the positive momentum of my career going.

I shook my head, believing that I wasn't as bad off as I really was. "I'm okay, I'm okay. I don't need an ambulance." That's what

I meant to say but it probably came out muddled and slurred because he offered the ambulance again. "Are you sure? To be honest, sir, I don't think you are thinking clearly. I should call you an ambulance."

I did not want an ambulance, and to make my point clearly, I decided to step out of the car and tell the nice constable in person. That would show him. I sat up and pulled on the handle to open the back door, but even those simple tasks brought waves of pain, nausea, and more flashes of light into black and back again. I fell against the open door and would have cracked my head on the cement if not for the quickness of the young constable. He dropped to one knee and, as if I was a little baby falling out of the crib, caught my head in one hand and the back of my neck in the other. He then slowly lowered me to the ground, supporting my head and neck all the way. After he set me down and ensured I was still alive and okay to be released for a second, he made the call.

A doctor shone several lights in my eyes, bright painful stabs of pain followed, and then he wrote a few comments on a chart. "Can you hear me"—he looked at the chart—"Mr. Desroches?" He pronounced the name incorrectly, saying the *s* and using three syllables instead of two.

I nodded, but that wasn't enough.

"I'm sorry, Mr. Desroches, but I need an audible response. Can you hear me?"

"Yes, I can hear you," I said, not being able to resist being a smart-ass. "Can you hear me?"

The doctor smiled. "That's good, Mr. Desroches. A sense of humor is a good thing, considering what you've been through. I understand the police will be wanting to talk to you, but I just wanted to make sure you are aware of your situation before you undertake any strenuous activity. Do you understand?"

I nodded, but then a second later, I remembered I was supposed to speak. "I understand, but I have to get back to work."

"I'm sorry, Mr. Desroches. When I said *strenuous activity* I was talking about things like talking, working, stuff like that. What is it that you do, if you don't mind me asking?"

It took me a second to remember, and in that second I also realized that there was more to this question than just the question itself. "You're testing me, aren't you? Testing my memory."

"Very good, Mr. Desroches. Your cognitive abilities are pretty good, unless you were a leading expert in quantum physics or one of the great thinkers of our time, in which case I'd say your cognitive abilities have diminished. But I am willing to give you the benefit of the doubt."

"You're a funny and strange man, Doctor . . ." I left the sentence hanging in a question so he would tell me his name.

"Reese. Dr. Reese. And I'm sorry if my humor offends in some way but I find it helps in these sorts of interviews."

"Don't worry about it, Dr. Reese. I could use a little levity at the moment."

"That would be an understatement, I believe," he said, his voice turning serious. "But please, could you answer the question?"

"What question?" I said, but when Reese moved to write something on the chart, I jumped in. "Sorry, I was only kidding. I remember the question. You wanted to know what I did for a living."

"Yes, that's correct," he said, and wrote something on the chart anyway.

"I'm a journalist. And I'd like to get back at it as soon as possible."

He nodded and chuckled. "I'm sorry, Mr. Desroches, but that probably falls into a category of strenuous activity."

"But I am talking to you, aren't I?"

"Yes, you are. But as you are probably starting to notice, your breathing is getting a bit labored and you're having a little trouble staying in focus." He was right. Just talking to him was wearing me out and I wanted to sleep. "But that's to be expected from someone who has suffered the injuries you have suffered. Based on the X-rays and the CT scans, I'm glad to see that your injuries, no doubt difficult for yourself to deal with at the moment, are relatively minor and will heal quite quickly, if, that is, you don't overtax yourself."

I heard and understood most of what he said but I had no idea what he was talking about when he said the words *X-rays* and *CT scans*. When had those occurred? And what about the ambulance ride? When had that happened?

Dr. Reese was still talking, saying something about a concussion, lacerations, and bruising, but then he reminded me that if I took things easy, I would be relatively okay. "But no more bumps on the head, okay, Mr. Desroches?"

I managed a nod, or at least I thought I managed a nod. The lights came back, first in one eye then the other. From a well I heard the good doctor's voice calling me. "Mr. Desroches? Mr. Desroches? Are you still there?"

I shut my eyes, shook my head, and I climbed out of the well. At least for a few more seconds. "The name is Desroches, Dr. Reese. De-Rossch. The *s*'s at the front and end are silent and it's only two syllables."

Reese nodded and wrote something down on his chart. "Good. Very good, Mr. Desroches," he said, pronouncing the name as if it was his own. "That's a good start but don't push it. I'm going to let the good constable speak to you but not for long, okay?"

I nodded. Or at least I thought I did. Whatever, the cop came over and spoke with me.

"So you never saw your attacker?" the constable asked again, writing in his notebook.

I shook my head. "He came at me from behind. I never saw him." In my head, I added, When he attacked me, because I was quite sure who had attacked me.

"And you say you have no idea why this attack occurred."

"I'm guessing I was mugged. That's what I thought was happening."

"But you still have your wallet? And your car keys? And if I might add, your car," the constable said without sarcasm. "I'm sorry to say that in most muggings, something is stolen, and in this case, nothing was."

I shook my head. "I had some cash in one of my jacket pockets. And an iPod," I added, lying. "I think he took that."

The constable nodded, again writing in his notebook. "There was no cash on your person, save for a few dollars in your wallet."

"There you go, then. I guess he did take something."

"So do you recall that he did take the cash out of your pocket?"

I shut my eyes and waited for a wave of nausea to pass. These episodes were starting to be annoying but at least they were getting shorter in duration and less intense. "I'm sorry, I don't really recall anything like that. After he bashed my head into the side of my car, it all is a bit fuzzy."

"I'm sorry to be bothering you, Mr. Desroches," he said in all sincerity, pronouncing my name clearly, "but we've found that if we take too long in questioning victims of crimes, especially violent ones like the one that occurred to you, we lose many of the details."

"I know. You're only doing your job. And I would like to help."
But only to a point, I added in my head. "It's just that I'm finding
it difficult to concentrate. I really didn't see my attacker."

"That's okay. Now if you don't mind, this won't be much longer,
but could you please tell me again why were you in that neighborhood at the time? To be honest, it's not a good place for someone of
your, how should I put it, demographic, to be."

Tell you again? I thought. I've told you this story before? I must
have been hit really hard because I had no memory of any previous
conversation with this guy save for the time when he was tapping
on my window. But I didn't want him or anyone else to know that,
because then I'd be forced to spend more time in this place and I
wanted to get back to the office and write my story as quickly as
possible. "I was on a story. I was interviewing someone for a story."

"Yes. A prostitute named Jackie," he said, looking over his notes.
"Unusual subject for a news story, don't you think?" Translated,
that meant, Are you sure you weren't there for her other services?

I shook my head. "Not really. I'm writing a story on the death of
another prostitute and Jackie was her friend. I was getting what we
call background information about the other girl's life. Trying to
fill the holes in a person's life and story. You probably understand?"

Whether he did or not, he nodded just the same. "And you don't
recall an address for this Jackie individual?"

"I do, Constable, but I'm sorry if I won't share it with you. She was
a source for a story, a difficult source if you understand my meaning,
and I would rather that she not be set upon by a number of constables like yourself. Nothing personal, but that would make things
even more difficult if I had to approach her again. As a source."

"I understand that, but as you probably know, the person who
assaulted you was probably someone she knows. Probably her pimp
who *(a)* was upset that you used up much of his employee's time

without compensating her or *(b)* set upon you because she made the suggestion to him that you might be a good mark."

I liked the fact that he was assuming it was her pimp that attacked me. It took the blame away from me and from the fact that I was a john or that I had impersonated a police officer. And it explained my reluctance in revealing Jackie's address. I went along with it. "If that was her pimp, then I'm guessing that the answer is *(c)*, all of the above."

The look of disappointment on the constable's face was obvious. To him, here was a victim of a beating, a beating that landed said victim in the hospital, and even though the victim was quite aware of who may have been behind said beating, he was unwilling to cooperate with the proper authorities in order to bring to justice those who were responsible for his injuries. "In all honesty, Mr. Desroches, it would make things much easier and simpler if you just cooperated fully with the Edmonton Police Service. You are the victim of a crime and it behooves you to help us to find those responsible."

I almost smiled at his use of the word *behooves,* but I held back. Instead, I just waved a hand and shut my eyes, my signal that I had had enough and to ask me more would be futile. Part of me felt relief when he finally got it and bid me good night. But another part felt sad. This constable was a decent person, and had done a lot to help me. In return, I had given him an annoying, unsolved case. I just hoped it would do him good and not embitter him.

18

❈

I spent several more hours at the hospital, most of it sleeping. I was questioned another time by the constable, and after he got the same answers, he placed his card at the side of the bed and told me if I had more information, I should call him. It was only a formality because we both knew I wouldn't call.

The doctor floated by another time, ran through the basic checks, and approved me for release. He also warned me against any strenuous activities and noted that if I suffered from another lack of consciousness, prolonged vomiting, or any other weird symptoms, I should return to the emerg or to a medical clinic for a checkup. Driving, operating large machinery, and any contact sports were verboten. He actually used the word *verboten*.

I thanked him for his fine work, gathered up my stuff, and left the hospital. Based on the reactions I received from passersby in the hospital, the driver and the other passengers on the bus downtown, plus the security guard at the front desk of the paper, I knew I didn't look good.

I thought about heading into a bathroom to check out the damage, but I pushed that aside. If I saw what I really looked like, then I would truly realize the extent of my injuries, and that would make me rethink the idea of going to work and finishing my story. But I didn't want that; what I wanted was to get this goddamn story done and out of the way. If I took time off to recuperate, I'd be going through my notes, and writing and rewriting the story in my head, so I wouldn't get any rest. It made more sense to finish the story and then rest.

The look on Whittaker's face said it all, anyway. It was a combination of shock, horror, disgust, with a bit of concern and compassion mixed in. And to her credit, after she asked, "What the hell happened to you?" she grabbed my arm and helped me to my desk.

I fought the urge to shake her off because in all honesty I needed the help. I sat down at the desk, glad that no one else, Anderson included, was at theirs. It was pretty early in the morning, most of the staff wouldn't be in till later. I entertained the hope that I could get the story done before any of them came in to work, but there was little chance of that happening. I had about two thousand words to write, a massive tome in the daily newspaper business. With my head pounding and the niggling little bits of pain from the minor wounds and bruises on my body, I knew writing this thing would be a major chore. If I got it done by the end of the day, then I would be pleased.

"Do you need anything, Leo?" Whittaker asked.

I was about to shake my head and get to work on the story but I realized that there were two things I needed. "Do you have any ibuprofen or anything like that?" I asked. "But no aspirin because the doctor said that could cause bleeding."

"Shit. Yeah, I got something in my desk from the time I had a root canal. You take it easy and I'll be right back."

I sat back in my chair and fought the urge to sleep. I saw that day's edition of the paper and a thought popped in my head. I flipped through the city section and was surprised that it was there, a short four-column-inch piece buried at the bottom of page B-6 underneath a 18-point hed that read "'John' Mugged." I laughed out loud as I read the story, which outlined how an unidentified man, "most likely a john looking for the services of a prostitute," police were quoted as saying, was attacked in the early afternoon yesterday.

The story quoted an unidentified EPS constable saying that "this further confirms that men seeking sexual services from prostitutes are risking attack from pimps and prostitutes" and also warned that there was a strong possibility a pimp and some of his prostitutes were targeting johns in this manner. That was a nice touch, I thought, because now some johns would think twice about trying to get a prostitute; it wouldn't stop them completely, but at the very least, activity in the areas known for pickups would drop, at least for a few weeks. I was glad that my attack at least had performed a weird sort of public service.

Whittaker came back with the pills and a bottle of water, arriving just as I was laughing at the story. "What's so funny?" she asked. While I downed the pills, I pointed at the story.

"Yeah, I wrote that myself. Came in late last night and if it hadn't had that john business, I would have set it aside." She gave me a funny look. "What's so funny about it?"

"The unidentified john was me," I said, pointing at my face and body. "That's what explains all this."

"Jesus Christ, Leo. You got mugged? What the hell are you doing here? Shouldn't you be in the hospital?"

"Just got out not long ago. I didn't want to go home so I came here. I got all the info on that story Larry assigned and I want to get it all done."

"But what were you doing out there, then? I mean, I'm not one to pry and judge, but shit, Leo, getting beat up by a pimp isn't typical newspaper reporter behavior."

"Tell me about it, but don't worry about it, Mandy, I wasn't trolling for hookers. I was actually talking to one for this story, and on my way back to the car, I got hit from behind and mugged. And it seems the EPS wants to discourage johns from picking up hookers and couldn't resist using me as an example. By the way, I was told not to drive for a few days so I left the paper's car on the street back where I got hit. Sorry."

"Fuck the car. We got plenty of cars," she said, which scored some points in her favor. "But are you sure you're all right? Because you look a real mess. Have you had a chance to look in the mirror?"

I shook my head. "Afraid to. If I see what I really look like, I might actually realize that I should go home."

"You should go home. I'll even drive you myself if you want."

"Thanks, I really appreciate that, Mandy, but I can't. I have a story to finish."

"Fuck the story, it can wait. Go home, rest for a few days, and then come back."

I told her that while that sounded good, I wouldn't be able to rest with the story hanging over me. She said she understood. "But if you're so intent on staying here and working, is there anything else I can get for you?"

I thought about it and realized that every time someone came in and saw me, they would demand to know what had happened, and I would have to go through the whole explanation about the mugging over and over again. I would never get any work done with that. I told Whittaker my thoughts and asked, "Is there an empty office someplace, is some editor or management type out of the office for today?"

She thought for a second and then nodded. "There's got to be someone in ad sales who's going to be out on calls all day. Even if there isn't, I'll get you space there. You have any problems working on the third floor with all the suits?"

"Better there than here. Suits are afraid to ask questions, especially if the person looks like they've been hit by a truck. Fucking reporters wouldn't let me rest." Whittaker nodded and got on the phone. In a few minutes, she found an office in ad sales, a nice quiet cubicle that had a door that could be shut. After getting me settled, she brought in another bottled water and her over-the-counter pain-killers. "If you need me, call me," she said. "And don't be surprised or offended if I drop in once in a while. I won't be checking up on you to see if you're working, I'll just be seeing if you're still alive, all right?"

I nodded but she didn't leave the room. "Is there anything else?" I asked.

"I know I shouldn't be prying but I can't help it, it comes with the territory; every so often I see you taking some kind of medica-tion, prescription type, and I was wondering what it was. That is, if you don't mind me asking?"

Part of me did, but it was only a small part. Every so often, someone would notice me taking my meds but would say nothing save for a continued awkwardness. Only a few would actually have the guts to ask me about them. I told her.

"Never heard of it," she said.

"They're for depression," I said, lying only a little.

She nodded, and for a couple of seconds, I couldn't read her face. Would she keep it quiet or would that become another bit of office gossip? "I take Effexor," she said with a grin. "It's pretty common." And then she left. I shook my head and got to work.

It took me all day to write the story, and the fact that I was in con-stant pain actually made the story sadder and more poignant. Of course that could have been the painkillers talking, but even Whit-taker and Larry noted that my story had something more to offer than the typical feature piece. "If getting beat up can improve your writing, Leo, I'm thinking of implementing a policy that requires all reporters that get into a rut be subjected to the same handling as that pimp put you through," Larry said in a tone that showed he wasn't completely joking.

"He wasn't a pimp," I said.

"Whatever. This is nice work," he said, holding a hard copy of the story. "Whittaker and I are going to edit the shit out of it, tighten some bits up and make other things clearer. Normally I wouldn't make such an offer, but since you went through a lot to get this story I'm going to ask if you want to read it and make comments on what we've done before we send it out?"

"Thanks but no. I'll read it when it comes out," I said. Larry and Mandy were solid editors and the one thing that I've learned in my years as a journalist is that good editors always make a story stronger. There was no need to double-check their work.

"You'll have to wait till Sunday because we're going to run it in the Insight section. We'll have her picture as the entire front page of the section."

"Her name is Grace."

"Right. Grace's face will be the entire front of the Insight section, with a small one as a teaser across the top."

"Great," I said quietly. "That's great."

"Anything else then, Leo?"

"Like what?"

"I don't know, any comments, any additions or suggestions?"

I shook my head.

"How about your personal life? Everything good . . . there?" It was, on the surface, an innocuous question but since Larry knew a lot about my background, it had deeper meaning.

"Except for getting mugged in broad daylight, everything's okey-dokey."

"You sure? You'll be fine?" Again, seemingly innocuous but he was wondering if this attack would push me into my old ways.

"I'm fine, Larry. Really. I'll be fine. I'm going to hurt for the next few days but overall I feel good about things. About the work I've done, about how I'm settling in here."

Larry nodded and for a brief second he smiled. "Good. I've only got two more things to say, if that's okay with you."

"You're the boss, Larry, so knock yourself out."

"Okay, first off. This is great work, Leo. One of the best stories I've read in the past few years in this goddamn place, and one of the best pieces I've read in my entire career. We are, that is confirmed, going to put you up for a bunch of awards this year."

"Thanks, Larry. That means a lot. Not the awards but what you said." And it did. Larry was a friend, but first he was a damn good editor. High praise from him meant something.

"Okay, now that I've been nice, I have to tell you that you look like shit, and in all honesty, looking at you is making me sick. So go home. Do you need a cab or anything?"

"No. I'll be fine."

"You sure? It's no problem, I'll pay it out of my own pocket."

"Thanks, Larry. But really, I'll be fine."

"Okay, then. Then get the fuck out of here. You're also scaring the entire ad sales department and we need those people working in order for guys like you and me to get paid."

19

With Grace's story written, edited, and set for Sunday's Insight section, and the fact that I had been recently assaulted, I was given some free time. It wasn't officially time off—I had to be in the newsroom during most of the day—but I wouldn't be assigned anything until Monday. That is, if I didn't come up with a story on my own. I was free to do that, but since everyone had agreed that my story was a success, and that I had gone the extra mile to get it completed, I was free just to sit on my butt, surf the Web, or read a book for a few days.

I was quite tempted to do the book thing, sit back with my feet up and bask in the glory of a well-written piece of work, but that weird energy of the newsroom kept gnawing at me. All those people furiously working, doing phoners and typing words, made it impossible for me to do nothing. But I wasn't keen to ask for an assignment, so I scratched an itch that had been bugging me for the last few days.

Two people, Grace's foster mom and Jackie, had mentioned a yellow pickup truck and the danger it may have presented to street prostitutes. To them, it seemed that somebody had been picking up prostitutes and killing them at an alarming rate, but the numbers from the police and our files didn't match. Was the yellow pickup just a fairy tale told by prostitutes to warn of bad johns or was there really someone driving a yellow pickup and killing prostitutes?

I pulled up those Infomart files that I had dug up, the ones of bodies found in a manner similar to Grace, and set those aside. And then in my notes, I found the name of that Mountie, the one who had been glad that Grace had been found in the EPS's jurisdiction and not his. He had said something that I couldn't recall but I thought I had written it in my notes. I flipped through and found it, just after Whitford's comments about giving Grace a face.

" 'Thank God means I get to go home and watch some hockey tonight instead of filing the paperwork on another one of these,' " was the quote I had in my notes. Like Jackie's, I had written this comment down afterward, and it may not have been word for word what he actually said, but it was close enough. What the hell did he mean by "another one of these"? He said there had been a few similar but did those match the ones that had been printed in the paper?

I found the number for the Strathcona detachment and when I found the Mountie I wanted and reminded him who I was, I asked him if he could give me information on those cases he had mentioned.

"Take a while," he said.

"Define a while."

"Couple of days. Depends if we get busy."

"So it's no problem."

"Shouldn't think so, but you might want to check with media folks in K Division. They like to be kept aware of stuff like that. In fact they'll offer to handle the request personally for you, but in the end, they'll come to one of our members here to do the actual work, so I might as well get a head start on them," he said.

K Division was the headquarters for the RCMP. They were based in Edmonton but they oversaw all of the detachments in northern Alberta. In most parts of Canada, every major city had its own police department. Some smaller cities and towns also did, depending on their need, budget, and desires. Provinces like Quebec and Ontario also had their own provincial police: OPP for Ontario and Sûreté du Québec, respectively. The rest of the country was served by the Royal Canadian Mounted Police, those famed Mounties who were descendants of the NWMP, the Northwest Mounted Police.

In 1873, the Canadian government, barely six years old, established the NWMP to provide a government presence in the Northwest Territories, the huge tract of land west of Upper Canada (Ontario) that included what now comprises the provinces of Manitoba, Saskatchewan, Alberta, and the area that is still called the Northwest Territories.

With so many European settlers moving into the area, the Canadian government wanted a modicum of law and order to be present in these new lands. They had seen how the western lands of the post-Civil War United States had become the lawless Wild West that we enjoy today in movies and on TV and their mostly British backgrounds couldn't abide such anarchy. So they decided to make sure that when people arrived to settle the Canadian west, there would already be a police presence. They also hoped that having a government presence in their open lands would make those wild Americans rethink any plans to increase the size of their country.

Another side effect of the NWMP was to stem the flow of the "demon liquor" from Montana into southern Canada, where it was wreaking havoc among the population of Canadian Natives. So Colonel James McLeod and 150 members of the newly formed NWMP headed west and a legend was born. The RCMP still serve in Canada. Almost every single town with a population over five thousand has an RCMP detachment and the members of the detachment serve the rural and smaller communities within that area.

The detachments are entities onto themselves, with a commander overseeing a complement of Mounties whose number depends on the size of the town and area they cover. K Division is the upper management of these detachments and provides centralized services like forensics, media relations, and support for crime too serious or important for a local detachment to deal with.

I thanked the Mountie for his time, found a number for the media contact of K Division. When I got hold of her and told her what I was requesting from the Strathcona detachment, she also noted it would take a couple of days. Maybe more if I wanted similar information from the other detachments in the surrounding area.

"Other detachments?" I asked, and then immediately remembered that Edmonton was surrounded by a series of detachments covering the suburban and bedroom communities, which included Sherwood Park to the east, St. Albert to the north, Leduc to the south, and Stony Plain and Spruce Grove.

Calgary, which was the other major city over a million in Alberta, had annexed many of its bedroom communities in the sixties and seventies, places like Bowness, Forest Lawn, and Midnapore, so it was mostly one big metro area. Edmonton had let these communities remain separate from the city itself. Therefore, it was surrounded on all sides by some of the larger communities in the province. There was talk of turning the entire Capital Region into a megacity, like what had happened to Toronto and its suburbs, but the feelings of animosity between Edmonton and its surrounding communities ran deep, despite the fact that a majority of the population of the other cities worked in Edmonton and made use of many of its services.

So there were four major detachments around Edmonton, not to mention the many rural towns within a fifty-kilometer radius. I told the fine RCMP media relations consultant that it would be great if she could get me information from the other detachments.

The info came in slowly. First, as expected, the Strathcona detachment, which covered Sherwood Park and the county around that city. My Mountie friend had compiled a list of four incidents similar to Grace's murder. Over the next few days, one detachment at a time, more information came in. I felt a chill start to set in. And with every new list, that chill got deeper. I had spent two years living on the streets, through a couple of the toughest winters this city had to offer in the last two decades, and there were only a few cities in the world that had colder, tougher winters than Edmonton. But the chill that settled into my bones after adding the numbers from the last list to the total of cases similar to Grace's was harsher than anything I had felt during those two years. What made it worse was that every single case was officially listed as "open." And that meant that not a single one had been solved.

20

✳

"You have to be fucking kidding me." That was the response from Detective Whitford when I asked him, on the record, if the Edmonton Police Service was investigating the possibility that there was a serial killer on the loose in the city.

"Is that your official response?" I asked into the phone. Like most of the other reporters on staff, I had no time to set up an appointment so that I could interview Whitford in person, so I had called him. At first, he wasn't keen on talking to me, but the higher-ups in the EPS had liked the story I had written about Grace. They liked the fact that at no point in the story did I lay any blame on the police for Grace's situation—although according to one of our legislature reporters, the minister responsible for Children Services was mighty ticked. The higher-ups also liked the line in which I noted that Grace's life story would have never come to light if it hadn't been for the assistance of some friendly members of the EPS.

"If your paper would print the word *fuck* and it doesn't annoy the shit out of our media relations, sure," he said with sarcasm. "But the chance of that happening is about the same as the chance that a serial killer is on the loose in Edmonton."

"So what is the official response?"

"The official response to your question about whether the Edmonton Police Service is investigating the possibility that there might be a serial killer on the loose in the city is, 'No.' We are not investigating that possibility."

"Why not?"

"Because based on our evidence, there is not a serial killer on the loose on the streets of Edmonton. And I cannot stress that enough. At the moment, the Edmonton Police Service has no evidence that there is a serial killer operating within the limits of the city or within the surrounding Capital Region. And to put forward such an idea does nothing for the public good. In fact, to make such a suggestion will only hurt the public good because it can create fear where no such fear is warranted."

"But what about the other cases that I told you about? What about all those women apparently killed in similar fashion and found in similar locations in areas around the city?"

"Having a number of incidents that are, on the surface, I might add, similar, does not automatically mean that a serial killer is operating. Police do not and cannot make these kinds of assumptions whenever there are crimes that may seem similar, because if we did, it would dramatically reduce our ability to undertake our investigations."

"How could saying that there might be a serial killer in the capital region reduce the police's ability to do their investigations?"

Whitford sighed. It was a sigh I recognized and used when I tried to explain how the media really worked to those outside the industry. People have so many assumptions about the newspaper business, about how reporters actually work, and I guessed it was the same with the police.

"Okay, let's say, just hypothetically, that police say that they are investigating the possibility that there is a serial killer. And I'm going to stress that I am being hypothetical here; I don't want this to come back and bite me in the ass the same way letting you into the tent did, okay?" I thought he was speaking rhetorically so I didn't respond. But he wasn't and after a pause, he added, "I need you to say okay, Leo, to confirm that I am only speaking hypothetically."

"Okay."

"Okay what?"

"Jesus. Okay, I understand that you are only speaking hypothetically, you are not confirming in any way that Edmonton police are admitting that there is a serial killer on the loose. How's that? Cover your ass enough?"

"It better. Okay, so we've established a hypothetical situation in which police are investigating that there is a serial killer loose. The problem with that is that now the focus has a tendency to go to one person doing all of these murders or ones that have similarities. It's not a conscious decision or action, mind you, but it does happen. At the same time, there tends to be more pressure from superiors to solve the case, to find a suspect when a case comes up that at first seems to be part of a large case. Then, if through further investigation it doesn't fit into that large case, unfortunately that case can be shunted aside and treated as secondary, as not as important as those that are part of the serial case."

"I get that, makes sense, but it also brings up another question: What do you say about criticism that police aren't treating these murder cases that seriously because most of them involve women who are sex workers, and a good number of them Aboriginal women? Is there any truth to these kinds of suggestions, that their lifestyle and race play a role in how much importance a case is given?"

"The lifestyle or activities of a person are completely and totally irrelevant when it comes to the importance we place on an investigation of a homicide or a missing person," he said. "And in all honesty, Leo, I am insulted by such suggestions, whoever has made them, because as a homicide investigator, I treat all of my cases with the same dedication. I put the same amount of effort into the investigation of every single homicide that comes across my desk. I couldn't sleep at night if I didn't treat every single case with the same amount of effort as the next."

"What about Allanah White? Did her case get the same treatment as any other homicide case?" Allanah White was a suburban mother of two, who one day several months ago didn't show up for work, despite the fact that her husband reported that she had left for work that morning and her car had been found parked in its regular spot at her office's underground parking garage.

By the end of the work day, there was a major investigation under way with search teams, sniffer dogs, helicopters buzzing the empty fields near her northeast neighborhood, and pleas from police and her husband on the TV news for any information. Her disappearance was the talk of the town and became national news a couple of days later when police, with the help of her husband, found her body in a shed in a field a couple klicks from her home.

For the next couple of days, the police released little information, except to confirm that the body they found was Allanah's. In the meantime, and despite the suspicions, her husband played the grieving spouse, giving interviews to anyone who would listen, crying about his loss, the suffering of his children, and stating his innocence. After a few days of quiet, police charged him with murder and he was awaiting trial. Most expected him to be convicted.

"I don't understand the question," said Whitford.

"Well, you guys seemed to have pulled out all the stops to find Allanah White, but in many of these cases I've told you about, the investigations seem to have been pretty perfunctory. At least when compared to what transpired in the White investigation. If you claim that every homicide investigation gets the same treatment, then how do you explain the differences in how Allanah White and these other cases were handled?"

"First off, let me just say that I was not involved in the Allanah White investigation so I cannot and will not make any comments about it, except that prior to the discovery of her body, the Allanah White case was being treated as an abduction, not as a murder. Hence the search," Whitford said, a tone of irritation rising in his voice.

"And second, I let me reiterate that I make the same investigative effort in every single homicide case that comes across my desk. I do not discriminate based on who the victim is, where they come from, what they look like, or any other differences. Every murder is a tragedy and deserves the same amount of treatment and investigation. And to imply otherwise is an insult to me and other members of the Edmonton Police Service."

"Not every cop is like you. Some cops don't have the same ethical commitment that you do, right?"

"If you're trying to get me to publicly criticize other members of the Edmonton Police Service, that's not going to happen," he said. "As far as I'm concerned, all members of the Edmonton Police Service undertake their duties to the best of their abilities."

"Yeah, but some cops have better abilities than others," I said, and then waited for a response. It was a typical interview technique, to make a comment but then say nothing for several seconds. Most people abhor silences during a conversation and do their best to fill them up with something. And usually, that's where a lot of reporters get their best comments. But Whitford wasn't a typical interview subject; as a homicide cop, he probably used the same technique to get suspects to slip up.

My silence was returned with silence of his own and it took almost seven seconds, a long time to have no one say anything in a conversation, before I gave up. "So again, despite the similarities in these cases I have mentioned, you or anybody else in the Edmonton Police Service refuse to admit that there is a serial killer on the loose in Edmonton?" I asked, continuing the interview.

"Sorry, Leo, I won't use the word *refuse* in my answer or respond to your question in any way that will enable you to quote me in a manner that tells people the police are refusing your suggestion," he said with a laugh. "Nice try, I'll give you that. But I will reiterate that the Edmonton Police Service is not investigating or putting forward the idea that there is a serial killer operating in the Capital Region. And we strongly urge members of the public not to become fearful and worry about such things because in Edmonton we believe that there is not a serial killer operating."

"You sure?"

"Listen, Leo, I know you are only doing your job, but off the record, I am a little worried about you."

"Worried? In case you haven't noticed, I'm doing a hell of a lot better than I was last year. I probably need a new place to live, but other than that, things are gangbusters."

"I know that, and I congratulate you for battling your demons and doing what you can to make your life better. But about this serial killer, I know you believe you have some evidence suggesting such a thing, and though I don't want to tell you how to do your job, are you sure your . . . uh, I don't know . . . your personality isn't making this thing bigger than it really is?"

"What the hell are you talking about? I'm fine, I told you that."

"Yeah, I know, but you have a tendency to chase after things that don't need to be chased after. Remember Charlie?"

His comment hit me like a punch in the stomach, a hard one in which the breath is knocked out of you and you feel like you're never going to take another one again. Charlie was a friend of mine from the time when I was a street person. He was one of the smartest people I had ever known, a former law student I had met in one of the many homeless shelters in the city. I was reading a newspaper and he came up to me, surprised that I was actually reading the newspaper and not flipping through the pages, glancing at the headlines and searching for the comics.

He was native like me, but unlike me, he looked it, had the darker skin, the long straight hair, the higher cheekbones, slightly broader nose, and almond-shaped eyes. Charlie also suffered from paranoid schizophrenia, and from time to time, he would disappear, sometimes for days, sometimes for weeks, sometimes longer.

One day a couple years ago, after realizing that Charlie had disappeared, I went in search of him. I met Whitford when I filed a missing person's report about Charlie and he was investigating the death of a man who matched his description. In fact, my little room in the basement used to be Charlie's.

"What the fuck does Charlie have to do with this?" I demanded.

"Did you find Charlie?"

"No."

"And why was that?"

"Fuck you," I hissed into the phone, trying extremely hard not to slam it down when I hung up on him.

21

✺

Whitford's comments about Charlie pissed me off so much that I went into "I'll show you" mode. The story about the serial killer was not like my search for Charlie. Someone was out there killing street prostitutes, I was sure of it. The list of cases and names did not lie. And if the EPS wasn't willing to accept the evidence and admit the truth, then I would find someone who would.

I went through the police-beat Rolodex and found the names of a few professors of criminology at the local U. The first two were actually sociologists who specialized in other areas and both suggested a professor whose name was at the bottom of my own list. His name was Blake Creighton. When I explained who I was, and outlined what I was looking for and wondered if he was the correct person to talk to, he said he was, quickly outlining his knowledge to confirm.

He first asked to meet me in person so he could get to know me and possibly explain himself better, but I nixed the idea. This was a straight-up hard news story and I didn't need any of the descriptive bits that I included in the longer piece on Grace. I just wanted his comments, so there was no need to meet him in person.

And it was already late afternoon and I wanted to get this story into the next edition. I had no time to drive to the southside, look for a parking spot near the U so I could meet some professor in a coffee shop or his office for an interview that I would have to transcribe from my notes once I got back to the office a couple hours later.

Besides, I was still feeling the aftereffects of being beaten up. My head throbbed constantly, my vision was fuzzy, and there was still a red tinge to my urine. Just getting to work was a struggle in itself. I didn't go into those gory details with the professor, I just told him I was on tight deadline for this and didn't have time to meet in person.

I outlined the information I had, told him of my serial killer theory, and asked him for an opinion.

"From a criminologist's point of view there are too many coincidences to deny the likelihood of a link here. When you have a number of dead women being found in and around in the city, usually in similar locations such as farmers' fields, ditches, and such, and these victims have been murdered in a similar fashion, it is not unreasonable to speculate that there is a very strong possibility that a serial killer is operating in the Edmonton area," he said matter-of-factly.

At my desk, I raised my fist in victory and in my head I shouted, Yes! With that comment, I not only had my story, I had my *fuck you!* for Whitford's comments about Charlie. As the good professor continued, I began typing the lead to my story: "Despite repeated denials from police, a serial killer is mostly likely operating in Edmonton, says a prominent criminologist."

"That's not to say that all of these women were killed by the same person, but there's a good chance there's one person responsible for a number of them," he went on. "And by definition, that's a serial killer, someone who kills more than three people over a long period with a cooling-off time in between the murders. The murders are usually committed in the same fashion and the victims usually have something in common such as gender, race, occupation."

"So the killer is actually looking for female Aboriginal street prostitutes?"

"Possibly, but the sad fact is that a large number of prostitutes in Canada happen to be Aboriginal. So mostly likely, this serial killer is targeting street prostitutes and it's just the odds that a majority of them are Aboriginal."

"I know it's an obvious question, but why prostitutes?"

"Prostitutes, by the nature of their profession, and the fact that they are willing to climb into an unknown vehicle driven by a stranger, are easy targets for a serial killer," he said. "And these women, who live what police call high-risk lifestyles, are not known to be as reliable in their comings and goings as members of regular society. So when one of them doesn't show up at work the next day, nobody's phoning her at home to check if she's sick or filing a missing person's report because she hasn't shown up for a couple of days or even weeks.

"It's usually only when a family member realizes that they haven't heard from so-and-so for a while that the police are made aware that someone might or might not be missing. And by then, if something of a heinous nature has occurred, odds are police will have little or nothing to go on because even if a body is found, the trail is really cold. Much of the evidence is lost, disturbed, or has been washed away by the elements. I don't envy the police in these situations."

"But why are police so unwilling to admit there is a serial killer? I've given them the same evidence that I've given you but all I get is repeated denials, 'there is no serial killer operating in the Capital Region,' over and over again."

"It doesn't matter where you go in the world, police are always unwilling to admit that there is a serial killer at work," Creighton said. "It's a highly explosive term, conjuring up images of Hannibal Lector, Jason from *Friday the 13th*, Ted Bundy and all that, when in reality most serial killers, despite the acts that they commit, are for the most part loser misfits who like to prey on the vulnerable for whatever reason. So you can understand why the police won't just come out and admit there is a serial killer on the loose in the streets of Edmonton.

"The term strikes terror into the heart of the average citizen and that's one thing the police don't want. They want people to be vigilant about crime but they don't want people to live in fear. At the same time, it puts a lot of pressure, political and otherwise, on the police to apprehend a suspect. When they don't do so as quickly as people hope and expect them to, that can have repercussions, not just throughout the police service but in all of their political dealings, such as with the local police commission, and their dealings with the general public, be it writing out a ticket for speeding or directing traffic. Quite simply, the public could lose faith in their local law enforcement and that would be a bad thing."

"But wouldn't it make more sense for the police to go public and suggest that there might be a serial killer at work? Wouldn't that make all those who fall into the high-risk category take precautions and also spur the public to provide tips that may lead to the killer?"

"Let me explain a couple of things Mr. Desroches. First off, they call it a high-risk lifestyle for a reason. That said, I have no doubt that street prostitutes are already aware of something happening and are taking whatever precautions they think are necessary."

I told him what Jackie had said about the yellow pickup truck and the warnings that were given.

"There you go. Frontline workers are already more aware of what's happening than those who are supposedly in charge. But to your comment about tips from the public, that's good but only to a point. If the Edmonton Police Service announced that they were looking for a serial killer and wanted tips from the public, do you know what will happen?"

"They'll get hundreds of them."

"More likely they'd get thousands. And while many would be made in good faith, there would be some provided for nefarious reasons, to get back at a brother-in-law someone doesn't like or at a neighbor who lets his dog bark too much. But even out of those made in good faith, only a few will actually lead somewhere and most likely they won't lead to the specific case at hand. Despite what Hollywood shows us, the majority of serial killers are caught because of luck. They forget to pay their parking tickets, like the Son of Sam, or they get pulled over in a routine traffic stop, like Ted Bundy. It's very rare that law enforcement officials capture a serial killer through their typical investigative processes. It does happen, but those kinds of cases are still quite rare. And that's not a slight against the police, it's just the way it is."

"Okay, having the police telling the public that there might be a serial killer may not be the best solution, but shouldn't they, at least internally, admit to themselves that there might be serial killer and establish some type of task force to deal with the problem?"

"Oh, no doubt there are probably some members of the Edmonton Police Service who do suspect that there might be a serial killer at work and are quietly working on it. There's nothing official and I bet there's a good chance that they haven't said anything about it to their superiors."

"Why the hell not?" I asked, a little too loudly.

"Well, that's just typical of any major public institution with a large bureaucratic side to it. The frontline workers may know what's really going on but on the higher and administrative side, nobody really wants to go out on a limb and admit something bad may be happening."

"But what if they are right, but they didn't say anything?"

"Well, they can admit that they didn't know at the time, that they didn't have all the facts or that the evidence at the time didn't reveal as much, and now with the new and correct information at hand, they are ready to move forward," he said with a laugh. "That's just basic politics. I'm surprised, Mr. Desroches, that with you being a journalist, you weren't aware of that."

22

✸

It was the kind of story that journalists live for. A giant headline:

Serial Killer on the Loose?

with a subhead of:

Bodies of 16 Women Found in Capital Region

Brent was assigned to help me by going through the list of sixteen names and writing a side piece with their names in chronological order starting with the first victim, Lydia Alexandra, who was found in 1988, to the most recent, Grace Cardinal.

And not only was our coverage a scoop, it made its own news. All of the local media outlets ran stories on it, using the information in the paper for their own story, but at the same time acknowledging that it had come from us. And the resulting blowback meant there were several follow-up stories, press conferences, and all the other fun things that reporters live for. Even though I had started the story, it had taken on a life of its own and all I had to do was keep riding it until it wore itself out. Every day for about a week I was writing something new related to it. Not of all of the stories were groundbreaking and some of them were just follow-ups on info broken by other media outlets—including a TV bit about how police had a list of sixty-three women who fit the profiles of the other victims and had been reported missing over the past fifteen years.

But through it all, the Edmonton Police still claimed that they were not investigating the possibility that a serial killer was on the loose. The media relations people, now the *only* police officials commenting on the story, kept to their talking points: "Despite the perceived similarities in these crimes, the Edmonton Police Service are not investigating the possibility that there is a serial killer operating in the Capital Region" and similar comments, reworded and reframed over and over to sound fresh but to mean the same thing.

After a week and a half, it was over. With all the media in the city clamoring for the story, we finally beat the horse to the ground and the ride ended. The story wasn't dead, it would linger in the background, but it would only start up again if the police arrested someone or another body was found.

And in that lull, I made the call that I had been thinking about for a couple of months. A few weeks ago, I had actually dialed it a couple of times before hanging up, but this time, I made it through until the first ring. After that happened I knew I couldn't hang up and let it go.

"Hello, Joan," I said when the phone was answered after the third ring.

There was a pause on the other side, maybe I heard a sigh, or I was just imagining it.

"Leo. I was kind of expecting you to call," Joan said, her voice showing no emotion, although she had plenty of reasons to be emotional about a call from me.

Joan was my ex-wife. We had met almost two decades ago when I was the editor of a small-town newspaper and she was the vice principal of the local elementary school. We married after a three-year courtship and stayed together for about seven years, producing two children, Eileen and Peter.

In the years of our marriage, I had two falls into gambling. The second one occurred not long after we moved to Edmonton so she could take an administrative job at Alberta Education. We almost lost our home. Both times she took me back, although following the second incident she took total control of our finances.

There would have been a third transgression into gambling for me in our relationship but I left before that could happen. She didn't chase me, not even for payment of child support, because she was smart enough to realize that she wouldn't get it. Sometime, somewhere in the haze of my fall, she divorced me and put all her efforts into raising our children.

"That's kind of unusual, isn't it, expecting me to call?" I said, trying to sound as casual as I could. At the same time, the hand that wasn't holding the phone was shaking and my bowels started clenching in nervous tension.

"Actually it's kind of obvious. I've been seeing your byline for the last few months, and then once checks started to arrive, I've been wondering when you would actually call. Thanks for the checks by the way, completely unnecessary, but any little bit helps, you know."

No, I don't know. You were the one who raised the kids, I thought. Out loud, I said, "Yeah, now that I'm working, I figured I should do something. I know it doesn't make up for missing payments all those years, but . . ." The tendons in my throat clutched, cutting off my words.

My relationship with Joan had been the most intimate one of my entire life; she knew everything, she knew all that I had done and all that I was capable of, for better and worse. And for years, she accepted it, forgiving the worst and putting all of her being into trying to help, trying to keep me on track with our life. But there's only so much a person can keep on their plate and she realized she had to choose between helping me or raising our children, and as per usual for her, she took the wisest course. I knew it probably hurt her dearly to cut me loose but I knew it also came as a relief.

Once again, she saved me by getting to the point. "So is this just a 'Hey, how ya doing?' call or do you have a purpose for conversation?" she asked.

"A little bit of both, I guess."

"Well, I'm doing good, the kids are doing good, and I see that you are doing good. What else?"

"That's it? No details? No catching up on what's been going in your life?"

"No," she said firmly. "That's all you get at the moment. State your business, Leo."

"That's pretty cold, Joan."

"Well, we do live in Edmonton. You should be used to it by now. But really, seriously, Leo, I'm glad you are back on track again and I really do appreciate the checks, I really do, but don't expect anything more out of me. I don't have it."

"Well, I was expecting something small," I said tentatively.

"Then get it over with and ask."

"I was hoping, now that I'm back on my feet and respectable again, I could see the kids, you know, maybe take them out for lunch, a movie, something like that."

There was silence for a long time. Joan was a great mother and great mothers are extremely protective of their children. I imagined her pacing the room with the phone in hand, imagined her giving the phone an angry look and a silent scream. Finally she came back. "That's a big thing, not a small one."

"Yeah, I know, but it's been a while since I've seen them and—"

She cut me off. "That's not my fault. Don't blame me for that. You made your own choices, Leo, and that was one of them."

"I know that and now I'm deciding that it would be good if I could see the kids. Only for a brief moment, an hour or two. And then if it works, maybe I can start to try and establish a relationship with them."

"God, Leo," she said, her voice cracking. "You are really pushing it here. Really pushing it."

"Yeah, but I felt I had to ask, even though I have no right to, I felt I had to at least do that."

There was another long pause, much longer than the other one. I waited it out, said nothing, let her make the decision without any verbal input because if I campaigned further, she would feel pressured and it would end in an instant.

"I can't make this decision right now. I can't. It's too big and important," she said. "And I'm going to have to ask the kids. They're both old enough to be a part of this decision, so you're going to have to wait. You will have to wait for us to make this decision. And in the meantime, please don't make any more calls about this until you hear from me."

"I can do that," I said, a little bit of hope rising inside of me.

"That wasn't a request. I don't want to hear from you at all until I get back to you. I want no passive-aggressive phone calls pretending to be about something else, you got that? And if I don't get back to you, then the answer is no."

She called me a couple days later. "There's good news and bad news, which one do you want first?"

"The bad, I guess."

"Okay. Eileen wants nothing to do with you. If you want me to quote her exact words I can but the gist of it is, No, thank you."

"What did she really say?" I asked. I hate getting things second-hand or via heresay. Getting the actual quote is always the best.

"You sure?"

"Hit me."

"When I mentioned your request to her she said, and like I said, these are her words and her punctuation: 'No fuckin' way. I can't believe you're even asking me such a thing, Mother. Not even if he was dying of some debilitating disease. I never want to see that prick again. No. Fucking. Way.' Those periods are hers, in case you were wondering."

"Jesus. Nice vocabulary on the kid."

"You asked. And after she said all that, she stormed out of the room and we haven't said much to each other since."

"Sorry. Hope she won't be mad long."

"She'll be fine. It's just that the topic of you is a very touchy subject."

"Again, sorry."

"It's a bit late for that. That's just the way it is. Anyway, the good news is that Peter is okay with it. He's a bit apprehensive but he wouldn't mind seeing you for a bit."

My heart rose to the ceiling. One out of two wasn't bad and I felt that if I made a good impression on Peter, showed him that his dad had it all under control and was willing to be an important and positive part of his life, then maybe he could convince his sister to give me a small chance. The probability of such an occurrence was still pretty slim but I had won against worse odds, so I was positive.

"That's awesome," I said with a bounce in my voice. "When can I pick him up?"

"First off, there are a bunch of ground rules and these are nonnegotiable. If you don't like any of them, then too bad. Suck it up or forget about it. Understand, Leo, I'm very serious here, very serious, and there will be no negotiations in this area."

"Okay, I understand. No negotiations."

"The first rule is that at no time will you pick him up at this house or drop him off here. I will not have you coming to our house and disrupting our lives with your presence. Already you've created a bit of a mess and I don't want it escalating further."

"I can meet you guys anywhere you want."

"Good, but before we decide on that, there are a few other stipulations. I will not, will not, you hear me, leave you alone with my son until I know for sure he will be okay and is safe. I'm honestly glad you are trying to get your life back, and truly hope that this time it will work, but when all is said and done, I don't trust you worth shit, Leo. There is almost nothing you can do to gain back that trust, but at the very least I can try to help you create a relationship with your son.

"I know what you and your father went through and I see a lot of you as a little boy in Peter. He's a great kid, bright, funny, and with lots of friends, and he's done really well, considering the history of his family. But he always seems to be missing something, like there's a tiny hole in his heart. God, it would kill him if he heard me talk about him in this way, but I can't help it, I'm his mother and he's my little boy."

Her voice cracked and I could tell she was speaking through tears at that point. "That's why he reminds me a lot of you, of a lot of those stories you told me about when you were a boy. It's pretty obvious that your relationship with your father, or lack thereof, played a major role in them. And maybe if I can do something to help improve the situation between Peter and his father, then maybe I can help fill that hole a little bit." It took her a moment to regain her composure, and when she came back, she was strong and unyielding.

"So while I'll let you see my son, you'll have to see him with me there first. There is no way I'm letting you take him out by himself until I believe he'll be okay. Okay?"

"Sounds fair to me." It was more than fair, I thought.

"So wherever we decide to meet, probably some coffee shop, I will be there with him and I will stay with him until both he and I believe that I can leave. At first I might move to another table nearby or whatever, but just be prepared for me to be there and for the possibility that you may not get any alone time with him. And that, as I said, is how it will be. None of this is negotiable."

"Yeah, I got that. But what if he wants you to go, but he doesn't want to stay in the coffee shop? What if he wants to go somewhere else, like maybe see a movie or something like that?"

"As long as you tell me exactly where you are going, how long it's going to last, and give your cell number so I can call you, that should be okay," she said.

"And one final thing, if at any time you do anything stupid or cause my son to be hurt or threatened in any way, you will have blown your chance with him. If Peter feels even the slightest bit uncomfortable with your actions, then that's it. We will no longer tolerate any connection or contact with you. I will tear up any and all checks that you send to us. I will change our phone numbers, and if you make any attempts to contact us in any way, I will go to the police and seek a restraining order against you. And if I'm in a really bad mood when that happens, I will go to your boss and get him to kick your ass."

"That's pretty harsh, Joan."

"Tough shit, Leo. Let me show you how serious I am about this," she said angrily. "As soon as your name appeared in a byline in the paper, I did some checking for myself and discovered a familiar name on the masthead, one Larry Maurizo, who I remembered from the paper in Olds. And that's how I knew how you got hired. And when you called me about the kids, the first person I called was Larry and I grilled him about you. He remembered me, of course, and he was quite helpful answering all my questions without flinching. In fact, he was more than willing to help me."

"Jesus Christ, Joan, you didn't have to take things so far."

"Yes I did," she said, jumping in. "These are my children we are talking about and there is nothing more important and precious than my children."

"They are my children, too—"

"No. They are not. They are not! You are only their father because we just happened to be married at the time they were born and you were around for a few years afterward. But when you left and never came back, that's when you ceased to be their parent. And when it comes to my children, I am highly protective of them, especially from their father.

"So I don't really give a fuck if you don't like the fact that I talked to your boss about you. And in truth, you should be thankful I did because until I talked to Larry, there was no way I was going to let you see your children. It was partly because of him that I'm going to let you see Peter. However, despite that, Larry is with me and agrees with my stipulation that if you fuck up in any way, you will lose all contact with them. I will protect my children at all costs. Make no mistake about that."

Part of me was angry at Joan for going over my head and talking to Larry about me. It seemed like an invasion of privacy to bring my family life and its difficulties to work, hanging over me like an unreported crime.

At the same time, I was glad that my kids had someone like Joan protecting them. She could be tough, but she was also very loving. When you have kids, you are given no guarantee on how they will turn out, but with someone like Joan looking out for them, Eileen and Peter had a better chance than most. And that's what I tried to focus on, that Joan was only protecting the kids, and I should be thankful for it.

So I apologized, and accepted all of her conditions. And we made plans.

23

❋

"Leo Desroches," I said, when the call came in.

"Mr. Desroches. We haven't seen you yet at class and I got to wondering if you were just humoring me the other day." The voice sounded familiar, a bit of the slur and dance on the words, but I couldn't place it.

"I'm sorry. Who am I talking to?"

"The name's Francis Alexandra. We met the other day at the Native Friendship Centre. You made a nice speech about your mom and then ran out of the room."

My face heated up at that memory, and at the same time I recalled the elder who had offered me a cigarette later on outside. "Yeah, yeah. Mr. Alexandra, I remember now. Sorry that I didn't recognize your voice."

"Actually, if you could call me Francis, that would be much better."

"Sure, Francis. No problem. What can I do for you?"

"Well, I seem to recall that during our nice talk outside the Friendship Centre, you mentioned an interest in attending Cree classes. And it's been a few weeks and you haven't attended yet so I was wondering if you were just humoring me."

"Actually I believe it was you who expressed the interest in having me attend the Cree classes."

He laughed, an easy, warm laugh. "Probably it may have been

my idea in the first place, that's been known to happen. But I do recall that you said you'd consider it and I was wondering if you had."

I hadn't. I had been so busy since that time that any thoughts about attending something like a beginning Cree class barely crossed my mind. And if it did, I probably just shunted it aside. I have never been good at big life changes or participating in activities that may compel me to rethink my life and my roots. When I was growing up, Dad was gone weeks or months at a time for exercises or whatever things the army did. And even when he was home, he wasn't really there because he was usually drunk, passed out on the couch within an hour of arriving. Mom worked as a clerk at a major department store, and even though her presence was the key stabilizing influence in our lives, she was the classic codependent.

Also, because Dad was in the army and we were forced to move every two or three years, we were experts at packing up and starting fresh, at least physically. Changing our addresses was second nature but that came with a cost. In order to keep things stabilized in a world that was always moving, we all had to remain in the physical and emotional roles in which we were cast. Doing things like discussing our feelings or moving out of our expected roles would only upset things and create chaos in our world. We may have moved in time and space a hell of lot more times than the average family, but none of us truly made any emotional changes. We were, me especially, stuck in the same rut we grew up in. It was something we were just used to.

So even considering learning a new language or "getting in touch" with my Aboriginal roots would be a huge step. I imagined myself at the Cree language classes, being the only adult in the room, surrounded by the little Crees, with their straight black hair and their smiling, dark eyes, giggling and whispering to one another as all kids do when someone does something stupid, especially an adult. I would be more comfortable reading a book at home or sitting in a casino, playing cards.

"Yes, ever since we talked that lovely fall afternoon, I've been watching your work. And I must admit you have been busy," he said. "The story on that poor young prostitute was very compelling. Quite sad but compelling. I know little about journalism and writing but in my opinion you are a fine writer."

"Thanks. I appreciate that." And I did. Normally when people comment about a story in the paper, even a positive one, they have some complaint about it: something was missed, they were misquoted, or if they weren't misquoted then their words were taken out of context or they didn't truly mean what they said when they said it. It was rare for someone other than another journalist to say something positive about the actual writing.

"Yes, but about the Cree classes? Any chance of you attending in the next little while?"

"You know, learning a second language at my age, I don't know, I don't think it's in me."

"You never know till you try."

"Yeah, that's probably true but they keep me pretty busy here."

"I'm pretty sure they must give you time off now and again. And besides, it might make a good story in your capacity as the new Aboriginal issues reporter."

The guy was relentless, just couldn't take a hint. His idea for the story was not bad, but at the moment I really didn't want to probe myself and make it part of a new story. There was no way I was ready for that kind of thing.

"You know, Francis, I think I'll just come straight out and say, although it does sound intriguing and it would probably make a good story, I don't think I'm ready to attend a Cree class right now.

Let's just say, life's a challenge at the moment. Maybe later but not now."

"Oh, sorry to hear that," he said, and if he was disappointed I couldn't hear it in his voice. "I understand. It's tough for people who were not raised in an environment that was open to their Aboriginal culture. They tend to choose well-trodden paths. Either they completely submerge themselves in it, accept everything they can about Aboriginal culture and, in a sense, reject their Western upbringing as being wrong and harmful. Or they've consciously or unconsciously bought into the concept that being native is something to deny and be ashamed of. They resist and reject anything to do with their Aboriginal heritage because of that. Or they feel they aren't native enough to be allowed to accept these new things.

"But one thing most people forget is that just because they are accepting this new side of themselves, it doesn't mean they have to reject the other side. And even though they haven't been raised in traditional or stereotypical native situations like living on a reserve or with parents who were open about their culture, it doesn't mean their Aboriginal experience is less valid than the experience of those who have. It's just another part of the whole Aboriginal experience.

"So maybe learning a new language like Cree may not be the right first step for someone like you," he went on. I was going to say something about how this wouldn't be my first step in being exposed to native culture and life, because in my past there had been some other experiences, but I didn't feel like explaining myself at the moment. So I let him continue. "But I think there might be another way, one that doesn't involve as much commitment as learning a new language but one that can be as powerful."

I sighed, knowing that I had to give this guy something or he would never let me go. "I won't have to dress up in any regalia, dance around, or do anything like that?"

"All you have to do is sit there," he said, adding, "and be open to whatever comes your way."

"No one will be asking me how I feel about things?"

"No. You only have to share your feelings if you want to. No one will be asking. In fact, if you don't want to say anything, you don't have to. Silence is fine."

My first reaction was to refuse. But I knew if I did, Francis would call me again and again. And if I kept refusing, there was the possibility that he might call Larry and complain. And I didn't want Larry on my ass. The only way to deal with this was to accept the invitation and see what happened. If it was interesting, I could move further. If it wasn't, I could say I tried, but it wasn't my cup of tea. "Okay," I said, a touch of reluctance in my voice. "I'm in."

We set up a date on the weekend. He wanted Saturday but that was the day I was meeting Peter. So we made it for Sunday.

24

✳

I forgot how Joan could always take my breath away. She wasn't what one would call a classic beauty, she didn't have the Botticelli features, didn't have the alabaster skin, a cute button nose, or all the accoutrements that men are told defines beauty. If you focused on her features individually, her wide eyes, her small mouth, her tall, big-boned body, you wouldn't look twice. However, if you took in the whole package, it was something to write home about.

She also had a presence, a charisma, created by her keen intelligence that caused almost everyone to watch her as she entered a room, even though they had no idea why, since she didn't possess the lean glamour of a supermodel or the hourglass figure of a centerfold model.

So when we started dating, there were a bunch of other men hovering around, teachers, a lawyer, a car salesmen, and a district agriculturist—typical small-town professionals—and they still attempted to be part of her life when we became an official couple. They cornered her at parties, asked her out for coffee after school, pretended to be her friend, and all the time she was oblivious to their attempts to upgrade their friendships. It was only after we got married that she realized the truth, because, one by one, her old male friends disappeared.

And even though she married me, I never understood why. But that feeling was typical for your average male who doesn't believe he is God's gift to women. You never understand why you were chosen, even when you are told the reasons. You are happy that you were chosen and sometimes you can go for a very long period without questions, but every so often you find yourself staring at your wife, wondering, Why? Why me? What made me so special that she chose me over all the others? What did I have that the others didn't? And then when she notices that you are looking at her, she can't help but wonder what the hell you are doing.

"What are you thinking?" she asks.

And the only thing you feel comfortable in answering her is, "Nothing."

Joan had a few more wrinkles and gray hairs than the last time I saw her, but nothing about her had really changed. She still commanded the attention of the coffee shop when she walked in and she still took my breath away, especially when our eyes met. A shiver of excitement ran through me when that happened, the same shiver I used to get as a teenager and some girl that I had a crush on happened to look my way.

Unfortunately, the look of disappointment on Joan's face also reminded me of those same teenaged crushes. No doubt those girls were disappointed that I was the one watching them, and Joan was probably disappointed that I had managed to turn up. I was also glad that the bruises on my face from my attack a couple weeks ago had faded. They would not have made a good impression. As it was, I was still sore and stiff in many spots but the headache was less intense and my vision was clear.

But I didn't dwell on that for long. Standing next to Joan was my son, Peter. If Joan's presence took my breath away, Peter stopped my heart. It had been almost five years since I'd seen my boy, and though I mentally told myself he had aged, I expected to see a taller version of the kindergarten kid I left behind. I was completely caught off guard by the person standing next to my ex-wife. I first thought he was just someone who had walked in with her, some skater kid in a hoodie, looking to pick up a coffee on his way home from wherever skater kids went.

But then I realized that this kid, this almost teenager, was my son. He had lost most of his baby fat and his face was much more angular, but at the same time, his body had filled in, giving him some heft and a presence similar to his mother's. His hair was even more unruly than I remembered, and as he looked up at me, there was none of the preschooler inquisitiveness in his eyes, none of that wide-eyed stare that every four- and five-year-old gets when confronted with something new and interesting. There was curiosity, of course, a hopefulness, but it was mostly covered with a layer of vigilance. That look broke my heart and made it soar at the same time.

When they arrived at my little table, I also realized how tall Peter had grown. When I last saw him, he was barely over three feet tall, the top of his head reaching my waist. Now, the top of his head was almost to my shoulder. I couldn't help but blurt out, "Look at you. You're so tall!," and that sent a blush across his face and caused him to shrink back toward his mother.

Joan did her best to break the awkwardness by offering a hand, but I made things worse by trying to pull her in closer for a hug or a kiss on the cheek. She held her place, loosening her grip to tell me that despite our past intimacies, we were now strangers connected only by our children and even that connection was tenuous. I had no qualms about admitting to myself that Joan probably looked at our relationship as the biggest mistake of her life. For me, it was the opposite.

We ordered some drinks and pastry—I made a point of paying for everything—but the combination of my nostalgia for our relationship, her defensive and protective stance, and all the other baggage that we carried around about each other made our conversation stilted and banal.

We talked about the weather, any old friends we happened to know, what kind of car she drove and if she liked it, and bits about our jobs. As for Peter, it was worse. He barely looked at me, and because I was so fearful of saying and doing something wrong, I questioned him like some out-of-touch relative, asking him stock questions about school, about his favorite subjects, what he liked to watch on TV. In return I got one- and two-word answers and nothing else. It would go down in history as the worst interview of my career, and then I realized that I was actually interviewing this kid, trying to get answers to a list of questions rather than trying to really get to know him.

So for a second or two, I looked him over, saw how he sat, saw that the hoodie he was wearing was faded with age and a bit tight on his shoulders, which told me that it was, probably much to the chagrin of his mother, one of his favorite pieces of clothing. And by noticing the logo on the front, I found my way in.

I asked him a question about the Oilers, the local pro hockey team. But instead of just asking whether he thought the team would do well this year or something as basic as that, I mentioned the name of a player the team recently signed and asked Peter if that player should be moved up from the third line to the second. He froze for a second, and for the first time during our meeting, he truly looked at me, wondering if he had heard the question correctly.

"What did you say?" he asked, puzzled.

"I asked if you think he should be moved up to the second line," I said. "I mean, he's been contributing much more than anyone else, but for some reason, they seem to keep holding him back, making him more of a checker when he's really more a playmaker. I think if they move him up with some scorers, the Oilers really have a chance of creating more goals than they have lately, right?"

Peter's face lit up, and for the next couple of minutes we went back and forth on the Oilers, the merits of this and that player, the state of the team, whether the number of teams in the league was diluting the talent base, all the stuff that Canadian hockey buffs obsess about. Even though I knew the lingo and some of the details, I wasn't as much of a hockey freak as my son, but then again, I wasn't a ten-year-old boy growing up in Edmonton.

Getting caught up in the comings and goings of the NHL was still as much a male rite of passage in Canada as drinking your first beer or touching your first bra strap. Joan cared nothing about hockey, and while her eyes glazed over with boredom, I could tell she was pleased that a connection was made between me and Peter.

And while we talked, I came up with a plan to ensure that Peter and I would meet again. "Ever been to a game?" I asked, knowing the answer. Despite Peter's being born in Edmonton and being a longtime fan of the Oilers, I was pretty sure that he had never been to a game. With even the cheapest nosebleed seats costing about fifty dollars apiece, it was not economical for families to go to a game. And with Joan not being a fan, she would consider such an expense frivolous.

When Peter said, "No," he gave his mother a quick and dirty look, and she tried to defend herself by explaining how much tickets cost.

I interrupted her. "You wanna go to one?" I asked Peter.

There was a moment of stunned silence, with Peter and Joan both staring at me as if I was crazy.

"Seriously?" Peter asked.

"No, this is not happening," Joan said at the same time.

I nodded to Peter. "No problem. You know where I work?" I

said, and he nodded, the look on his face showing me that he made the connection. "I can make a couple of calls and it should be no problem."

"Like live at the Coliseum?" he said, shocked and surprised, now looking at me with frank admiration. "That would be fucking awesome."

"Peter!" Joan snapped in her teacher voice.

"Sorry, Mom," he said with only a bit of humility in his voice. I did my best not to smile, remembering my own childhood when we were around friends, away from our parents, and we would swear like sailors. It was good to see that some things didn't change between generations. "But could I go to a game?"

Joan said no over and over again but she was fighting a losing battle. She knew her son inside and out, so even though she didn't like hockey, she knew that going to see a live Oilers game was probably one of the biggest dreams of his young life. And to deny him this would reverberate throughout the rest of their lives. At the same time I could see her seething anger just below the surface. This could have been the perfect excuse for her to cut Peter out of my life completely, but I knew that her love for our son, and her knowledge that this might become a turning point for our relationship, was more important.

As for me, I knew I was being completely manipulative and would no doubt get an earful from Joan about it later. But I also knew that Peter's first meeting with his dad after not seeing him for years would be more memorable than he'd thought possible. For a few short hours I would be his new hero and that was just perfect, even if there were deeper repercussions.

Finally she acquiesced, and the way Peter smiled, the way his whole face lit up, the way he looked at me as if I was the greatest person in world, made my heart burst with the same delight that I had felt on the days he and his sister were born, when I first held him in my arms and realized that this was my child and that any and all of the preconceived notions I had had about children and child rearing were lost in a moment of pure joy. I just basked in the smile of my son and hoped that in time, I would get more and more smiles. And maybe he would talk to his older sister and one day she would smile at me in this way, too.

25

❊

The next day, I was at the Native Friendship Centre. The doors were locked and since there were no windows in the concrete block of a building, I couldn't tell if anybody was inside. I knocked and the sound of my pounding echoed inside the building. Still, nobody answered. I checked my watch. I was a little late, but to be honest, I was secretly pleased that the door was locked because even coming here was a big step for me.

And now that the door was locked and nobody was answering, I had my excuse to step away. I was free to falsely congratulate myself for at least trying. To continue with the charade that I was really looking forward to this, I kicked the door in frustration. "Fuck it," I said, and began to walk back to my neighborhood, a couple klicks away.

As I walked away from the door a large pickup pulled into the lot. It spun in a half doughnut, spraying me with a bit of gravel. The passenger window rolled down and Francis waved at me. "Leo. Sorry to keep you waiting," he said. "Come on, let's go."

I walked up to the truck but didn't get in; I leaned against the door, sticking my head halfway through the open window. "We aren't going in?"

He shrugged, only a tiny movement of the shoulder and a tilt of the head that could be saying a million things, anything from Sorry, to I don't know; from Land? Man cannot own land, to The white man had more guns and apparently a tougher God so we just had to do what we had to do to adjust to the genocide. No white man I know has ever shrugged in that way. It reminded me of my mother and how she always responded when I asked if she knew if Dad was going to be home in time to drive me to hockey. "This was only our meeting place," he said. "Get in."

"Where we going?"

"You'll find out," he said, smiling. "Get in." I hesitated for a second, a bad feeling sliding through and past, but then I realized I might have had some residual feelings from Jackie's comment about avoiding yellow pickups. I shook it off and climbed in.

"Excellent," he said. "You're going to like this."

We headed down 111th, to the west end of the city. Francis's pickup was clean and in good shape on the inside, although the shocks bounced every time we hit a bump. That could have been the state of the truck or the state of the Edmonton roads. The cycles of bitter cold and dry summer heat Edmonton faced year after year wreaked havoc on the city streets. The city had several dedicated crews with the sole job of patching potholes and cracks in the streets, but they always had a tough time keeping up. And the heaving of roads as the frost rose from the ground every summer didn't help. After a few minutes of nobody talking, Francis finally broke the silence.

"I hate to be the bearer of bad news but the honest truth is that there are a number of people in the community who are, let's say, a bit disappointed in the stories you've written so far. They haven't really fallen in to the category of stories that they were expecting from the new Aboriginal issues reporter."

"Is this just you talking or is this really a concern from the community?" I asked a bit angrily. I hoped that this wasn't his main reason for meeting with me. "Because you did say you enjoyed my writing about the young girl who was murdered."

"Yes, I did enjoy the writing, although not the topic of the story," he said. "However, I am not one of those who are disappointed in your stories. I was just giving you the heads-up that there are people upset at these stories and that some have expressed an interest in contacting your superiors in order to let their views be known."

"I can deal with a few complaints," I said, although I didn't completely buy his explanation. There might have been some others concerned about my story but I bet he was one of them. "It's all part of the job. But just for fun, what are they saying about my stories?"

"I think the phrase is they aren't 'reflective of the true nature of the urban Aboriginal in Edmonton.' Their words, not mine."

"They don't like the fact that there might be a serial killer hunting native women in the city and that the police in and around the city were completely unaware of that possibility because many of these victims were native? They would rather that kind of news be kept quiet and that the deaths of these women continue to be dealt with with indifference? Is that what they want?"

"Nobody wants that, and though many are appreciative of how you uncovered that news, there are also many others who were hoping for more positive stories from you. Stories that would focus on the more positive aspects of being an urban Aboriginal."

"Ah! A series of feel-good stories, showing positive role models like a successful native businessperson, politician, artist, musician, somebody like that?"

"Exactly."

"And we're supposed to pretend that all those other natives, the ones that live on the street, the ones in the foster-care system, or just those who have more difficulties than the average person, don't exist."

"Of course not. We should do what we can to help those people, but there are those who were hoping that an Aboriginal issues reporter would not just cover the less typical Aboriginal issues such as homelessness, addiction, land claims, and so on."

"And the more positive stories would be better."

"To some, yes."

"That doesn't make sense."

"Leo, you have to understand that in many ways, the native community in Edmonton is no different than any other community in the city. So you can't expect them to act any different. Human nature doesn't make sense and one thing people have a tendency to forget is that natives are, at the core, still human," he said with a laugh.

"We don't have a higher understanding of goodness, badness, spirituality, nature, or anything. We're not all drunks living on the street, but then again, we're not all shamans with an innate sense of the natural world. We're pretty much like most everyone else in this country except for one difference."

"And what's that?"

"It doesn't matter what kind of native you are, whether you were raised in a reserve or not, whether you were exposed to the culture of your people or not, or whatever your life experience, every single Aboriginal person in Canada, in North America, suffers from a great wound. The wound of losing everything, of being forced out of the lives you lived and the homes and the land you lived in for thousands of years because the Europeans came across the Atlantic and took over the country.

"It's a cultural wound similar to the wound suffered by African Americans because of slavery and the wound suffered by Jews because of the Holocaust. I have it, you have it, the people who want you removed as the Aboriginal issues reporter have it. The difference is in how natives deal with it.

"For example, there are those natives, some of whom are those who want more stories about positive natives, who have a tendency to ignore the wound. They believe it's not good for natives to rehash the past. The future of the Aboriginal peoples is in the future and we can't remain in the past. This attitude is understandable because there are also many natives who revel in the wound, who believe that your status as an Aboriginal is equal to how much you have suffered because you are Aboriginal.

"Someone like you, who probably never lived on or visited a reserve, isn't truly native because even if your life was hard for whatever reasons, you haven't endured the typical native suffering.

"But both attitudes are flawed because if you ignore a wound, it just festers and will only kill you in the end if you leave it too long. And if you keep poking at the wound, never allowing it to heal, it will also kill you in the end. The trick, of course, is to find a balance between the two, to realize that there is a wound, to accept that the wound is bad, almost a mortal one, but to also realize that the wound can and should be healed so you can move forward. And when the wound is healed, you must never forget it."

"That's it? As simple as that?" I asked. It was typical pop psychology, probably true in a sense, because no one could deny the suffering that Aboriginals around the world had been through. But it was also some of the same language that I had heard when I sat through those Gamblers Anonymous sessions so many years ago.

I also knew that usually when people talk like this to someone they've just met they are doing one of two things: *(1)* trying to convert me to their way of thinking, or *(2)* using the lecture as a roundabout way of telling me something else. I figured the first choice because despite what he said earlier, I would bet that Francis wasn't as completely happy with my story as he claimed. He was one of those who hoped for more positive stories about urban natives and no doubt he would have liked to have been the topic of one of those stories. I didn't fault him for that; it was a normal reaction. Everyone believes their story is important enough for the newspaper or that they know of a story that is.

"No, it's not that simple," Francis continued. "Not everyone is as fluent in language as you or me, and even if they are, they lack the emotional awareness of themselves. They lack the language to describe what they are feeling and the emotional capacity to change their lives. People like those natives who live on the street, like those drunk Indians everyone complains about, like those girls who end up dead in a field outside the city, people like . . . Oh, here we are."

It was a small acreage on the west end of the city, just near the outskirts, an area where the suburban sprawl was starting to eat away at the outlying wilderness of the city. There were a few other trucks and an old camping trailer set near a clump of trees and he parked next to them. He shut off the engine, and before he climbed out, he turned to me and smiled. "Come on. I think you're going to like this."

I climbed out, curious to see what I had been invited to. I could hear voices quietly speaking somewhere in the trees, but instead of heading toward them, we went into the trailer. Francis handed me an old bathrobe and I stared at it for several seconds.

"What's this for?" I asked.

"I know it's a bit unusual but for this ceremony it's suitable to remove all our clothes and wear this," he said. "However, since it's your first time, no one will mind if you want to keep your underwear."

He then turned and started to remove his clothes. By then I had a fair idea of what was ahead and started to get undressed. And though I was keen and intrigued about attending my first sweat, I couldn't help but replay the last part of our conversation. He never got to finish the sentence but I knew what he had been about to say: "People like you."

26

There were five men, all around Francis's age and dressed in similar robes, gathered around a fire pit.

"Hey, fellas, sorry we're late," Francis said with a laugh. "Traffic was a bitch."

They turned at the sound of Francis's voice and he introduced me to the first man, Noah. He was one of the older ones, tall, with salt-and-pepper hair tied into two long braids and an expansive stomach that Buddha would have been proud of. I really didn't want to reach out, open my robe, and expose my almost naked body in order to shake the proffered hand, a mammoth callused paw that should have belonged to a bear, but I had no choice since he was also offering something in the other hand: something wrapped in a bit of yellow cloth. I hesitated, looking at Francis in confusion.

"Tobacco and cloth. It's the standard offering. Normally they would give them to me since I'm going to be leading the sweat, but since it's your first, they wanted to give 'em to you. Go ahead, take them. This time, it's bad form if you refuse."

Shocked that I might be insulting this elder, I quickly reached out, one hand to shake and the other for the gift, but he enveloped both of my hands in his, a warm and welcoming vise. I was shivering in the crisp fall air, but he looked as comfortable as if this were a warm summer afternoon. "Thank you, Leo, for joining us for this sweat." Noah said, his voice deep and rich. "We promise to be gentle." There was a soft chuckle from the group and a bit of a grin as Noah squeezed my hands a bit tighter.

My face turned red with a slight embarrassment but I still managed to respond. "Thank you. It's all I can ask for."

The group laughed and Noah smiled, showing all his teeth, many of them black. Then he released me, stepping aside and tapping me on the shoulder. One by one, the other elders were introduced, shaking my hand and offering a pouch of tobacco wrapped in cloth: Jeffrey, like Noah with braids and a large stomach but younger; Louis, short hair, about my height but skinny; Daniel, braids and skinny like Louis but a bit shorter and with a boxer's nose; and finally Lucas, older and looking a bit like Francis, but white.

Francis also offered me tobacco and cloth but then took all the offerings out of my hand and placed them in a pile near the door of the lodge, next to a small shovel. The lodge was about four feet high, a dome covered with stained blankets and carpet remnants. A long flap of carpet hung over the opening. "Okay, fellas, thanks for coming. We'll be heading in, Leo will go first since it's his first, and then I'll sit next to him and you guys come in whenever you're ready. Louis, if you don't mind, will you tend to the grandfathers?"

Louis nodded, and as a group they removed their robes and tossed them over a lawn chair by the fire pit. Francis put his arm around me and shepherded me to the door of the lodge. He flipped the carpet to reveal the opening and made a sweeping motion, left to right, with his hand.

"When you move in the lodge, whether you're coming in or going out, you have to move in a clockwise direction. Since I'm leading the sweat, I'll be sitting right across the pit from the door and I want you to sit to the north, which, if you're facing the door, I'll be on your right, got that? I want to keep an eye on you during the sweat, make sure you don't pass out or anything." He gave my shoulders a squeeze, removed his robe, draped it over his arm, and held the same hand out for mine. "Ready, Leo?"

I didn't know how to reply. I was a mix of emotions. I was looking forward to this sweat, looking forward to experiencing something totally new, elated at being invited to participate in this spiritual event, but also apprehensive.

I didn't know what was expected of me, I didn't know if my presence would temper the celebration, didn't know how I would react to the heat. I had been in saunas before but I had no idea how hot it would get in a sweat lodge. I hoped my body could handle the heat and that it or I didn't do anything stupid to spoil the experience, not just for me, but mostly for everybody else. And even though I had made a joke about it, I hoped that I would hold up.

I nodded in response to his question and he smiled. "Everyone who enters the lodge gets a smudge. Takes away the negative energy and brings in the good," he said, taking a piece of braided sweetgrass from a pouch and lighting the edge with the fire that heated the stones. Then he took the bit of smoldering sweetgrass, flapped it gently so the end glowed brighter and more smoke rose from the tip.

Based on one or two other experiences with Aboriginal ceremonies that I'd seen, I knew I was supposed to pull this smoke toward me, rub it into my hands, over my head, to my heart, and to any other part of me that I felt needed healing.

Francis went first, and when he held the sweetgrass near me, I did what he did. He smiled and then handed the braid of sweetgrass to one of the other elders so they could smudge themselves.

Francis flipped the carpet from the opening, and before he went in, he told me to wait a few seconds before following. As I did, I wondered if someone from the Catholic Church had visited the New World centuries before Columbus. And then, after I figured enough time had passed, I pulled off the robe, tossed it aside, and bent down to crawl through the door.

The ground was hard like concrete, but already the air was pretty hot, my skin tightening and any coldness in my body melting away. There was a moment of blindness as I passed from the outside to the inside but then the light became a soft glow of twilight in the lodge. In the middle of the lodge there was a hole with a single rock glowing red and emanating heat.

Francis sat opposite the door, beside a small bucket partly filled with water. He gestured to his right, which I figured was my spot, a place marked with a medium-sized white towel and a water bottle. I crawled around the lodge, in a clockwise direction as Francis had said, stepped over him and sat down, turning to face the door. I settled in, crossing my legs. Francis nodded at me and pointed at the towel.

"Since this is your first time in a sweat, we're only going to do a few rounds, but even so it's going to be extremely hot. Some people can handle it, some can't, and if you feel yourself getting too hot during a round, just wet the towel from the water bottle, drape it over your head, and bend down toward the cooler air."

The rest of the group entered, circling around the lodge, but Francis kept talking, leaning back to let them pass. I did the same and they sat down just to my right. "We'll be opening the door after each round and it's okay, Leo, if you want to step outside and cool off. It's perfectly normal, a lot of us do that. And drink plenty of water to keep hydrated. You got that?"

I nodded, feeling my body tense up with the unusualness of the experience and the closeness of the space. I resisted the urge to touch the walls in order to test their strength. I occupied my hands by pouring some of the water over the towel. I wanted to be prepared, not

fumbling around in the dark for the bottle, interrupting the ceremony with my clumsiness. I closed the bottle and set it underneath
my knee for quick access and then placed the towel on my lap, the
excess water dripping down my thighs and into my crotch.

Most of the elders had settled in already, one carrying a drum
and a wooden stick. The stick had a piece of what might have been
suede sewn on one end and the drum was the size of a small tam-
bourine and smelled faintly of rotten meat.

"Just relax and let yourself go," Francis continued. "I'm not going
to say much, but if I do, it'll be in Cree so don't worry about it. Don't
think too much or force yourself to try to get something out of this,
just experience the moment as it comes. Okay, there's no goal you
have to reach, no vision that has to come, but if something comes
then something will come. But most importantly, try to stay in the
moment and accept the experience, be it just a physical one or something else." He gave me a bright smile, his teeth glowing in the light
from the door, and winked. "You ready, Leo?" he asked, placing a
warm hand on my shoulder.

I took a deep breath and nodded. Francis lifted his hand and
shouted toward the door. "Okay, Louis, you can bring in the grandfathers." A second passed and then Louis came in, carrying one of
the rocks with the shovel. He dropped it into the hole and then repeated the act until there were four rocks in the hole.

Francis took the birch branch and shook it twice over the rocks,
a spray of water pelting down. It burst into a cloud of steam with a
sharp hiss and in an instant the temperature and humidity jumped
considerably. Louis sat down with his back to the door, facing Francis. He gave a short nod that Francis returned and then Louis
reached behind and pulled the flap over the door, blocking the outside light.

The suddenness and depth of the darkness was so intense that it knocked the wind out of me for several seconds. My eyes blinked rapidly, searching for any sort of reference point. It took a few seconds but I soon found the silhouettes of the elders, the distinctive shape of Francis next to me. But when I heard his voice, the quick dance of Cree, the direction from where his words came and the image of his shadow didn't correlate. My brain, so keen on finding something in the darkness, had generated false images based on where I thought everybody was supposed to be. When I heard Francis speak again, another blasting hiss, and then the sudden red glow of the rocks from the water, I knew I had been completely wrong about where I had been and was now lost.

The heat from the rocks felt like someone had opened an oven, and it knocked me back enough that I bumped my head on the lodge wall. Beads of sweat gathered across my forehead and started to stream down the side of my face, over my eyebrows, and into my eyes. I blinked my eyes in rapid succession, but was unable to differentiate when my eyes were open or closed.

The heat kept rising, a heavy humidity that crept over me, weighing me down. I breathed through my mouth, almost gasping, the hot air reaching into my mouth to scorch the back of my throat and sear my lungs. The pain spread across my chest, my heart striking against my breastbone. I instinctively moved back to escape the heat, but the farther I leaned back the hotter it became. I stopped breathing and a lightness rose up inside of my head. There was a second when I drifted away, but then Francis spoke again, bringing me back.

In that second, I remembered his advice and felt the damp towel on my lap. I snatched it up and pressed it against my face, the cool wetness dispelling the heat. I put the towel over my head, my body cooling slightly, and then held it in place so that part of it hung over my face. I bent over, ignoring the pain in my back as I stretched to get as low as possible. It was still hot down there, but the intensity of the heat was reduced. I peered up and could see the rocks glowing a soft red, but that was all. I cocked my head and found the locations of the others in the lodge by listening to their breathing. The sounds were even and steady, as if they were sleeping.

I felt a wave of embarrassment rise over me because compared to them I must have been as noisy as a colicky baby. But I tried to push the embarrassment away, telling myself that these men were elders with countless years of sweats behind them and I was just a virgin. And whether they were judging me was not something I could control; I could only control how I felt, and I was now pleased to have things under some control and felt ready to face the rest of the sweat.

I took a deep breath, slow and soft so as not to overtax my body, and then sat up, wiping the sweat from my face with the towel. It was no longer cool so, as quietly as I could, I poured some fresh water from the bottle over the towel. When I had the bottle closed and back underneath my knee, I held the damp cloth against my mouth and nose and took in several wet, cool breaths. I held that posture and then they started singing.

It started with the drum, soft distant thumps that seemed to spring from the forest outside and around the yard. At first I thought it was a two-step rhythm, one heavy, one soft, like a heartbeat. It was, in fact, simpler, one beat over and over again. It circled the lodge for several rounds and then moved toward us, the tentative footsteps of a shy creature.

For a long time, it felt like the drumming would stay outside forever, the sounds curious of our presence but uncertain of our intentions. But suddenly, without warning, it charged forward, breaching the walls of the lodge, moving among us like another invited guest to the sweat. The drumming echoed all around, pounding off the walls, filling the space with sound and penetrating our skin, flowing back and forth through our bodies with every beat of our hearts.

27

✴

There was a voice mail for me Monday morning, short and to the point.

"I saw your stories about the serial killer and I thought you might be the guy to help. I'm a retired member of the EPS and I got some info you might be interested in." He gave a number and that was that. Intriguing as hell, and if he had something new that would bring the story back to life for a few more days, then all the better.

I immediately called him back.

Retired detective Mike Gardiner lived in a quiet neighborhood that was probably on the northern outskirts when it was first built in the fifties, but would now be considered a central neighborhood.

He greeted me at the door with a smile and a military handshake, a strong grip that lasted exactly one and half seconds. He wore a pair of plaid shorts and a light brown cardigan opened to reveal a white muscle shirt underneath. He may have once been a cop but those years were long behind him. There were a lot more lines of his face and gray hair when compared to the constable photo that I found in the morgue at the paper, along with about thirty to forty pounds of additional weight. He had been retired for almost twenty years so that was to be expected.

After a brief introduction, Gardiner invited me into his home, a typical three-bedroom prairie range bungalow with the living room in the front, kitchen in the back, and three bedrooms down the hall. He pointed at a well-worn, floral-patterned chesterfield backed against the front window for me, and then took a seat in the matching armchair set next to a fake fireplace.

There was no artwork in the room, just a few well-cared-for plants and a timeline of photos, either on end tables or hanging off walls, that started at the edge of the mantel and made a clockwise circuit of the room. The early ones were easy to spot, yellowed with time and showing a young Gardiner and wife, a leggy brunette, smiling in their wedding clothes, and then successive additions, three kids it seemed, first as infants then progressing through the years all the way to graduation.

Then the cycles started to repeat, with another wedding shot, and some new photos of a couple of infants growing into toddlerhood. And that's where it ended because that's probably where Gardiner's life sat at the present. I also noticed that somewhere after the high school graduation section, the photos of one kid, a boy, stopped appearing.

"Sorry about not dressing up for ya," Gardiner said in a scratchy voice, bringing me back to the now. "It's been a while since anybody paid me a visit because of police reasons. Besides, I was never one for pomp and circumstance and all that, even when I was on the force. Don't get me wrong, I kept my uniform clean and pressed but I figured since we were all cops, part of the same team, I never really got why the 'sir yes sir' was such a big deal.

"'Course that got me in trouble a few times, kept me from getting a couple of promotions because—what the hell did they call it once? Yeah, 'At times Constable Gardiner shows a discourteous attitude toward superior officers' which meant I told a couple of supervisors to fuck off. But anyway, you didn't come here to hear an old cop reminisce about the old days, did you?"

I couldn't help but smile at the old cop, projecting myself in his life, but knowing that when I reached his age there would probably be no photos on my walls and end tables, just empty spaces and, maybe if I was lucky and strong, with my career to fill in the blanks. "You're the one who called me, remember?" I said, and while he nodded to show me that he heard the question, he didn't answer.

"I can tell by the way you were checking out my living room, running through the photos, that you were adding more to the file, building the character that sits in front of you and wondering if that will help you make a connection in the interview." He turned his chair on a swivel to point at a spot on the wall directly across from me, just above the console TV. "And I noticed that you stopped here for a second and you probably wondered why there are no more photos of the boy."

"And you retired from the service when, Detective Gardiner?" I asked, trying to keep things light. "'Cause when I checked, there was an announcement fifteen years ago, but from the way you're talking, it seems like last week. You wanna be the good cop or bad cop in this interview?"

He chuckled but there was also a flash of grief and something else. Anger? Embarrassment? "The answer to that conundrum is simple: drunk driver."

Anger. That was the addition. Anger at a drunk driver for killing his kid.

"I'm sorry, it must—"

He waved my concern away. "Don't give me your pity, 'cause despite our jocular attitude so far, we hardly know each other. Just let me ask you this, before I let you get on with your interview, you have any kids?"

I first thought about lying but he would see through that. "Yeah. I have a son and daughter. They live with their mother."

"Thought so. So you know you better be prepared for the worst because despite the odds, bad things can happen and do happen. And even though cops like me did our darnedest to educate people and kids in school about the evils and stupidity of drunk driving, there are always those few idiots who never learn." He again pointed to the teenager smiling in his high school graduation gown. "And my son was one of those idiots. And even though I loved my son to pieces, I just thank God that his was a single MVA so that he didn't kill anybody else."

Shame. That's what that extra look was. Not anger, but shame. Shame toward his son and shame for himself because of his son. Must have been tough for a cop to deal with, his son driving drunk and killing himself. I wondered if his retirement came close after the accident, but then I pushed the thought aside because we already knew who killed his son. We didn't know who killed Grace Cardinal and that's why Gardiner had called me here, to possibly help with the story.

Maybe sensing my desire to move on, Gardiner cleared his throat. "So enough reminiscences from an old ex-cop. As you said, I called you and I'm about to tell you why."

I pulled out my notebook and flipped to the page where I had written down the info he had given me over the phone. Gardiner sat up straight at the sight of my notebook. Despite the differences in our professions, there are similarities, such as the use of a notebook. From his reaction, I could tell that he missed the job. "Yeah, you said it was an investigation you undertook about twenty years ago? Pretty vague 'cause you must have undertaken many investigations in your career."

"Yeah," he said, taking a sip of his beer. "I'm sorry I was so vague on the phone but as you'll discover pretty quick, I have my reasons. First off, I have to tell you that I am no longer a serving member of the Police Service, haven't been for, as you said, fifteen years, and am not representing that Police Service. Also, some of the information I may give you comes from an official investigation file which should be in the archives of the EPS but, for reasons I won't tell you, isn't.

"And because there are possibly one or two illegal acts here, I am demanding, not requesting but demanding, that my name not be used in your story. You can call me an unidentified retired member of the EPS but you cannot use my name, badge number, or even my rank in your story. Do you understand?"

"I can see you've got the ability to pique one's interest because that's a hell of a thing to ask, especially since you called me and I haven't seen any of this information you are talking about."

"I don't give a fuck. You either agree to what I'm asking or leave my fucking house right now. Empty-handed. Do I make myself clear?"

It's not really a good policy for reporters to make deals like this, especially before they have an idea of what the story is about. I could have walked out right then. Could have shaken the old cop's hand, thanked him for his interest in my story, and moved on with my life. But the way he was talking, I couldn't resist.

The potential for a good story was big, but even if there wasn't a story here, I couldn't pass up the chance to learn what was in the possibly illegally obtained file and why this old ex-cop was so concerned about having other people not know that he was the one who had given me the information. "We have a deal. If this file is interesting enough for a story, then I won't tell anyone who or where I got it from."

"Not even your boss, your editors. No one knows."

"I hate to tell you that if there is a story here and if I write something about one of your old investigations, chances are someone will be able to figure out where it came from."

"I don't give a fuck if somebody figures it out," he growled at me, in a tone that made me glad I hadn't been on the receiving end of attention from this guy when he was a cop. "You can't use anything that can identify me in this story or tell anyone where you got the file from."

I waved my notebook at him. "Okay, nobody will know, not even my editor who will be pissed, but I can deal with him," I was lying because there was no such thing as a Deep Throat source that journalists didn't share with their editors. The days of backing up a story with a nondisclosed source were long gone. You could write that in a story—the same way I did when I didn't mention Whitford's name as the guy who let me into the crime-scene tent—but you'd better make sure that when your editor asks you who that unnamed source is, you tell them.

"However, if this story results in legal problems for me," I added, "and I'm faced with the choice of going to jail or giving up my source, I can't promise I won't tell. I'll do my best not to give you up but if they push, I'll have to give in."

Gardiner leaned back in his chair with a short laugh, all the anger and tension gone. "Relax, Mr. Desroches. I don't think anyone is going to threaten you with jail time. You may take some heat from the fuzz when you run this story, and you will run this story because I know you won't be able to resist it, and there will be a bunch of cops who would love nothing more than to find a reason to run you in, but you should be fine.

"Even though I've been retired for a while, I know how the old boys work. And for the most part, they are a bunch of old dogs who bark but have no teeth. They'll complain to your bosses, maybe file a grievance with the press council and get the police union to write a nasty letter to the editor, but you'll be fine." He stood up and I expected him to pull a file from underneath the cushion of his chair but he just motioned to me to stand up and follow him down to the basement.

28

✳

The furniture in the main area of the basement was new, that modern Ikea style of wood and soft fabric. It fit the room. This part seemed newly renovated, white drywall along the walls and the ceiling, with a soft gray Berber carpet along the floor. There was a wood-burning brick fireplace along one wall and a large flat-screen TV along the other.

We walked past this room through a door into the rest of the basement, which was unfinished and housed the laundry facilities along with furnace and hot water heater. I followed Gardiner through here, stepping around piles of clothes organized by color and material, till we got to a thick wooden door with two heavy-duty dead bolts keeping it locked. Gardiner reached into his shorts pocket and pulled out a couple of keys, opened the doors and, before we stepped in, reached around the corner to flip a light switch.

The air in the room was stale, as if it hadn't been used in years. But it was tidy. There was a small desk tucked into a corner, with an old wooden office chair in front of it. The desk was flanked by two three-drawer filing cabinets and the top was clear except for a can full of pens and pencils, a short stack of legal pads, a clock radio with the correct time, and a black rotary phone. It looked like Gardiner had furnished his room with items absconded from the set of that old TV cop show *Barney Miller*. There was no other chair in the room, no other place for anybody else to sit, so it seemed that no one else in Gardiner's family ever came down here.

And while the living room upstairs was filled with family memorabilia, this room looked to be a shrine to his career in the Police Service. The walls were filled with photos, everything from his academy class shot to grip and grins with various dignitaries, and candid shots from the job and social events, showing a young Gardiner with other people who were probably fellow cops. It was not surprising that all the people in the photos were men; even now female cops are still a minority in the service but in Gardiner's time they were probably rarer than a passenger pigeon.

Along with the photos were citations, medals, framed thank-you letters on letterhead from schools and small businesses, everything that a good cop collects in a solid twenty-five-year career. There was even a pressed uniform hanging in dry-cleaner plastic and I bet if I looked in the bottom drawer of the desk, I'd find his old service weapon. The ammunition would be here as well, still in its boxes, but shoved behind a stack of files in the back of one of the locked cabinets. It was obvious that Gardiner was one hell of a pack rat and I didn't envy this collection the way I envied his collection of family photos upstairs.

Gardiner grabbed a handful of pens and pencils out of the can and then dumped the rest of the contents on the desk. Along with a few coins and lenses from old sunglasses was a set of keys. He picked them up, sat down in the chair, and unlocked the filing cabinet on the right. He bent over to open the bottom drawer and flipped all the way to the end to get what he was looking for. Without turning, he reached around and held the file out to me.

"This is what I told you about," he said as he closed the cabinet, locked the file, and then dropped the keys back into the can with the pens and pencils. The chair squeaked as he turned to face me.

"Case number 1349–987," he said as I read the number on the file. I also noticed that the folder wasn't something that he'd bought at a stationery store; it was the original Police Service file folder. I slowly opened the file and saw that none of the papers inside were copies; these were the original reports, complete with notes and several black-and-white eight-by-ten photos, long-angle surveillance shots, each one showing a typical john-and-hooker shot: a vehicle stopped on the darkened street, the girl bent over to peer through the passenger window. In a couple of shots, the vehicle in question was a police cruiser.

"Yeah, that is the original file you have there," he said, answering my unasked question. "You won't find anything like this in the archives, I can tell you that. This is something that nobody would miss, anyway, so when I took it, I didn't think I would get in trouble. Showing you is another story, but go ahead, read it and let me know what you think."

I slowly flipped through the pages, noting that Gardiner may have been relaxed in his demeanor as a cop but he was ruthless in his paperwork. It was a typical indictment report, a series of statements, records, and notes that a cop files with the Crown Prosecutor office when he believes charges should be filed.

Everything in the file was organized by time, with the first reports of a minor assault against prostitutes at the beginning followed by roughly scrawled statements and interview notes indicating that some of these assaults may have involved members of the police service, or at the very least, young men in plainclothes carrying badges and holstered weapons, and the further interview notes and statements saying that some of these police officers were using these prostitutes as informants, gathering information on their pimps and drug deals they may have known about.

So far, that was nothing unusual; prostitutes are regularly used as informants. But the next few pages showed the relationships went deeper. And darker. Two statements stated that the informant relationship was only the beginning and these so-called cops were threatening communication for the intent of prostitution (the typical charge because officially prostitution isn't illegal in Canada. It's a typically Canadian quirk. You are allowed to pay or charge someone to have sex with you, however, if you actually verbalize the offering of and asking for sexual services in exchange for money, then you have broken the law) and other criminal charges in exchange for sexual favors, for themselves, for friends, and also for extortion purposes. If any of the prostitutes refused these offers, then charges were filed against them or, sometimes, they were assaulted, sexually and/or otherwise.

Those statements painted a bleak picture of police corruption and brutality, but the cynic in me believed that the statements from the prostitutes were false and designed to be a means of getting back against the cops who were only doing their duty to make the city streets safe and free of things like prostitution. It all came down to who are you going to believe, the woman who sells her body on the street, usually to get money for her drug habit, or the guy who rides in the cruiser risking his life for making our city a better and safer place? Most everyone would believe the cop.

But one of the statements was highly detailed, listing incidents, threats of charges, assaults, parties, blackmail attempts, along with dates, times, locations, and the badge numbers and cruiser numbers of the members involved. This statement was further backed up by Gardiner's work.

His investigative skills seemed to be pretty solid and he had a plethora of information to back up the prostitute's statement; duty schedules matching the dates of some of the incidents with the badge numbers, motor pool request matching the cruiser numbers

FALL FROM GRACE   ❋   199

listed, arrest reports connected to threats, a sidebar report about a member of the Police Commission, who was critical of the police service, being caught in the backseat of the car with one of the prostitutes in question, plus a couple of invitations to stag parties, offering special entertainment, that coincided with some of the parties the prostitute had listed. Gardiner even had what he had termed "an undercover report" in which he attended one of these parties and cataloged events and possible charges.

The guy sitting in the chair in his basement was one of two things: a hell of a cop, or a rat, depending on which side one landed on, who believed the prostitutes and then backed up their allegations with a solid case, including photos.

When I turned to the page that listed the recommended charges and the names of the cops he recommended should be charged, my heart stopped. I read it a second time, this time much slower, making note of each name on the list. A couple of them almost knocked me on the floor. I looked up at Gardiner, shocked at what was either incredible bravery or stupidity. "Were you serious with this?"

He nodded, giving me a long, slow blink. "Very serious. I never recommended charges without a solid case and this was one of the most solid cases I ever made. As you may or may not know, some cops in the service are idiots, they think they are immune to the real world and can play by their own rules."

"I don't know many of these names, but these two, I think everybody knows who these guys are. They aren't your basic cop."

"Not anymore, yeah, but back then, these guys were a bunch of gung ho constables, fresh out of the academy and being trained by old school cops who had learned from even more old school cops that this is the way things are and how one does the job. Whoever they are now is immaterial. Back then they were just stupid constables, and from the look on your face, I know you know the type."

I knew the type and had come across cops like the ones named in the file, but they were a minority. I also knew there were police like Gardiner or Whitford or the thousands of others who did their jobs with honor and respect. Police officers who took seriously their oaths about protecting the public and the city they lived. But the other truth of the matter was that there were countless times when good cops let the behavior of the bad ones slide because to call them to task or complain about them was to be labeled a rat. So in the end they were all tarred with the same brush when the bad or stupid ones transgressed.

But Gardiner's list was something else: something worse. Gardiner's list of "gung ho constables" fresh out of the academy included not only the recently resigned chief of police but the now-serving chief. This was a hell of a story that would blow through the city like a nasty winter blizzard, grinding it to a halt and creating a backlash that would reverberate for months, maybe years.

But I was not at all sure I wanted to be the one to write it. The reputation of every cop, even the good ones, would be tarnished by this. And every cop, even the good ones, would hate me for writing it. I wanted to take this file to Gardiner's fireplace, toss it in, and roast a couple of marshmallows in its flame.

"You can keep that if you want. Nobody wanted it when I wrote it up," Gardiner said, which was probably the understatement of the year. "Not even the Crown Prosecutor. I thought that fucker would have a heart attack when I showed him my report. Actually, the look on your face matches his, although he stopped breathing for so long I thought I would have to give a bit of mouth-to-mouth."

"You actually filed this with the Crown?"

Gardiner gave a dismissive grunt. "This was one of the best cases I ever made in my career, so of course I filed it with the Crown. Nine months of work, poking into every cranny, buddying up with guys who made me puke, who made me feel ashamed to call myself a fellow member, and backing up all statements with a solid case and then recommending charges to the Crown. That's what cops are supposed to do, isn't it?"

No wonder he missed several rounds of promotions; this was the biggest fuck-off you could give a superior. But Gardiner's words told me he was the bravest and the dumbest cop I had ever met. He had found fellow members involved in criminal activity, and instead of turning his back on it, filing it under "boys will be boys" or redrawing the thin blue line, he came forward with it. He didn't care if the people being abused by the system were criminals themselves or living an unsavory lifestyle. He didn't care if they would call him a rat, didn't care about his chances for advancement or about being ostracized by every single cop in the country, he just did his job.

"But since I was not an official member of Internal Affairs and therefore not officially sanctioned or approved to conduct such an investigation, and since I didn't go through official police channels, the Crown said they couldn't file charges. The defense, they said, could get it all thrown out of court, but I knew that was a load of bull. They were just afraid; no doubt somebody in their office was involved in some way or had attended one of those special parties and they would look bad."

"So why give this to me?"

His eyes took on a faraway look and it was several seconds before he answered. "You know, there are three basic rules of being a good cop," he said, technically to me but the distant tone in his voice told me that someone else was supposed to be the recipient, a younger cop, his dead son, himself, his God, I didn't know. "Rule Number One is that bad things happen."

I nodded 'cause I had heard that before. Journalism has a similar rule: Bad things happen and that makes good news.

"Rule Number Two," Gardiner continued, "is that you can't change Rule Number One."

He drifted away again and after a few more seconds, I nudged him with a clearing of my throat. He came back, as if his soul had visited faraway friends and then transported back into his body. "Huh? Yeah, right, Rule Number Three is that you still gotta try. Even though bad things happen and you can't change that, you still gotta try. Every cop knows that, every good cop, I mean, with all the shit they see every day, with all the anger, violence, stupidity, and senseless waste of human life, you still gotta try."

"What about bad cops?" I asked.

"Bad cops," he said, tapping his finger against the file, "always forget about Rule Number Three. They forget they gotta keep try-ing."

Reluctantly, I tucked the file under my arm, wondering if I should just toss the fucker the first chance I got. Gardiner seemed lighter as he stood up, his back a bit straighter as he saw me to the door. We shook hands at the front door, me trying my best to ignore the file in my hand. "Uh, thanks for your help," I said, but I was lying.

Gardiner knew it. "Yeah, and fuck you, too," he said with a laugh. "Don't worry about it too much, Leo. I also gave this to you because I liked how you said, Fuck you, to the department when you wrote the story on whether there might be a serial killer. I liked the way you showed them that they weren't doing their job, that a cheap-ass reporter could do a better job than them. And even though I was a cop, I liked that. You weren't afraid to step into the shit and I hope you aren't afraid to step in this shit. But I won't be bothered if you don't. You look like you got enough baggage already, so like I said downstairs, you can do what you want with the file, toss it, burn it, whatever. I don't really care."

He was telling the truth but only part of it. There was a part of him that wanted me to do something, to take over his case and ensure that justice was done, whatever justice a "cheap-ass reporter" could deliver. But I couldn't help but wonder if it was worth it for me to try. Sure, it would make a fantastic story, but would it do me any good?

29

✳

I had never seen Larry look so shocked and scared at the same time.

"Where the fuck did you get this?" he asked, seconds after reading Gardiner's file. He stared at the folder with disgusted fascination and terror, as if it held information telling him exactly where, when, and how he would die.

"Do you really want to know?" I replied. We were sitting in his office with the door closed. No doubt this fact was creating much speculation in the newsroom since Larry never closed his door, even if he was firing someone.

"Not really, 'cause I don't want my ass dragged to a courthouse and then tossed into jail for contempt of court, but since I'm in charge and I'm the one who made the crazy fucking decision of hiring you, I have no choice."

I didn't insult Larry with any sort of "this is only between us" or "you can't reveal this source to anyone" comments before I started. We were both longtime professionals so I told Larry about Gardiner, who he was and how he got hold of me.

"I don't like this," Larry said with a shake of his head. "I don't trust this fucker."

I shrugged. What could I say? That I didn't trust Gardiner, that I didn't trust his true reasons behind giving me the file? Of course

I didn't trust him, despite the fact that I may have respected him in the short time that I had spent with him.

No doubt he liked the fact that I made the EPS look bad in the serial killer story and he wanted me to help them look even worse. It was obvious that he, even so many years after his retirement, was still nursing a grudge against some members of the EPS brass and wanted to use me to issue another "Fuck you, sirs" to his old superiors. Some of them, of course, did deserve it, based on the file sitting on Larry's desk, but I wasn't ignorant of the fact that he was using me, for whatever reason.

Despite all that, it was still a hell of a story. Any questions in the newsroom about my capability as a journalist would be immediately dismissed. My reputation would be renewed with a vengeance and Larry would look like a genius for hiring me. Both Larry and I knew that, but we had to find a way to get the story out without crossing any legal or ethical lines that would get us in serious trouble.

"Okay, first things first," Larry started. "Does anyone else know about this? Has this fucker given this story to anyone else?"

"I don't think so."

"You don't think so? Or you don't know? You gotta be fucking clear on this one, Leo, because how we play this story depends on whether we have time on it or not. If we have time, we can hold off on it for a little bit and make sure we do this right. But if we don't, if someone else has the information, then we have to run it tomorrow. Understand?"

"This isn't some copy of the file, Larry, it's the fucking original that he kept in the back of a locked filing cabinet in a locked room in his basement," I said, tapping my finger on the file.

"So while he never actually told me I was the only one who got this, I'm pretty sure I'm the only one. And even though we both know that gambling's really bad for me, I'm willing to bet my job that no one else in the media has seen this file. In fact, I'm pretty sure that you, me, and that old cop are the only ones that have seen this file in a long time. Some folks may have seen it years ago, but I'll bet you that they've done their best to try and forget about it. This is going to fuck them up."

"No shit, Sherlock. Tell me something I don't know," Larry said, taking a deep breath. "Okay, I agree with you on the fact that none of our competitors know about this, so please no gambling, Leo. You've been on the right track for the past few months and I'd really hate to see you fall off it.

"But first things first. As you said, this is an original document that we have in our hands. I have no idea what the legal status is for original police documents. Is this stolen property? Are we criminally liable now that we have it in our possession? Or will we be okay if we give it back? And since no one was really charged, how do we write this so we don't get sued for libel?"

Larry grabbed his phone, punched in a number. "This is Larry Maurizo, I need someone from Legal and I need them now," he shouted into the phone. "And don't send me some assistant or a flunky, send me Weinel, the head of the department. Yeah, now! I need her in my office in the next ten minutes. If she gives you any shit, tell her the next person I'm calling is Bill King, and I'm also going to demand that he be here in the next five minutes."

He slammed down the phone. "Fucking lawyers. They always think that their job is the most important." Of course, the same could be said about journalists, but in a company like this, we were. Without reporters, there would be no newspaper. I also had no doubt that the ad sales guy felt the same way.

"Is it really necessary to call in the publisher?" I asked.

Larry already had the phone in his hand and the look on his face asked if I was an idiot.

The publisher of our paper was a relatively young guy named Bill King. His full name was William Lyon MacKenzie King. No fucking joke, the same name as Canada's tenth prime minister, the guy who was not only prime minister during the Second World War and Canada's longest-serving prime minister, but an eccentric, unmarried loon who owned a crystal ball, a Ouija board, and took political and spiritual advice from the spirits of his dead mother, FDR, Leonardo da Vinci, and several of his dead Irish terriers, all of them named Pat.

He was considered one of the great political leaders in Canadian history. Despite the lunacy of his namesake, publisher Bill King was down-to-earth, a former journalist turned lawyer turned publisher. Unlike previous publishers, King liked to hang out in the newsroom talking to reporters, especially those in the sports and entertainment sections, departments he never worked in during his writing career, but probably always wished he did.

It was typical; almost all people coming out of journalism school hope to work in the sports and entertainment sections. And when I said King was relatively young, I meant he was a few years younger than me, relatively young to be a publisher of a major metro paper. He came into Larry's office, sans suit jacket, tie askew and sleeves rolled up—his normal look—and when he saw me, he smiled.

"Hey, Leo. How you doing? Nice work on the serial killer story. Got me a bunch of nasty calls from the mayor, the head of the Police Commission and the police chief, but heck, that means we're doing our jobs, doesn't it?"

There was no sarcasm in his tone; he was offering a true compliment. He turned to Larry and asked him what the big deal was. Larry handed the file to Bill, but said nothing. Bill shrugged, picked up the file, and began flipping through the pages. The jocular look on his face quickly disappeared and he looked at me.

"Jesus, Leo, what the fuck did you dig up now?"

"Keep reading," Larry said. "It gets worse."

King's face went through a series of changes, reflecting shock, anger, dismay, and then finally it melted into one of resigned sadness as he slumped against the wall of Larry's office. "Holy shit. What the fuck are you guys trying to do to me? If you think the mayor and the police chief are mad at me now, this is going to fucking kill them."

"What's the problem, Bill?" Larry asked, leaning back in his chair, arms behind his head. "I thought you said if we pissed off the mayor and the police chief, we were doing a good job?"

"Do you have any fucking idea who these people are on this list? Do you?"

"Well, there's the present chief of police and the recently retired one, but they were only listed as people who were associated with some of these cops so they shouldn't be too upset. No doubt almost every single young cop at the time associated with some of these guys, so he should have no problem with this because he's done nothing wrong. At least not officially."

King shook his head and rubbed his eyes with his fists. "You have no idea what you really have here, do you? You think this is just some old investigation into wrongdoing by some young cops twenty years ago, but the truth is that, like reporters, cops also get old and they move up in the structure of their organization and get into positions of power. Just like you and me, Larry. We were young journalists once, journalists like Leo here, but now, because of education, ambition, and political gamesmanship, we're part of the command structure." He waved the file in front of Larry's face. "This is exactly the same."

"So some of these guys got promoted," Larry said. "That's to be expected."

"It's nothing like that," King said, slapping down the file and turning to the page where the names of constables that had been investigated were listed. He pointed at one. "That name. Do you know who that person is now?"

We both shook our heads. I knew only a few cops, like Whitford, a constable or two, the chief, the reps to the Police Commission, and a couple of folks from Public Affairs, but that was about it.

"That is the deputy supervisor of Operational Support Division." He pointed at another name. "That is a supervisor of the West Division." And another. "That is the head of the Property Crimes Division." And another. "That is the Assistant Deputy of Administrative Services."

And he went on and matched a bunch more titles to names. "I'll bet that if you continue down the list, you'll find sergeants, lieutenants, deputy supervisors, and the like. You think this is just a story into an old investigation of some young constables, but in reality what you have here is an indictment of the entire command structure of the city police department."

About twenty-five years ago, a tornado about a mile wide tore through the east end of the city, killing twenty-nine people, injuring over two hundred, and causing almost a billion dollars in damage. I didn't live in Edmonton at the time but news of the tornado played everywhere.

One of the most common comments about the tornado was that most people in Edmonton had no idea that such a thing could happen. Tornados killing people and destroying property happened only in Midwestern states like Oklahoma, Kansas, or Nebraska, and in small towns and farming areas, never in a northern Canadian city with a population approaching a million people.

But everyone was wrong. While tornadoes were more common in the U.S. Tornado Alley states, the prairie provinces of Canada were also susceptible, and in Edmonton, one of the major cities in the Prairies, we should not have been surprised. Bad things do happen.

That July tornado was the biggest natural disaster ever to hit the city. And probably the biggest news story of the last half of the twentieth century for Edmonton, probably tied for first with the trade of Wayne Gretzky to the L.A. Kings, which by odd coincidence occurred almost a year to the day after the tornado.

This story, while not on the caliber of the those two, would be in the top ten. That was, if it ran.

The head of the paper's legal department arrived a few minutes later. She was a no-nonsense woman named Karen Weinel, dressed in a blue business skirt and jacket that seemed to be the dress code for female politicians across the country. "The first thing we have to do," she said, after I filled her in on the situation and showed her the file," is return this file to the police department."

"Return it? You've got to be kidding," Larry almost shouted. "This is the biggest story this paper has seen in years and now you want us to return the file?"

"This is an original Edmonton Police Service file that I have been told was taken without permission from the files of the Edmonton Police Service. In short, it was stolen. And so if you do not return this file in a reasonable amount of time, then we run the risk of both Leo and yourself being charged with possession of stolen property," Weinel said matter-of-factly. "And because Bill has been made aware of this file's existence, then there is a good chance that he would be charged as an accessory to the fact."

"What!" King barked, his voice breaking in surprise. "They would never charge me."

"If we run a story on the contents of this file, it will almost certainly damage the reputation of the Edmonton Police Service. They will not be happy, and that is an understatement. Someone, somewhere in the system, will find a way to get back at us. You can bet on it."

"This is the Edmonton Police Service, not some small-town sheriff's department from a bad movie," King said, indignant.

Weinel and Larry both shook their heads at the same time. "Obviously the Overtime debacle taught you nothing," Weinel said.

Damn, I really felt like a dunce—everyone in Edmonton news over the past decades knew about that. Everyone except King, that is. So Weinel, who had less to lose, filled him in.

The Overtime was the name of a sports bar in the south area of the city, but in the early part of the century, it became the center of a police case that showed how far the local police department had fallen.

It all began with a columnist from the other daily in town writing an article critical of the police's photo radar system. A sergeant in charge of this section was so pissed off by the piece that he accessed the police database to get info on the columnist's vehicle and then told officers in his section to keep an eye out for it during an overall drunk driving investigation.

In November of 2005, said vehicle was seen outside the Overtime bar while there was a media event of some type occurring. Undercover cops, who were supposed to be watching drivers who were known by their record to be dangerous drivers and at risk for driving drunk, were pulled away from that and sent to the Overtime to watch this columnist. And while they were doing that, they also happened to notice that in attendance was another person they didn't like, a member of the Police Commission who was critical of the police from time to time.

The plan was that the undercover cops would watch to see how much these guys drank and then report back to other uniformed cops who were outside, hoping that at least one of their targets would climb into his car and then, boom, a reputation would be tarred with a drunk-driving conviction.

Unfortunately, the radio chatter between the two groups of police was picked up by another reporter from our paper who was back at the office, trolling for stories by listening to the police scanner. When he heard what was going and the names of the targets being bandied about, he called the cell of his fellow journalist at the Overtime and let him know what was going on.

The columnist made the commission member aware of what was happening, and although witnesses said that both men were not drunk, both took cabs home. The police even followed the columnist to his home to confirm that he actually got there. If there were any plans for the police to continue to target both of these individuals, they were immediately halted when both papers ran a story about the situation the next day.

Despite the uproar, every single cop in the Overtime saga, except for the one who implemented and supervised the investigation, was cleared of any wrongdoing by an internal police inquiry. They found there was nothing really wrong in how the investigation was conducted, because in the end, even if they thought something was amiss, or not right, they were only following orders. The sergeant who initiated the investigation in the first place only received a ten-hour suspension.

"He wrote one column," Weinel said, holding up an index finger.

"Just one, in which he suggested that photo radar was designed to raise money and may not deter people from speeding because you get no demerits. That's it. He never even said anything about the members of the police who were given Oilers tickets and trips to Vegas by the company bidding on the ninety-million-dollar contract to provide the photo radar equipment.

"All he did was question whether photo radar actually deters speeding, and he was targeted by someone in the police department.

"And if you run this story, you must be prepared for the possibility that someone will target this paper because of it. Most likely Leo here, because it will be his byline on the story. So to minimize that risk, we must act in good faith and return this document to the police, as soon as possible.

"The law states that if a person who comes into possession of stolen property arranges to have it returned to the rightful owners, or contacts the proper authorities about the property, he should not be charged. And since the rightful owners and the property owners are one and the same, we only have one call to make.

"Leo, you said you received this file only a couple hours ago, so as long as we contact the police within a half hour and arrange an immediate handover of it, we should be fine."

"But if we don't have the document, then we can't run the story," I said.

Weinel sighed. "I'm sorry if I'm telling you guys how to do your job but when I said you had to return the document, I didn't say you weren't allowed to make copies. As long as the police have the original file that was taken from their archives within a reasonable period of time, then in no way can anyone be charged with possession of stolen property."

"But what if the police ask me where I got this file from? What do I say to that?"

"Say what you want because based on the date of this file, I believe Gardiner may be beyond the statute of limitations. That said, you never know. They might charge Gardiner with possession of stolen property. You decide what you think is best.

"From a legal standpoint, you are not obligated to tell the police any details about how and where you received this document or who gave it to you, no matter how they'll try to tell you otherwise. If you feel uncomfortable with giving a name, I would recommend that you say you received it from an anonymous source and then reiterate the fact that you are returning the documents.

"There will be no need for you to undergo any sort of interrogation because of it. You know, in fact, I believe I should be present when this handover occurs, that way we can confirm that a handover has occurred and I will be able to support Leo here in case things get out of hand."

"How the hell will things get out of hand?" Larry asked.

"I have no idea, but it's my job to realize that such things may happen and to assist our staff members if they do," she said, placing a hand on my shoulder. "Don't worry about it, Leo. It will all be fine."

I smiled because I was not worried about getting in trouble because of something as minor as this: I had bigger worries. I also had a more important question. "Thanks. But in the end, will we be able to run this story?"

Weinel nodded. "I see no reason why you cannot run this story, albeit with a few limitations." Before anyone could ask the obvious questions, she continued.

"Because none of the people on this list were charged with any crimes, only named in the investigative file, you cannot identify them in any way. You cannot name them, cannot give their proper titles and place of standing in the Edmonton Police Service because that would identify them."

"What about the two chiefs? The story loses a lot of its bite if we don't mention that."

"Yes, I'm aware of that, and in my opinion I would say it would be okay if we mention their names, especially since they aren't the actual targets of the investigation, just that one was named as one of many associates of the constables listed and the other was the superior of the investigating officer whose name appears on a memo recommending charges not be filed.

"From a legal standpoint, I would highly recommend two things appear in the story. First, when you initially mention the name of either the present and/or former chiefs of police, I would suggest that you include a line stating that neither of these people has been charged with any crime either relating to this investigation or any other, if that is the case.

"And second, I would suggest that, at the very least, someone attempt to get an interview with either the present or former chief, or both, to get their side of the story. If they agree, then you can question them about the file, and if they don't agree, then you can at least say you tried but were refused. That's what I would recommend."

Larry nodded, his big smile rising. "We'll also make sure that we have a shooter on site so he can take a photo of one of these guys during the interview. That's a nice front-page image, if you ask me."

I couldn't care less if there was a shooter or not. I just wanted to get the story in motion. Weinel shrugged. "You may lay it out as you wish, but I would request that, for legal reasons, I get to see the story before it goes to press."

Larry gave her a thumbs-up. "Sure, Karen, you got it. Thanks for all the advice."

"That's why I'm here," she said. "But first, as I said earlier, we must arrange the return of the file and get that out of the way."

"Should you arrange that or what?" King said, breaking his silence.

"I believe it would be best if Leo made contact with someone in the Police Service and handed over the file. Doesn't have to be anybody in a position of authority, just someone that Leo knows and has a bit of trust with."

They all looked at me expectantly. I had a pretty good idea who I could contact but I knew he wouldn't like it.

30

✹

It had taken a lot of convincing to get Detective Whitford to even talk to me on the phone, but when I told him it was extremely important and he was the only one in the EPS I could turn to, he relented. Another reason why he was a good cop; despite his personal feelings, he knew the important thing was that someone needed his help and it was his job to offer that help.

Detective Whitford burst into the police interview room, looking angry and annoyed. "This fuckin' better be . . ." he started to say as soon as he opened the door, but when he saw that I was not alone, but with Karen Weinel, dressed in her finest newspaper-lawyer ensemble, complete with legal briefcase, Whitford came up short. He spent several seconds taking in the scene, and once he adjusted to the new situation, he sat down across from me at the table. He was no longer angry but he was still annoyed, probably even more so.

"Who's the legal help?" he asked me, as if Weinel wasn't even in the room with us.

I was about to introduce Weinel but the lawyer beat me to it, reaching across me and the table with her hand. "Karen Weinel. I'm the head of the legal department at the paper. I've heard many positive things about you, from Leo here and other reporters at the paper."

Whitford took a whole second looking at Weinel's hand. Like

many cops, he was distrustful of lawyers, especially those appearing across the table in a police station interview room. But then he grabbed it and gave it a shake. "Nice to meet you, Ms. Weinel, but you'll pardon my bluntness when I ask, What the fuck is this all about?"

"In the course of investigating a story, Leo here came upon, let's just say an awkward situation, in which he came into possession of property of the Edmonton Police Service. And when I became aware of the situation, my advice to him was to return this property in order to prevent any charges resulting as a consequence of his possession of this property."

Whitford's entire body loosened up so completely that it looked like somebody poked a hole through his skin and let out all the air. His face softened into a relieved smile. "Thank God. For a second, Leo, I thought you had done something wrong and you had brought a lawyer along so you could confess to me."

Although I wasn't insulted by that assumption, Weinel was taken aback. She went into defending-lawyer mode. "Mr. Desroches is a respected member of our staff at the paper and we find the assumption that he had done something wrong irresponsible."

I waved Weinel down. "It's okay, Karen. Whitford and I understand each other, and in all honesty, it isn't wrong for Detective Whitford to assume that I may have done something wrong."

"What!" Weinel said, shocked, but Whitford ignored the outburst.

"Not wrong, just maybe misguided." Whitford leaned in close, still grinning. "So somebody gave you something, eh, Leo? I sure hope it's not an old service revolver or something like that. Those things are dangerous and any community police station would have taken it in, no questions asked, except where you found it and when. You didn't have to call me."

"It wasn't a gun," I said. "Theoretically, it's not as dangerous but I'll let you be the judge of that."

"All right. I'll admit that my curiosity is piqued. What is this police property?"

I turned to Weinel, who was carrying the file in her briefcase, but she was still in a state of shock at my previous admission. I had to call her by her first name twice to get her attention. When she finally snapped out of it, I told her to get the file. She reached into the case, brought it and a sheet of legal foolscap out, handed the file to me, and I handed it to Whitford.

"An old police file, that's it?" he asked. I nodded.

"At this moment, I'd like to state that I have witnessed Leo Desroches hand over said item to Detective Allan Whitford of the Edmonton Police Service," Weinel said, writing the same thing on the legal sheet. She called out the date and time and also wrote that on the sheet.

Whitford chuckled. "Like a gun, you could have dropped this off at any community station, to any cop you met on the street, and there would have been no questions asked. You didn't have to call me, 'cause it's only an old file. Hate to say it but we lose a few of these every year. Some gung ho cop takes one home to do some overtime and then forgets it, stuff like that. Most of the time they're really minor cases, misdemeanor things that a typical member can't get done in their typical shift and they got to go home and feed the kids."

I nodded but then shook my head. "This is nothing like that. This one wasn't taken and accidentally left at home. This file was taken and kept on purpose. And now I'm returning it. Read it and find out."

Whitford opened the file with a sigh that said he had better things to do with his time and was only doing this as a favor to me.

But his mood changed within a few seconds. He looked up at me, staring into my eyes like an experienced homicide detective sizing up an obviously guilty murder suspect. I leaned back in my chair and my heart rate jumped a couple notches. I felt an uncomfortable desire for water.

When Whitford demanded to know where we got the file, I wanted to tell him everything, about Gardiner, about his file, about my bank robberies. But Weinel stepped in and came to my rescue. "At this moment, we'd prefer not to share that information."

"Why the hell not?"

"Well, precisely because we knew that a file containing such information as this one holds would create such a reaction from the Edmonton Police Service. And that's why—"

"You're returning the file in this way," Whitford completed the thought. "You're worried about retaliation in some way from members of the police service. And that tells me that while you've returned this file, you've also made copies and are prepared to write a story on this, am I right?"

I nodded. "This meeting was only requested in order to return the file. This is not an interview."

"Yes, Detective Whitford, we are not interviewing at this time, only returning the file in good faith to its rightful owners."

"There'd be no fucking reason to interview me anyway, 'cause the instant I leave the room, I'm taking this file to Internal Affairs, telling them who gave it to me, and then walking out the door. And when I get back to my office, I'm going to contact my immediate superior and tell him about it. And then I'm going to type out a report outlining all that shit so I can cover my butt to them. And then I'm going to forget it ever existed.

"But as a friend, Leo, I have to warn you that despite your efforts to reduce any chance of a retaliation, take care of yourself," he continued. "A large number of EPS members, including myself, won't like it when this story runs. Our reputation sucks at the moment; it's going to suck even worse when this shit hits the fan. And certain members will blame the messenger rather than look deeper."

"Excuse me, Detective Whitford," Weinel said with indignation. "Are you threatening Mr. Desroches here? Because if you are, then—"

Whitford cut her off. "I am in no way threatening Leo with anything. I'm not that kind of cop. However, I am not blind to how some members function, and since Leo is a friend of mine of sorts, I'm just making him aware of the possibilities. He'd be stupid not to understand that."

31

✿

As per Karen Weinel's suggestion, I contacted the Public Affairs Department of the police, told them in detail the information I had, and asked for someone, hopefully the chief, to respond. A day later, he did, agreeing to a sit-down interview in his office. We were not alone. In the room with us was the head legal counsel for the police department, the manager of public affairs, the chief's personal lawyer, and Karen Weinel.

The chief was blunt, yet respectful toward my questions. He stood up for the members of his department, denied any personal wrongdoing, and chided Gardiner for his sloppy detective skills, his lack of professionalism, his theft of police property, among other things. Although he didn't mention Gardiner by name, he said that my source was a disgruntled ex-detective with a history of disciplinary charges on his record, most for insubordination.

He also said that since no charges had been filed in the past, there was no reason to investigate further. The police counsel added that even if the police did investigate, most of the charges claimed in Gardiner's report were past the statute of limitations.

I interviewed the head of the police union, who supported his members; more vocal members of the Police Commission who suggested that the chief might have to resign, a Crown Prosecutor who said the investigation looked flawed, and a criminal lawyer who said the investigation seemed fine and that charges should have been laid.

I tried to contact people Gardiner had named in his file but they referred any questions about the case to Public Affairs and the chief. I contacted the mayor, and while he also declined to comment, he noted that he supported the chief and the good job he was doing.

I wrote up all of this, along with Gardiner's accusations, and waited two days while Karen Weinel and her legal department dissected the story. The changes they made were minor, the removal of a name and a couple of quotes from the Police Commission politician that could be deemed libelous.

When that was completed, Larry rubbed his hands together with glee as he sent the page off to the printer. The story broke the next day and we waited for the city to come to a grinding halt. It didn't.

Sure, the other media outlets covered the story and there were even a few requests from other media to interview me, but we rebuffed those. I hated talking to reporters. They had so many questions and I really didn't have all the answers. And while there were calls of outrage from various sides of the story, it didn't seem to bother the average Edmontonian.

Maybe it was the fact that Edmontonians were very forgiving of their leaders. One mayor, William Hawrelak, had not only been forced out of office twice for shady business dealings, he had been reelected seven times, becoming Edmonton's longest-serving mayor. The city's largest and most popular park was even named after him.

A few other things worked against the story. The Oilers had won only two games in their first ten, the local CFL team, the Eskimos, was heading to a Western Final, and the temperature had dropped into the minus twenties with nary a hint of snow. It didn't matter what news was breaking, sports and weather will always trump it.

Especially in a city like Edmonton where the two major topics of conversation at this time of the year are sports and weather.

I, too, had more important things to worry about. After the Gardiner story faded, I asked Larry if there was any way the paper could spot me some tickets to an Oilers game. He contacted Bill King, who sent down two tickets in the paper's corporate box, left over from the time it had been a minority partner in the team. Normally, the folks in ad sales had dibs on these seats to reward advertisers, but when Bill King found out I was looking for tickets, he sent down the corporate seats.

I then contacted Joan and set up the hockey date with Peter. We met at the same coffee shop, but this time Peter was glad to see me. He was wearing a brand-new Oilers jersey and a bright smile.

That smile got bigger when he discovered that we were sitting in a corporate box. "Fuck!" he gasped. And then he quickly apologized.

I gave him a cliché ruffle of his hair. "Don't worry about it. We're just two guys at a hockey game so if we feel like swearing, no one's going to give a shit."

His face was one of shock and glee at that statement. When I was a kid, I loved those times when I used to hang out with my dad when my mom and sisters weren't around. Dad figured he could turn his filters off and swore the way he did at work, which was a lot. I thought it was one of the greatest things ever; too bad our times like that were few.

And when the Oilers scored the first goal of the game, after Peter and I celebrated with the rest of the crowd, he looked at me and smiled his beautiful smile, his whole face shining brighter than the fake fireworks they shot off after the goal. "The guys at school are going to fucking die when I tell them about this," he said. "This is fucking awesome, Dad."

When he called me Dad, I realized that there were some things bigger and stronger than any of my other addictions. I knew then that I had to do what I could to get him to call me that again and again. If I could achieve that, then all would be fine in the world. But even if I screwed up and never saw him again, I would at least have had that one moment.

But when the first intermission came up, something inside of me kicked in. When I heard that buzzer go and the sound of the Zambonis coming out to clean the ice, I was transported back in time, to when I was a kid and my dad had taken me to a hockey game.

Back then, there were no Edmonton Oilers, no NHL hockey team in the city. In fact, the only NHL team in Western Canada was the Vancouver Canucks. And even then, most Canadians still weren't used to it. The idea that cities like Edmonton and Calgary would have NHL teams was a dream that no one really had even started to imagine.

We were living in Calgary at the time and the closest thing we had then to a professional hockey team was the Calgary Centennials, a scrappy Major Junior A team. Major Junior A hockey was the pinnacle of amateur hockey in Canada, similar to the NCAA in the U.S. for sports like basketball, football, and so on, but without all the academic trappings.

The players were between sixteen and twenty years old and many were NHL prospects. And prior to the NHL expansion in the eighties, Major Junior hockey was the best hockey one could find in Western Canada.

Going to a live Junior A hockey game with all the noises, the smell of popcorn, frying fat of the concessions, and the overlying haze of cigarette smoke was intoxicating to a seven-year-old kid. And even though they were still only teenagers, the players were stars. With no professional hockey in town, local sports coverage in the winter focused on the Centennials. Players like John Davidson,

Danny Gare, Bob Nystrom, and Mike Rogers, players who would later go on to great careers in the NHL, were known throughout town.

At the game, I was just like Peter, bouncing in my seat, shocked that I was actually here. The game was held at the Stampede Corral, an old brick hockey arena seating about six thousand people located in the middle of the grounds where the annual Calgary Stampede was held. Although the building was much dated even then, being in it made me feel as if I was at bigger and more famous rinks like the Forum in Montreal or Maple Leaf Gardens in Toronto.

Coming to the game with only my dad was a rare treat for me. Almost everywhere I went with my dad, even to see Stampede Wrestling at the Victoria Pavilion, just right next door to the Corral, my sisters always had to tag along. But even though they had insisted on coming to this game, my old man stood his ground.

"Sorry, girls. This is a man's thing," he said. "If Leo wants to play in the NHL then he's going to have to see how the big boys play."

So I was overjoyed beyond belief being not only on an outing with just my dad, but in the stands of the Calgary Corral to see the Centennials take on their provincial rivals, the evil Edmonton Oil Kings. So many years later, I remembered little about the game itself; I couldn't even recall what the score was or who won.

My biggest memory of the game was my dad buying me a Coke and one of those boxes of Lucky Elephant popcorn and then us finding our seats for the start of the game. The sounds of the game was something else, the buzz of the crowd, the thundering organ with its traditional hockey songs, the sharp scrape of the skates on the ice and the crack of the puck as it careened off the boards after a shot from the point.

I also remembered the speed, the quickness with which the game developed. Although the hockey was not up to the caliber of the NHL, most of us in the stands had only seen the NHL on TV. And the one thing that TV can't do, even in these high-definition days, is capture the speed of the actual game. I made a mental note, as much as I could at seven years old, that if I wanted to play in the NHL, I'd better work on my skating.

Those first five or seven minutes of the first period were pure joy. And then my old man shrugged, said he had to take a leak, slapped me on the shoulder, and left. For the first few minutes, I was so into the game, I barely registered that he was gone. But after a while, I began to notice he had been away longer than it normally took to take a piss. Okay, he had to take a dump, my seven-year-old mind theorized. My old man loved to take a long time taking a dump at home so this was no different.

When the buzzer sounded for the end of the first period and the old Zamboni came out at the east of the rink, I realized that he wasn't coming back. He hadn't left me behind for the night; I knew he was out there somewhere in the stands, in the concourse, talking and smoking and drinking with his friends, and he would drive me home after the game, but he wasn't going to spend any more time with me.

I got my ticket to the game, my drink, my popcorn, my quick first part of the first period with him, and that was it. I would get nothing more. Even at the age of seven, I had come to know my dad and his habits pretty well.

But that didn't mean it didn't hurt.

And that's what I kept going over and over again, during my time with Peter at the Oilers game. I never left his side, except to briefly go to the bathroom and to refill our drinks and food, and I engaged him in brief conversations about the game and the Oilers generally, but I wasn't really present. Most of the time I was a seven-year-old, back in the Calgary Corral.

On the way back to the coffee shop, I was on edge. I knew he had to get back, that Joan was waiting, and if I was too late, she would end it all, cut me off from contact with my family. But there was something else I needed to do. I needed to purge my body of that memory, needed to find someplace I could go and bring things to a head, but there was no way I could show up at a casino with Peter. They wouldn't allow him in and I couldn't leave him in the car. There was only one other place I could go, and leaving him in the car wouldn't seem so bad because it would only take a few minutes.

"You know, Peter, we should get back to your mom ASAP, but I've got a headache, and if you don't mind, I need to stop at a store somewhere and get some Tylenol or something," I said as casually as I could. "However, I could drop you off with your mom first, if you want?"

Peter, being the wonderful kid that he was, shook his head. "That's okay, Dad, get what you need. It shouldn't be no problem."

But there was a bit of a problem. Since it was a Saturday, most bank branches weren't open. And even though I knew that, I kept looking. I gave Peter excuses about the other strip malls not having a drugstore or something stupid or whatever. He may have thought that something was out of sorts, but to be honest I wasn't really paying that much attention to him. I was too focused on what I thought needed to be done.

At the third strip mall, I found a kind of replacement, one of the payday loan places. It probably had money just like a bank, and since it was a chain, I figured it probably gave similar training to its staff concerning robbery.

I parked the car, leaving the engine running and climbing out. "You hang tight here, Peter, I won't be long," I said. And before he had a chance to argue and to ask to come with me, I dashed away.

I made like I was heading to the drugstore but I had parked facing the street so he couldn't really see the storefronts.

As I made my way to the payday loan store, I pulled my ball cap out of my pocket and slipped it onto my head. I pulled the brim down to partially obscure my face. I pulled the outside door and was about to step in when I stopped.

That seven-year-old boy during that hockey game years ago came back to me and I saw myself sitting all alone in that big hockey rink while my old man was doing his own thing. And then I saw Peter in the front seat of the car, innocently waiting for me.

I wondered what would happen to Peter if I got caught this time. How long would he sit until he realized that something was wrong? How would he live knowing that his father had taken him along on a bank robbery? And what would Children Services think about that? Would they deem Joan unfit because she had allowed me to take Peter to a hockey game?

"May I help you?" I heard someone ask.

I turned to the sound and saw that one of the clerks had noticed me standing in the doorway. I waited for a second and then shook my head. "Oh, sorry, I think I forgot my wallet." And then I left the building, dashed through the parking lot, and back into the car.

Peter sat there as if nothing was wrong. He smiled when he saw me. "You okay, Dad?" he asked, and there was genuine concern in his voice and his face. I wanted to hug my boy forever, but instead I nodded and smiled back.

"Yeah, I got what I needed."

We said little on the drive back to the coffee shop, a few comments about the game and how we should do this again, although I warned him that it wouldn't always be hockey games, that it was only a special occasion to impress the shit out of him. He laughed at that, especially at the fact that I said *shit*.

When Joan spotted us arriving at the coffee shop, I could see her face and body relax. "Sorry for being late. The game went a bit longer than expected, right, Peter?"

He nodded and went into a excited monologue about where we sat, what we ate, who scored, how the ref made a bad call in the second period and all that. I looked at Joan and nodded at her. Her look was neutral. Despite the joy in her son's voice, she still didn't trust me. I didn't fault her for it. Heck, I barely trusted myself.

32

✳

Even though I knew the police and prostitute story was dead, I couldn't let it go. The fact that there was now a police document stating some members of the EPS had abused and blackmailed city prostitutes in the past made me wonder if one of them had taken things too far.

It was a big leap to imagine a city cop might be involved in one of these murders; Edmonton cops had had their problems over the past decade but killing a prostitute, or one of them being a serial murderer, was unthinkable. Even crazy.

But that was the way my mind worked sometimes. A small thought would be planted for whatever reason, a connection would be made that seemed logical, and even though it wasn't really something to worry about or it didn't really have a basis in reality, it would keep poking and jabbing at me until I had no choice but to pay attention and act.

This time it was probably due to some residual feelings from my recent outing with Peter and my close call at the payday loan place. And it reminded me of the way I'd obsessed over the search for Charlie. Since I hadn't been able to stop myself that time, why would this time be any different? So I read Gardiner's file over and over again, looking for anything that would keep this story, and possibly Grace's story, alive.

On page 5 of Gardiner's file I found something that kept me

going. It was alleged that a Constable Simon Meredith had set up a party for some of his fellow EPS members and used threats of physical violence to get a good number of young prostitutes to attend. It was further alleged, based on a thirdhand account, mind you, that the same Constable Meredith had beaten one of those prostitutes, breaking her nose and choking her to the point of unconsciousness before he tossed her aside.

I ran Meredith's name through the Infomart, expecting to get nothing. I told myself if I did, I would call it quits until something really substantial came up. What I found only convinced me to continue. Meredith's name did come up a few times and most entries had to do with appearances before police disciplinary committees for his behavior while on duty. He had even been charged with assault a couple of times, once for an off-duty bar fight in which another patron's arm had been broken, and another time when he used his Taser three times on a guy sleeping in a rooming house.

Both times, the charges were dropped. The first, because witnesses, most of them also off-duty police officers, testified that the other guy had started the fight. As for the guy Tasered in his sleep, the court believed Meredith's testimony in which he stated that he thought his life was in danger because the sleeping man was reportedly a robbery suspect, and if he woke him in a regular fashion, the suspect would strike out with a weapon. So he decided to use the Taser, even though there were no weapons found at the scene and the guy had no prior record and nothing to do with a robbery.

But the only witnesses to the event were Meredith, the guy who got Tasered, and another homeless guy who was sleeping in a neighboring bed. And since the two homeless guys didn't show up for the trial, Meredith's testimony was the only thing to count and the charge was dismissed by the judge.

It was obvious that Meredith had problems with violence. I

found his name and address in the phone book and went to see if he would talk to me. Maybe, I thought, he would confess to killing prostitutes and I would be the hero of the day again.

He was splitting wood in his backyard, the sound of each chop echoing through the neighborhood like a sharp gunshot. Even though it was barely minus 15 degrees Celsius, and I was wearing my winter jacket, gloves, toque and long underwear, he was sporting only a pair of torn jeans and a T-shirt with the EPS crest just below the right shoulder. Because of the cold, his body was steaming and with every swing it exploded into a cloud of angry mist. He split every piece of wood with one swing but at no time did he grunt.

I watched him for several seconds, wondering how to approach him, how to broach the subject of the death of several prostitutes without being too accusatory. Especially for a recently retired cop, he looked as fit as a recent graduate from the academy. He was also holding a very large ax. I wasn't even sure if there was a story here, a sure sign that I might have been chasing another ghost.

To get his attention, I cleared my throat, and if I surprised him, he didn't show it. Without letting go of the handle, he set the ax head down on the ground and turned. His face was inquisitive but there was no animosity or anger, as I had been expecting. He was just curious about who this dude was in his backyard.

"Are you Simon Meredith?" I asked.

He blinked and swung the ax over his shoulder. "Who's asking?" I introduced myself.

"I don't read newspapers," he said with a grunt. "Most of it's just crap. Even in the sports section no one knows what they're talking about."

"That's fine," I said, pulling out my notebook and pen. That gesture got a reaction. His face narrowed into a scowl and he shifted the ax to the other shoulder.

"I recently wrote a story about an old investigation into a group of police constables who were alleged to have blackmailed prostitutes for a number of reasons, and unfortunately, your name came up a number of times in that case and I was wondering if—"

He slammed the ax into the stump so hard that the handle shook and quivered. He took one step toward me, his hands squeezed into fists so tight that his knuckles were white. A puff of steam rose off his body.

I did my best not to step back because guys like him, guys who are prone to violent reactions, are very similar to dogs. If you run, then chances are they will chase you down and tear you to pieces. However, it also wasn't smart to stare down an angry dog, but you had a better chance of getting hurt if you ran. I was also somewhat happy that he put down the ax.

"I've got nothing to say to you," he said through his teeth. "So get the fuck off my property."

"You sure?" I said, trying to sound the way I thought another cop investigating him would sound. "It would probably be better if you told your side of the story. Without it, you might come out looking pretty bad, whether you did anything wrong or not."

He took a deep breath and I could tell that this was part of some anger-management training he probably was ordered to take. "Listen," he said, each word sounding like the life was being squeezed out of it. "I told you I have nothing to say to you. I also told you to get off my property, and if you don't do that within the next ten seconds, you're going to be in big trouble."

This was a sign that I should have just walked away from this guy, because he wasn't going to comment on anything, and since he wouldn't, there was no story here. But I couldn't help myself. "Are you threatening me, Mr. Meredith?" I wrote some gibberish in my notebook, probably one of the worst bluffs in my life.

"I don't make threats," he said. "And if you're still on my property for five more seconds, you're an official trespasser."

By the look on his face and the information I had about his background, I realized that was probably true. Meredith was one of those guys who didn't worry about little niceties like threats. He acted, usually with violence. And the fact that he was a recently retired cop and I was here on his property without invitation made me understand that it was time to leave.

I flipped my notebook closed and turned away. And though I did my best to play it cool and walked away as slowly as possible, without turning around, my heart danced in my chest and my brain told me to run as fast as I could because I was about to get an ax in the back of the head.

After that I decided the story was dead, at least for the moment. It would surface only when another body was found in a field or if something completely unrelated to my efforts broke.

There was nothing more for me to do but to put myself back into the assignment mix, and write the stories that were the backbone of the print-journalist job, pieces that were relatively easy to research, easy to write, and didn't create a tempest when they were published: stories about car accidents or minor criminal incidents, most of which got cut from the newspaper because of time and space requirements. The high of a major scoop was a wonderful experience but my run-in with Meredith convinced me that even addicts need a little downtime.

This went on for a couple days or so and I usually left the paper at a decent hour. Even so, by the time I stepped out of the front doors, it was usually already dark and the cold had settled in for the night. Even though there was no snow on the ground and it was still officially fall, winter was making its move. The air was biting, and the wind gnawed at the skin. Still, the night sky was clear, many of the stars still visible even with the light of downtown. I walked through the streets, hunched over, cursing the wind and thanking the stars for my decision to wear long underwear.

Nonetheless, I mentally kicked myself for forgetting a toque; having my head covered would have made a difference. I also yearned for and at the same time did not want the falling of the first snow. A first snow would not only bring a bit of warmth to the air, it would also finally relieve me of this misery of waiting. Until it snowed, this cold would drive the city crazy because there was always a lingering hope. But, if the snow came too early then we could be stuck with months upon months of the white stuff, and by the time March came around, we would be sick of it, the yearning for color in our lives so powerful that many would book a trip to a more tropical clime or, if we couldn't afford that, take to watching golf on TV to get a remembrance of the colors of summer.

This night I didn't stop across the street from the casino. I had arrived at a point where its presence no longer tempted me so I trudged past it and out of downtown, making my way through the vast open lot between 104th and 105th streets.

They were waiting for me in the middle, a spot in the field where the lack of light created a zone of darkness. The car was unmarked but, with its four doors and black unwhitewalled tires, it was obviously a police car.

The two cops who climbed out of it were in plainclothes and pretty nondescript, about thirty or so, not too big, not too small. But they moved with that typical police swagger that showed they were not only quite comfortable with the power of their authority, they got a big charge out of it. And even though it was night, they both wore large aviator sunglasses that covered not only their eyes but their eyebrows and the tops of their cheeks.

These guys weren't just police officers, they were Cops with an emphasis on the capital *C*. There's a big difference between police officers and Cops. Even between cops and Cops. Police officers and small *c* cops are relatively good people; all civilians no matter where they live or how much money they have, are treated equally across the board. They don't swagger, and if they wear sunglasses, they take them off when inside or at night.

Cops with a capital *C* swagger as much as possible, and get a hard-on from their authority, using it to push people around. The guys that beat Rodney King in L.A. were Cops. Those guys who were on Gardiner's list of EPS members who liked to coerce prostitutes to provide them with special services and party favors for their friends were big *C* Cops.

As they walked toward me, I said nothing. With Cops it's best if you keep quiet because they are looking for any excuse to make things difficult. As is typical when any police approach a subject, these two split left and right, one moving toward me while the other hung back.

I stopped, instinctively taking my hands out of my pockets to show I had nothing to hide. Despite their swagger, I wasn't worried too much about these guys. I figured they were probably looking for some homeless person to roust, and once I made them aware that I was just another working citizen, they would probably let me go, maybe with a warning that I was taking my life into my hands by walking through such a dark, dangerous area at this time of night. That feeling wouldn't last.

"Took you long enough," the first cop said, the one who was closer to me. "We've been waiting for about an hour and a half for you to show."

"Yeah, that's not very considerate of you, especially since it's a cold night," said the second cop, hitching his belt like some dime-store sheriff. "You must have been working late, writing lies about good police officers just trying to do their job, am I right?"

My body started to shake and my heart pounded. It was damn cold out but I could feel my head getting hot and my forehead starting to sweat. Any thought that this was a random encounter disappeared. I was being targeted and there were only two ways to deal with this: run or face them down. I wasn't that good a runner so I figured since these guys were so much into power, I could probably turn it on them. I did my best to temper my shakiness.

"This is a big mistake, fellas," I said, hoping that my voice wasn't cracking. "I'm not some nameless street person that you can push around. I'm someone with standing in the community, someone with a name, and if you think I can be intimidated by your Ge-stapo tactics, it's not going to work."

I wasn't sure what kind of reaction my tone would cause; in my mind I hoped they would back down, or after a few minor threats on my character, they would leave. I never expected laughter. It wasn't pleasant laughter but that kind bullies use when they're having fun but no one else around them is. The first cop looked over his shoulder to the other one. "He thinks we're trying to intimidate him," he said. "That's a laugh because intimidation is the farthest thing from our minds."

"Yeah, nobody is here to intimidate anyone."

My reaction was mixed. I relaxed slightly because of their words but at the same time, the situation was still tense and threatening. "That's good to hear because this is not the way civilized people operate. If there's a problem, you should take it up with my superiors 'cause, like you, I'm only doing my job."

"You're nothing like us," the second cop said sharply, "because unlike you, our profession is an honorable one. We don't spend our time figuring out how to ruin the reputation of fine public servants."

"I'm sorry you feel that way but I'm just doing my job, trying to make the world a better place."

The first cop smiled. "Well, that's a coincidence 'cause that's exactly what we're trying to do, make the world a better place. And one way we can do that is to take care of people like you." He stepped forward, hands on hips.

I should have run when I had the chance. I stepped back, tripped on something, and fell on my butt. The cops laughed and the second one stepped away from his car. Both of them moved toward me.

"You guys are making a big mistake, " I stammered. "I won't be intimidated."

The first cop stopped about five feet from me and knelt. He rubbed his nose with the back of his wrist and spit on the ground in front of me. "You really must be stupid because I keep telling you and you're not getting it: We're not here to intimidate you, you fucker, am I right?"

There was a pause, about a few seconds, but it felt like eternity. The second cop reached to his belt to pick up what I expected to be cuffs. I figured that they would take me in roughly, figure out some lame charge like loitering or say I looked drunk and disorderly, and when they tried to help me, I got abusive, hold me for a few hours and then let me go.

I was about to say something again about this being a mistake and then I saw the second cop wasn't holding cuffs, he had a square box that had two red LED lights shining toward me. I tilted my head and squinted to get a better look. I thought they were about to take my photo, and the lights were to eliminate the red eye from the flash. A second later there was a pop, like someone pulling a cork out of a wine bottle, and then two small mosquitolike stings hit me in the chest. A second later, a charge of power surged through my body, another blast of light, but this time in my brain, not in front of my eyes.

At first I thought I was having a heart attack, but any conscious and conventional thoughts evaporated as every muscle and nerve in my body burst to life, exploding in a ruthless, agonizing jolt that caused me to jerk like a fish dropped onto the deck of a boat. The pain came an instant later, intense and relentless, tearing me apart from the inside.

I screamed for it to stop, a harrowing howl of anguish, but there was no sound. My brain tried to flee into a protective fissure but there was no place to hide. I was trapped, held against my own will by my own body in a hellish universe of pain and torture. The last thing I noticed was my bladder losing control and warm liquid running down my left thigh.

33

✵

Lights . . . first bright white, then muted, as I was moved into a tunnel or placed in a cell. Voices, maybe . . . yes . . . loud, as if they were right next to me, grunting with effort but laughing, giggling actually, like children when they know they've done something wrong, but don't care. There was no real body sensation, mostly just light and sound. And when it became dark, the voices became muted and hushed. And rushed. Like they were in a hurry. And then, seconds later, they came back, loud, in the cell or whatever, with me.

I couldn't move, couldn't really think. My brain was a swirl of thoughts, a surrealist's dream of colors, lights, noise, voices, ideas, but none of them really staying for long. I recalled Dad for a brief second, lying in bed, unable to move, unable to communicate for months after his stroke, and realized that this was what he must have felt, this was his world for a time.

There was a body, I knew that, and there was a memory of how it worked, how that hand moved, how to scratch that leg or say that phrase or turn my neck, but there had to be a short somewhere, because I could no longer do those things. The only thing I could do was watch and wait, and hope it would all come back. And even though something told me that there had been violence of some kind to get me in this state, just like the sudden onset of Dad's stroke, I didn't feel threatened. The violence was over, it seemed, replaced by lights and some sound.

I was calm, probably because I was focusing on an image of my mother, who had cared for my dad, even though she said she never would, during those difficult months.

She played the martyr to the hilt, telling the world that her toil and suffering was worse than Dad's stroke, and she was probably right in some respects. We were all out of the house by then, and for six months or so, Mom took care of Dad as if he was a newborn baby. The rock of our lives, Mom was, and she fed him and carried him, changed him and cleaned him, and watched him regain his body like the arrival of a prairie spring, a thaw so gradual and sluggish that one day seemed indistinguishable from the next, but suddenly there was melting that you never noticed before and a lessening of weight, as you realized that you'd been peeling away layers without paying attention. I was sure that I would follow my dad and regain my body; I just had to be patient and await the release.

Motion.

The sensation surprised me when I became aware of it. First a few quick jerks, a small climb, and then a steady rolling, my balance shifting left and right from time to time. It was darker now, only lines of light, bright ships of radiance speeding by us, above in the heavens. The voices talked briefly, a language I knew I should understand but couldn't. The words were like the traits of a close friend, but I could no longer place the face. After a while, the voices stopped, and I watched the ships of lights moving above us.

The tingling started in my extremities, the tips of my toes and fingers, and spread through my body. That sensation you get when you fall asleep on your arm or your hand, and then awaken, was being experienced by my body. My muscles tweaked and twitched, recouping their lives and testing their limits. The edges of my vision were blurry, but there was enough clear focus in the center to determine my location: I was lying on the backseat of a car, a sheet of cold plastic pressing into my chin. We were still in the city; I could tell by the streetlights passing overhead. I could see the tops of two heads over the edge of the front seat, silhouettes in the dark, behind a sheet of Plexiglas that stretched across the entire width of the car.

"Jesus Christ!" I shouted, and jerked to a sitting position. My head whirled, the lights started spinning, and a surge of nausea assaulted my stomach. I doubled over, retching, heaving. Only a trickle of burning stomach acid and drool dripped out of my mouth.

"Son of a bitch," a harsh male voice shouted. "If you get anything on that fucking seat, you're going to get another taste of the Taser."

"Relax, man," said another voice, this one older and more relaxed. "Sounds like only dry heaving to me. It's got to be expected, remember when we got Tased? That's why I put the plastic in the backseat so it'll be easy to clean up once we're finished with this fucker."

The retching stopped and I could see and feel that clear plastic covered the entire seat. It was clipped onto small plastic hooks along the door and the edge of the seats to keep things in place. I sat up, saw the equipment underneath the dash, the glass separating the front and back, and the short hair of the driver and the one riding shotgun.

I looked outside, it was still dark, and we were driving through an industrial area, the long, low buildings of various businesses stretching to nowhere, the gestalt breaking only when we drove over a railway track. All the lights were off and the roads were deserted. My heart dropped as in a roller coaster. I fell back onto the seat, horrified and resigned, yet glad it wasn't a weekend.

Picking up undesirables such as the homeless, drunks, the mentally ill, and others, driving them around for a while only to abandon them at the edge of town or in an isolated part of the city, was a time-honored tradition of the Canadian police establishment. It saved on time and paperwork for the cops involved because they could administer punishment to a troublemaker without the bureaucratic hassle of filing charges and running somebody through the system.

For those on the receiving end of this treatment, the consequences varied. For many, it was only a frustrating, time-consuming experience because the police knew that for these people, most of the services they used were located in the central part of the city, and for someone to hike back was fucking annoying and tiring, especially in a city like Edmonton. The population of our fine prairie city might be barely a million folks when you include suburban communities like Sherwood Park and St. Albert. But without an ocean, mountains, or any other natural barrier preventing its expansion, Edmonton was one of the biggest cities, at least in area, in North America, bigger than Chicago, Toronto, or Philadelphia. So having to walk from an industrial zone in the boonies to downtown was no stroll in the park. Especially in the middle of the night when there was no transit running.

But for others, this kind of treatment led to more dire consequences. A couple of summers ago, some cops with a paddy wagon picked up random homeless folks along Whyte Avenue, Edmonton's hip bar and retail district, and drove these folks around for several hours, with no air-conditioning, food, or water, the outside temperature hitting 32 degrees Celsius. Only when some lady in a suburb complained about a group of homeless people walking through her neighborhood did the city discover that this practice was routine. But despite the heat stroke and dehydration, those guys were lucky.

In Saskatoon a few years ago, a couple of constables made it a regular practice to pick up street people who were causing trouble and drop them off in an industrial zone. At first, everyone was surprised to find a couple of homeless guys frozen to death so far from downtown, and thought that someone, a bunch of kids was the typical thought, was targeting the homeless and taking them for rides.

Only when another street person recalled seeing one of the victims in the back of a police car did some people realize that it was the police who were doing the targeting, not civilians. And even though two people died as a result of these police actions, none of the constables involved was charged with a major crime. They were given some minor slap on the wrist.

So there was nothing I could say to these cops now. Pleading and begging wouldn't make any difference to these guys. And with the weather having turned cold, I was in big trouble. Again. The only small consolation was that if something happened to me, it wouldn't be my fault this time. And maybe that would help my kids, Eileen and Peter, feel a bit better when they found out I was dead. I sure hoped so.

Instead of being a pathetic homeless fuck, freezing to death on the streets like I almost did a few years ago, I would be a murder victim. There would be no shame because it wasn't my fault, and maybe, I hoped, somewhere or sometime in their lives, they would feel a need for justice. At least they would have that little bit. It wasn't much, but it made me feel less afraid. Less angry.

The car drove on for a few more blocks, and just before a large, empty field, it made a left turn. I tried to spot a road sign, to get a sense of where I was in the city, but I was unable to do so. I could have been in any of the industrial areas of city. There were several in Edmonton, in each quadrant of the city, but because of the dark, the identical buildings all around, and the fact that I normally stuck to the central parts of the city, I had no idea where I was. I could be anywhere.

The road near the field continued for a few kilometers until it ended in a T intersection. The car turned right. Most of the strip-mall type buildings were behind us, leaving only large work yards, surrounded by high fences that were topped by barbed wire. I spotted a few gates, but they all seemed to be locked. I was a long way from anything that I could break into, on a two-lane road, with deep ditches on either side.

The area was completely open to the wind, with no buildings to hide behind, nothing to protect me. In normal weather, I could probably have walked the few kilometers to the strip mall area, broken into one of the businesses, called 911, and waited in the heated building for the police to respond to the break-and-enter call. But it was at least minus 20 degrees Celsius, not as cold as it could get in the dead of winter here, but it was enough, especially with the wind-chill. I would last an hour, maybe less, since I didn't have my jacket, only a sweater, and no gloves or toque.

Where did I lose those? Did they take them off me? I wondered.

They must have, in order to make the cold work faster on my body. I still had a pair of long underwear under my jeans, but the odds were still against me surviving for long in the cold.

These guys had picked their spot perfectly. But first, I decided, those pricks in the front seat would have to get me out of the car, and they would have to kill me before I would let them do that.

The car stopped in the middle of the road and the driver popped it into park. "This is where you get out," he said, without turning around so I couldn't see his face.

I said nothing, just sat in the middle of the back, my arms crossed in front of me. I knew one of them had to get out and open the door, because the locks in the back couldn't be opened from the inside. The guy in the passenger seat slipped on his gloves, and without saying a word, got out of the car and flung open the back door on his side of the car. "Get out," he commanded.

"Fuck you," I replied.

"I said get the fuck out."

"Fuck you."

"Son of a bitch!" He leaned forward, his hands above the door. "I'll fucking drag you out of there!"

"Come and get me, you motherfucker! I dare you!"

He stopped and backed up a step. The driver gave a short guffaw, but did nothing to help his partner. "Hurry up," the driver said. "You're letting out all the warm air."

The other one stood up straight and grabbed his belt to adjust it. It was the typical intimidation routine, but I wasn't scared of him. I had nothing to lose. He placed his right hand down by his right hip, clicking open a holster. "Listen, you piece of shit! I'm sick of fucking bastards like you fucking up the world, so you get out of this car now!"

"Fuck you!"

He pulled his gun out, getting into the two-fisted stance seen on every cop show and movie since forever. He leveled the pistol at my head. "Get the fuck out of the car now!"

"Come and get me, you fucker!"

There was a short click, like someone turning a key in a lock, as he flipped off the safety. Then there was a longer, deeper click that echoed so loud in the cold, clear air that I flinched, thinking he had shot me. But he had only cocked the pistol.

His voice was a monotone hiss and his phrasing came out as several one-word sentences. "Get. The. Fuck. Out."

The lack of emotion in his demand showed that he was ready to shoot me, but I didn't care. I was already dead. I knew that. There was really nothing I could do about that now. I would either die on the backseat of this car, or freeze to death on the side of the road, and I decided that I wasn't going to let them take the coward's way. I wasn't going to let myself go down easy. They would have to take an active role in my death, get actual blood on their hands, by shooting me. I spat at him and taunted him, trying to force his hand.

"Go ahead! Blow my fucking head off! Blow my fucking brains out! I don't care! It won't bother me, 'cause I'll be dead, and even if you dump my body in the street out here, you'll still have to explain the blood, brains, and DNA all over your backseat! Plastic can't protect everything, and you can detail it all you want, but something's going to be left behind. You should know that. Something is always left behind, and you'll be fucked!"

The tip of his pistol dropped for a second, came up again, held for a second, and then dropped again, this time for good. "Goddamn it! Son of a bitch!" he shouted as he rose out of his stance. I let out the breath I was holding, my hammering heart starting to slow with the realization that I had won this part of the showdown.

"Fuck this shit," the other cop said from the driver seat, and another set of mosquito-type stings struck me in the neck. Everything erupted in another blast of fire and jolt of agonizing energy. My body stiffened like a board, but this time the attack was much shorter, only a brief second, and I was released, my resistance destroyed. I was dragged out of the car, flopping like a fish, and left on the side of the road. Lying on my back. My body twitched in a series of aftershocks. Daggers of pain danced about my body, turning my skin inside out, it seemed. Arctic air, burning like acid, burst into my lungs and throat, as I gasped for breath.

My eyes blinked with tears as the pain dissipated, as my brain switched from its primitive mode into something more human. I saw that the sky was clear, the stars scattered across the dark night, and the moon bathing the air in a pale blue glow. There was no sound, except for the distant crackling of ice crystals in the air. The car was long gone, or at least I thought it was. I had lost all sense of time. But I couldn't have been on the ground for too long, because I was still alive and the cold was tearing at me with more vengeance than the Taser. Still, I didn't move. I just blinked and stared at the beauty of a clear winter sky.

34

❋

Get up!

No.

Get up!

No. I don't want to.

If you don't get up, you'll die.

I don't care if I die.

Of course you do.

Get up!

No!

Get up!

Leave me alone!

You can make it.

I said, Leave me alone, Grace!

You can do it, Leo. You can make it.

What the fuck do you know, you stupid Indian? Did you make it? Huh?

Don't worry about me. Worry about yourself. Get up. You can do it.

No. I can't.

Yes you can. But only if you get up off this road.

What's the point, Grace? What's the point?

The point is to live.

You didn't.

I know I didn't.

They don't tell me how to live my life. Or how to die.

But I didn't have a choice.

Sure you did. You could have stopped walking the streets. Cleaned yourself up. Gotten a real job.

It's not that easy, Leo. And you know it. Besides, it wasn't my fault. I was murdered.

So was I.

But you're not dead yet. I was dead before I hit the ground. You aren't. You can still get up.

But I don't want to get up. I want to stay here.

No. You don't. Nobody does.

You're too young to know, but sometimes people do.

And I'm always going to be too young. But I know enough, I know that you don't want to give up.

You don't know shit.

What about your kids? They know you're alive.

So what?

So stay alive for them, Leo. That's the least you can do.

But I keep fucking it up, over and over again, so what's the point?

You don't want to end up like me. I'm dead, so what's your excuse? What's ours?

I don't understand?

What's your excuse for lying here in the middle of the road and not getting up?

I'm tired. I'm tired of it all.

But that's still not an excuse.

But what's the point of it all?

The point is to get up. Just do that and figure out the other stuff later.

———

I got up. I sat up in the middle of the road.

There wasn't too much in the way of windchill out here; it was worse downtown with all the high buildings to funnel the air into harsh gusts. But the cold still ripped into me, scratching and slashing at my exposed skin like jagged shards of glass. I was up, but I had to do something quick, or the weather would kill me right where I was. I couldn't stay where I was, because I was in the middle of nowhere. I had to move. The strip mall area was only two or three kilometers away, so it was possible, but I had to fix things first before I did.

I pulled off my boots, undid my pants, and took off my jeans, placing them underneath my butt. And I took off the socks, followed by the long underwear. I ignored the cold that thrashed at my exposed legs, and pulled the long johns over my head—the lingering scent of urine and sweat seeped through the fabric—and tied the legs once around my head and a couple times around my neck.

The cold diminished the instant my head was covered and my face protected. My breath misted against my face. With eighty percent of body heat escaping through the head and face, I knew I now had a better chance.

Once my head was covered, I wasted no more time. I pulled on my jeans and slipped on my boots. I pulled the socks over my hands, and once I stood up, I shoved them into my pockets. I headed in the direction of the strip-mall buildings, using the feel of the concrete of the road as a guide, because I was blind. I tried not to think of the bone-chilling air, tried to ignore my legs. I was angry with the cold and my shivering body, and focused on one step at a time. One foot in front of the other.

I took ten steps but worried I might trip or walk into the ditch, so I peeked one eye through the pee-hole to see where I was. The buildings weren't any closer, but I was still in the middle of the road. I wasn't worried about my two assailants coming back, because they were cowards who had done their deed and were long gone. I didn't worry about any traffic coming my way, because if anybody else came down this road, they would see me before I saw them, and I'd be saved. Nobody would drive past me in this weather.

My exposed eye started to tear, and my tears started to freeze, so I closed the pee-hole and continued walking. I walked twenty steps before I looked again; still no closer. Over time, I became comfortable with my sense of direction and less worried about walking off the road, so my steps increased between each look, to thirty, forty, fifty, seventy-five. The buildings seemed to be getting closer, but my tears that froze instantly made it difficult to see.

My body stopped shivering and the burning in my legs and toes faded until I could barely feel anything below my waist. Walking became more difficult with every step. I jogged a bit, but that only aggravated the remnant pain in my ribs from the time Jackie's neighbor beat me. So I went back to walking. My shoulders and neck throbbed with the pain of keeping them hunched against the cold. Breathing was almost impossible.

I did make it to the strip-mall buildings, and even though I felt a brief gush of relief, I knew I was only halfway there. I had to get into one of these buildings somehow and I knew there were would be no unlocked doors. This was the industrial equivalent of the suburbs, and all doors would be locked.

The only way to get in was to break in a door, but the ones at the back were strong safety doors with no glass. The front doors were all glass, which I could probably kick in with my boots, but they, too, had another inner safety door that a tank couldn't get through. The only breakable material was the large picture windows at the front of each business.

But these buildings were well taken care of, so there were no rocks, no large pieces of debris lying around I could use to smash a window. My pocket contained only my wallet, keys, and some coins, but the coins only clattered off the glass and fell to the sidewalk.

I thudded the side of my fist against the glass but it was like hitting a brick wall. The only reaction was pain in my wrist that radiated into my shoulder and almost knocked me flat. The glass was thick and the little sticker at the bottom right-hand corner told me it was "SAFE-T Glass, Industrial Strength Against Breakage." I kicked the glass but it only vibrated slightly. I threw my body against it and the glass flexed and vibrated and bounced me back. I fell on my ass, but got up quickly, tore the long underwear off my head, and threw myself against the glass again.

"Break, you fucker, break!" I screamed, body-checking the glass over and over. It vibrated like a leaf in the wind but it wouldn't break. I screamed like a karate freak and did everything I could, threw my body, kicked with my boots, drummed with my hands, but the glass only shook in response. It wouldn't break.

"Goddamn it. Goddamn it!" I screamed, banging my fists against the glass until my strength gave way and I collapsed in a heap at the base of the window. I slugged it a couple more times, but I knew I was defeated. There was no way I was going to get into these buildings, no way I was going to be warm tonight. There was nothing for me to do but to let the cold come in and take me.

I pulled myself into a ball, and once my body cooled down from all the banging activity, the cold struck. I put both hands into one sock to share the warmth, my skin colder than the hand of death, because the hand of death wasn't really cold. Only the weather was cold, and the hand of death, once it came, was warm and inviting, like sleep. My eyes closed and I drifted. The warmth came from inside and, even though I knew it wasn't right, I didn't push it away. I fell into it, and it became warmer. I accepted it without reservation and without regret, except for a wish to have seen my kids one final time.

35

❋

When I was a kid, I didn't deal much with bullies like those two cops who dropped me off to die in the cold. Things were different for army brats. Moving to a new school was never a problem for me; you could expect a new school every two to three years. And while there was a bit of minor bullying, every kid was in the same boat. You could be the biggest kid, the fastest runner, the best hockey player, the smartest one, the best looking at the school, but there was no point lording that over people because that could change in the space of a week or two. Your dad gets posted and whatever standing you had in the old school is gone. Or a bunch of new kids get posted in and they are now bigger, faster, smarter, or prettier.

But one time, after we returned to Edmonton from Germany, Dad figured it was time for me to learn French. Instead of enrolling me in the DND elementary school a five-minute walk away, I was sent to a city public school that had a French-immersion program.

I figured it was going to be no big deal to take a bus to this new school where there was going to be a bunch of new kids. But most of these kids had known each other from birth and they had already drawn their lines of demarcation. Every clique was set, every kid had his role and would be stuck in the role, unless he had some major life-altering change, till he graduated from high school.

So when I tried jumping into a game of keepaway before the bell rang, the kids froze with shock when I grabbed the ball and started to run. In the army base, there would be a pause—"Who's the new kid?"—but the game would go on. Here, the game stopped dead. Nobody moved, and when I turned and saw what had happened, I froze, too.

Thinking this was part of the game, I waited, and tried to figure out the aspect of play that came next, but nobody said anything, they just stared at me like I was some type of leper or alien. We stood there for at least thirty seconds until it registered that I wasn't welcome.

Mostly out of spite, I held onto the ball for several more seconds, and then tossed the ball to the ground. It rolled to the feet of another boy, and when he picked it up, the game started again.

I went over to the fence where I had placed my lunch box and sat down next to a bunch of other kids who seemed to be coloring. I smiled at them but they shook their heads and walked away without a word. This was a very weird school, I thought.

It got worse in class. Since I was in grade three, I lined up under the teacher holding up three fingers when the bell rang. She shouted out something but I couldn't really understand her, but it seemed like three. And I was right because when I sat down in the classroom, at a seat near the back, my name was called and I shouted, "Present."

The class giggled at that and the teacher frowned, but only for a second. She then smiled a bright smile and pointed at me in a jocular yet admonishing tone. When she spoke, I understood nothing. It was just like the trips we took to Quebec; people spoke, even to me, but I couldn't understand a word they said. Why don't they speak English? was my typical thought during those trips. And it was the same with that teacher. Why doesn't she speak English?

When I didn't answer, her bright smile turned into a frown and the admonishing was no longer jocular. She kept asking me questions, which I knew by the inflection in her voice, but I had no idea what she was saying. Just to make her happy, I replied once, saying, "Yes," but instead of nodding, she harrumphed and shook her head. The entire class laughed out loud. Finally the teacher spoke to me in English, accented like Dad's. "Leo, if you are unable to participate in the class, then please sit quietly for the rest of the morning and don't interrupt us."

She turned away from me and started to teach whatever lesson was up for the day. I spent the morning drawing in my notebook, filling up the page with one complete line, a confused scribble that straggled across the page, while the various members of the class whispered, giggled, and pointed.

At lunch, I found a spot by myself and started to eat my baloney sandwich. While I ate, a kid I recognized from my class came up to me. He sat down. "Your name is Leo, right?"

"Yeah, so what?" I said, wary. I wasn't sure if this guy was one of those who had laughed at me but I wasn't taking any chances.

"Well, my name is Michael," he said, saying it the English way, not Michel, the French way, which sounded like a girl's name. He offered me a cookie. A peace offering? A sign of friendship? I took the cookie, glad to have met a new friend and offered him my banana. He took it with a smile, peeled it, and started to eat.

We said nothing, just ate, me the cookie, him the banana. When he finished, he tossed the peel in the garbage can by the corner. "Pretty good shot," I said.

"Yeah," he said. "It's true, then, that you can't speak French?"

There was nothing for me to say except, "Yeah." Still, a nervous feeling came over me, like it was before I was going to throw up.

"So if I said . . ."—and then he said something in French—"you wouldn't know what I'm saying?"

"Nope."

"And if I called you . . ."—he said a few words—"you wouldn't know what I was saying?"

"Nope."

"Okay," Michael said. And as fast as he had sat down, he stood up and went over to a group of boys who were watching us. Michael was the biggest of them all and he whispered to them, pointed a few times, and they nodded.

After a minute or two, they came over, smiles on their faces. I thought, great, Mike's going to introduce me to new friends and I'll be part of the group.

Instead, they made a half circle around me, and after a second, they pointed and started shouting those words that Michael had said. And they laughed. And pointed. And shouted those words I couldn't understand. And then some new words.

Then some new kids joined them. And then, despite the protestation of the teachers, the whole lunchroom joined in the shouting, pointing, and laughing at me. It was then that I knew that even though I couldn't understand the words, I understood the hatred and anger. Never in my life had I ever been the butt of such bullying. No way would something like that happen at a school full of army brats. I felt my face get hot, tears streaming down my cheeks. My head was spinning in grief and anger. But instead of running away, I calmly closed my lunch box and moved to walk away. Michael stood in front of me, laughing and shouting.

I hit him.

In the face.

With my metal lunch box.

Nothing told me to do it, I didn't even plan it, I just did it. The sound of metal cracking bone echoed through the room. Michael's nose exploded in a gush of blood and he went down, out cold. There was a stunned second of silence in which I felt happy and light, and then people started screaming and teachers started running. Some-one grabbed me and took me to an office, and even though they talked to me, yelled at me, in French and English, and even though Mom and Dad came by and yelled at me, Dad in French and English, and Mom in English, possibly even Cree, I said nothing. I didn't think of Michael, I just looked at my lunch box and wondered how I could fix the dent.

A few days later, I stood in front of the class at the DND school, telling the students my name and that I had just moved from Germany. When I sat down, the boy next to me asked me what part of Germany I had just come from. When I told him, he asked me if the chocolate factory was still there and if you could still find salamanders in the ponds in the woods.

I said yeah.

36

✳

In the distance, a blazing white light moved closer until it stopped right in front of me. A second later, a disembodied voice spoke to me in a language I should have understood, but could not. There was another sound, an insistent hum, a high-pitched wail. The voice spoke right in my ear. "Hey, you!" it shouted in an accent that was not quite French. My world started to shake, and the cold started to creep back in. "Wake up, wake up. I know you're in there, wake up!"

I lifted the cumbersome weight that was my head, and turned it toward the voice. My eyes opened like the peeling of an orange and stared into the face of Jesus, or someone who looked like Jesus, the way Jesus really looked, with brown skin, short curly hair, a scruffy mustache and beard, and a prominent nose that was long yet flattened at the edges. White light behind him formed a halo around his head.

I blinked twice and reached out with my hand, the cold returning to my body like a vengeful army after the sack of its country's capital. The shivers began in my internal organs and then spread throughout my body.

The face smiled in pure benevolence. "*Alhamdulillah!* You are still alive! Still alive. Can you walk?"

I nodded and tried to push myself up, but I couldn't feel my legs.

I stumbled. Hands reached out and pulled me to my feet. I groaned as sharp pains stabbed me in the thighs. My legs stiffened and held me up, but I wouldn't have been able to stand without those helping hands. They pulled me, steering me toward the light and the humming noise. A cloud of smoke drifted to the sky behind the lights. I moved forward, grunting as jabs of pain struck with each step.

"Does it hurt?"

I nodded. "Very much."

One hand left me and slapped me on the back. I almost fell but caught myself. "Excellent. Pain is good. Pain is good. If you feel pain, then you are still alive. Still alive."

Yes. Still alive. I am still alive. Someone has come to save me, I thought. It took me a second to realize that the bright light came from the headlights of a car, and the insistent hum wasn't the conversations of the Saved in heaven, but the alert given by a car when a door is open while the engine is running.

I stopped and turned toward my benefactor. "Thank you. Thank you."

He pushed one hand into my back to move me forward and placed another on my head to push me down. "Get in the car first, and then thank me. It's warm inside."

The passenger door opened, and as I moved to crawl into it, I heard another voice, this one filled with distress. "What are you doing? You can't do this! This is unheard of!" But no one responded to the voice, so I thought it was some kind of cold-induced hallucination, my hypothermic body playing tricks on my mind.

My new friend pushed me into the car. The softness of the seat was so exquisite, the friendly warmth blasting from the vents so breathtaking, I raised my arms in exultation and collapsed in a feeling I hadn't known since the birth of my children. Life was the most incredible experience in the universe, because without it, there would be no light, no joy, no pain, nothing but darkness and cold. Not even a glimmer of hope or despair. Just endless nothing.

But there is life and I am alive to see that!

A few seconds later, my savior climbed into the car, shutting the door and silencing the hum. He reached forward, grabbed a plastic cup from the holder, and held it out to me with both hands, like a priest offering the sacrament to a parishioner. "Drink this," he said.

I recalled a line from church, and while taking the cup from his hand, completed the ritual. "This is the cup of life." I pulled the cup to my mouth, bathing in the misty heat that rose from it. The scent of coffee was a powerful aphrodisiac, and I pulled it into me like a monk giving up vows of celibacy. The heat burned my lungs, but I didn't care. After an eternal olfactory orgasm, my lips reached out in a kissing pout to touch the silky softness of the liquid. There was a quick, sharp burn, and my lips snapped back, but only for an instant. They reached out again, tentative but insistent, and touched the surface. My lips parted, and my tongue reached out between them to caress the coffee. It was hot, but I pushed forward and plunged into the cup, taking a sip and feeling the warm, delicate liquid swirling in my mouth.

Eddies of heat and pain circulated through my mouth as the liquid touched my cold teeth and my cavities. After a second, I swallowed, welcoming the soothing warmth down my throat and into my yearning stomach. A surge of warmth radiated through my body, ending in a climactic shiver. I drank again from the plastic cup of life.

A harsh voice came from the backseat. I tried to look, but the tears in my eyes and the refraction of the light prevented me from seeing more than a silhouette. "This is outrageous. Don't you realize that I have a flight to catch, and you stop to pick up some bum off the street? I'm going to file a complaint."

My driver friend turned toward the backseat, his face burning with the fury of Christ attacking the merchants at the temple. "Get out of my taxi! Get out!"

"What? You can't do this!" the male passenger said.

"Of course I can. The Taxi Commission allows me to refuse or eject passengers if their behavior is threatening to the driver or anybody else, so you can just get out right now! Get out!"

The driver leaned over the front seat into the back and I thought he was going to physically attack his passenger. I opened my mouth to stop the violence, but nothing came out. The driver's fury was frightening and I had no strength to speak. The passenger probably thought the same thing, because I saw him scramble to the other side of the seat to escape. But we were both wrong. The driver wasn't attacking; he just reached over the seat back to grab the back door handle and fling open the door. A gust of cold air blew into the warm taxi and I shrank down into the seat to hide from it.

"There you are!" shouted the driver. "Now get out of my taxicab!"

The passenger stayed where he was. I could feel him shivering, from fear or cold, I couldn't tell. "You can't leave me out here, I'll freeze to death."

"So what? You'll freeze to death. That's what you wanted me to do to this poor man, to leave him in the cold so he could freeze to death, so we can do the same to you."

"Okay, I'm sorry. I get your point."

"No you don't. Get out of my cab!"

"No. You can't. I won't go."

"If you won't go, I'll throw you out myself!"

"No, please. Please don't," the passenger said, his voice breaking. "You can't leave me out there." I wasn't sure what to do. I really didn't like the anger in the driver, but then again, the passenger had been so obsessed with his own life that he was quite content to leave me

to freeze to death so he could keep his schedule. Maybe he did deserve to be left behind but I couldn't let that happen.

"Let him stay," I said quietly.

The driver looked at me for a couple of seconds and then nodded. He reached back and shut the door. "You'll make it to your
bloody flight," he finally said, turning toward the wheel, backing the
taxi up, "but only because this man saved your life. Remember that
when you climb into your comfortable business class seat, that this
man that you wanted to leave behind decided not to leave you behind. You remember that the next time you have to decide between
you own damn convenience and someone else's life." In a few seconds we were headed down the road.

"I don't believe you, I don't understand," the driver muttered.
"This man would have died if we hadn't stopped, he would have
died, but now he is alive. A man's life was at stake, and you were wor-
ried about something as silly as missing a flight. How sad is that?
How sad? We have saved a man's life. Can you not understand that?
A man's life has been saved."

The driver went on berating and shaming his passenger, and the
words faded into a wonderful sound, the murmur of wind through
summer leaves, the distant breaking of waves against the shore. I
held on to my cup of life, sipping from its elixir, watching the streetlights take me back into the world of the living.

The driver dropped me off at the Grey Nuns hospital, at the far
south side of the city. He offered to escort me in, but I assured him
I was fine. He accepted my refusal with a thankful nod.

"I don't want our friend to be late for his important flight," he said
sarcastically, throwing an angry glance at the person in the backseat.
"But take care of yourself. Make sure those doctors take good care of

you. I know they are busy, but make sure they see you. I don't know how long you were out there, so you might have caught something or created some sort of condition." He reached into his jacket pocket and pulled out a card. "Call me when you can," he said as he handed it over. "Let me know how you are feeling or if there is anything I can do for you."

I took the card and shoved it in my jeans. Even though this man had saved my life, I wanted to leave as fast as possible and forget everything about that night. I just wanted to be someplace safe. I thanked him for saving my life, but when he finally drove away, I didn't go all the way in. I sat in the lobby until I knew the buses were running and caught one back to my neighborhood.

37

❋

I phoned in sick and stayed in my room, sleeping and weeping. My phone kept ringing, no doubt someone from the paper, either Whittaker or Maurizo demanding to know where the fuck I was, whether I would be continuing with the stories, or Anderson wondering if I was okay. Probably all three, with Maurizo angry that I was somewhere gambling my life away and that the chance he had taken on me had blown up in his face. And he was close to being correct.

The urge to say fuck it to it all was so strong, and one time I got out of bed, put on my clothes to head out and do just that. But there was a banging on the door upstairs, someone shouting my name and jerking on the doorknob. I thought it was the police back for me so I fell back into bed, waiting for the heavy thud of police-issue boots to come down the stairs in order to finish the job that had been interrupted by that wonderful cabdriver. I slipped into a long depressive sleep.

When I woke up, I went through the motions of heading for the casino again, until finally I remembered that little kid who had just moved from Germany and how he dealt with those bullies at the French immersion school. But these were a different kind of bully; they were, in fact, the persons of authority to whom you were supposed to report bullies.

It now was too dangerous to live in Charlie's old basement room. If the cops who picked me up the other day knew my route home, they knew where I lived. I couldn't make things easier for them to find me. The time had come for me to find my own place, an apartment that was more suitable to a white-collar worker than to a semihomeless street person on government assistance for mental health reasons.

As soon as I had time, I would search the classifieds and find a decent place to live, preferably near downtown because that's where the city's transit system worked best. If you went too far out of the core, transit service was provided but it was sketchy at best, with buses running, even during rush hour, only every twenty to thirty minutes.

I figured on the area west of 109th Street just north of the river as my best bet. It was filled with apartment blocks of various size and all the services needed for such an area. I might have been a bit older than the demographic of the area but it also included Edmonton's tiny gay community so a single, almost middle-aged man wouldn't stick out. It was a big step to take, to admit that I had finally turned the corner, but it was mostly for practical, life-preservation reasons.

When I finally stepped out of the house, the cold snap had ended. It was even warm enough for me to walk to the office, but I would no longer make that walk. It was too dangerous. I headed a block north to 107th Avenue and grabbed the first bus downtown.

When I arrived at the paper, I experienced something I had never known at a big city newsroom: a moment of silence. It was short and abrupt, like a shot from a gun, and almost as surprising. I froze, at first not sure why it had happened and wondered if it was directed at me or if it was just a coincidence.

And when I discovered the truth, by how every face in the newsroom was looking at me, or in the process of looking at me, my gut reaction was exactly what one should feel at the sound of a gunshot, to run and escape from the incident as quickly as possible.

But I checked that emotion and moved forward, knowing that the silence wouldn't last long.

It didn't, because it was replaced by whispers that no doubt had to be about me. But even those whispers wouldn't last long because while journalists are notorious gossipmongers, there is also the compulsion to move past the immediate event, my appearance at the paper, and move on to a more important compulsion, the deadline.

Of course, a good number of the staffers continued to watch me, many of them surreptitiously, while they typed out their stories for the day, but many others filed my appearance away for future reference, something to look into once their main story, the one on their computer screen, was completed and filed.

The reaction of the newsroom to my arrival and the sight of Whittaker dashing into Larry's office a second later also confirmed another suspicion of mine: I was fired. Sure, I had broken a couple of big stories in the past few weeks, but no doubt the reaction from the higher-ups and the political fallout because of these stories, and the evidence that my gambling problems were back, had been weighed over and over again by Larry until he had decided that it just wasn't worth it to keep me on.

I was good because of the work I had done and the stories I had broken, but the reality of it—something I had no trouble accepting—was that I was lucky. Not only was I lucky enough to have been the first person on the scene where Grace was found and that Whitford had decided then to let someone from the media into the tent, but I was lucky to have been given the assignment in the first place. I wasn't chosen to cover that story because of my ability, I was just the only crime-beat reporter in the newsroom who didn't have an assignment or wasn't in the washroom at the time or getting a coffee from the cafeteria.

The truth of the matter was that while big stories were broken by decent hard work, it was just like finding a serial killer, a lot of it comes as a result of luck. You get the right assignment at the right time, someone gives you a tip or, in your efforts to find information about another story you stumble onto something else out of the blue.

Woodward and Bernstein only broke Watergate because they were crime reporters who fell into a minor story about a break-in at the famed hotel. Neal Sheehan broke the Pentagon Papers story for the *New York Times* because Daniel Ellsberg gave him the Pentagon Papers. Sure, these reporters worked hard and long to develop these stories, but without a lucky start, someone else would have broken them instead.

Any one of the staffers here could have found and written the stories I wrote so I was really nothing special. And because I had been hired as a scab during the strike, the union wouldn't make much of a noise. My only hope was that Larry would instead banish me to the copy desk, but if that happened, I wasn't sure it would be less hellish to be fired.

I was content to sit at my desk to plan what items I wanted to take home, but Larry stormed out of his office, quickly followed by Whittaker like some royal retainer, and shouted across the newsroom as if he was Lou Grant on a caffeine high. "Desroches! Get your ass over here!"

The entire newsroom turned at the sound and I could only shrug like a silent-movie comic and trudge over. Larry's entire head was red with rage and Whittaker was smug beyond description. I refrained from any smart comments because that would have been stupid and uncalled for. I had plenty of respect for Larry, plenty of gratitude for how he had given me a chance and taken me in when no one else would have, so making a flippant remark like, Hey,

Larry, what's up?, would have been insulting to both of us. I simply entered his office, stood at the edge of his desk until he was ready to speak. Whittaker followed us, quietly shut the door behind her and leaned against it, as if standing guard.

When Larry settled in his chair, he motioned for me to sit. I did, but again said nothing. I would give Larry the chance to speak first. And when he did speak, his tone surprised. It sounded gentle and caring, like one old friend inquiring about another's health. "You okay, Leo?"

I nodded. "Yeah, I'm fine. Had a bit of the flu but—"

He waved my comment away, telling me that he knew I was lying. "Fuck that. I'm being serious. Are you really okay? Is everything all right?"

"I said I'm fine, Larry. It was only the flu." I kept the lie going because with it I could see some way out. I wouldn't have to tell anyone what had really happened to me, because in the end everybody always assumed something else, like my gambling, was the reason I had missed work.

"Come on, Leo, I'm a friend here," Larry said, his voice rising in annoyance. "Just tell me if I'm going to lose you to gambling, because if I am, it's better for all of us if we cut our losses right now."

I sighed, falling into the act that he expected me to play. "Sorry, Larry, I had a slip but I managed to get it together before I completely lost it."

"Yeah, I figured something like that must have happened," he said. "And when you didn't answer your phone, I headed over to your place the other day, but you weren't home. I figured you were at the casino or something."

Even though his reasoning was completely off, I was shocked and touched by this display of friendship. He actually cared enough to come look for me to stop me from going to the casino. He was the one who had been banging at my door, not the police. I felt a pressure behind my eyes and they began to mist over.

"No need to feel ashamed over what happened," Larry said, taking my tears as shame rather than an emotional response to his efforts. "But next time something like this happens, I want you to realize that you do have friends in this newsroom, and instead of wallowing in pity at one of those bloodsucking video lottery terminals, come into my office and talk to me. And if I'm not here, talk to Whittaker 'cause she's a member of AA and knows something of what you experience.

"I hate to use a cliché but, as a group, we've seen it all. Take your pick, gambling, drugs, booze, whatever, probably a third of the people out there have had some difficulty with something, and for the most part, we're actually tired of watching good reporters fuck themselves over. So next time, don't go off half cocked all alone, just hang out here and find someone to talk to."

"So I'm not fired."

Larry and Whittaker both chuckled, which meant that the topic had come up. "Not this time, but next time, yeah. You only get one chance and that was yours. If I get the hint you're falling back on gambling, I'll either bounce you out the door or put you back on the copy desk. You tell me which one is worse and that's the one I punish you with. You got me?"

"Yeah, I got you."

"Seriously. I am not fucking around. We are here. And next time, you either find me or someone else to help or you'll be out. Understand?"

I nodded, glad that some good had come from my gambling, that I wouldn't have to explain what had really happened.

"Okay, then," Larry said, clapping his hands together. "Whittaker, I'll give you the honor of filling in our boy on what's been happening while he's been playing games of chance."

Whittaker nodded and tossed a copy of the front page on the desk in front of me. It was yesterday's edition and the hed screamed the whole story:

Prostitute Killer Captured?

"What the fuck?" I stammered, quickly reading the story. It said that acting on an anonymous tip, police had questioned an inmate at the Edmonton Max who had been serving time for one conviction for attempted murder and several for living off the avails of prostitution. Simply put, he was a pimp who had almost beaten another one to death a few years ago. After he'd been subjected to some questioning, the story said, the police had charged him with two of the murders I had listed in the serial-killer story.

"Jesus," I said, shocked by this development. "Are they charging him with others?"

"Don't know," Whittaker said with a shrug. "Police aren't saying much."

"Not surprising," I said, but the look on both Whittaker's and Larry's faces told me there was more to this story. I gave them each a look and then held out my palms. "What am I missing? What are you two holding back?"

Larry smiled the biggest smile I had ever seen from him. "He wants to talk to you."

"Who does?" I said, but the instant I said it, I knew exactly who he was talking about. I blinked because this was something completely out of the blue. I came to the paper expecting and accepting the fact that I was going to be fired and now there was a possible serial killer who wanted me to interview him.

"Maybe you should put me on the copy desk. That would be more fun," I said.

"No chancey, Mr. Whalen," Larry said, mimicking a catchphrase from an obscure wrestler in a long-canceled local wrestling program. "No chancey."

38

Justin Conlee didn't look like a serial killer, but then again, what does a serial killer look like? In movies and books, we expect a serial killer to be clean-cut and neat, almost to the point of fastidiousness; we expect serial killers to be cold and shrewd but with a touch of unexpected charisma that's at once intriguing and repulsive.

Justin Conlee was nothing like that. He looked like one of those working-class guys you see hanging around a small-town bar, nursing his beers not because he doesn't like to drink but because he only has ten bucks left and he needs to keep five to buy a pack of smokes for tomorrow. He was the kind of guy who, even though he was approaching middle age, wore his hair long as some type of residual youthful rebellion and sported a tattered Fu Manchu mustache that he doubtless thought made him look tough.

But in reality, especially since he was forced to wear his prison-issue jeans and light blue shirt buttoned to the top, he looked sad, like the loser he really was. It was hard to believe that this man had been charged with the murder of two prostitutes. I knew guys like him—hell, I could have easily become one. They, with their entrenched ideas of what made a man, felt as if the world had let them down. And because of that, they had a ton of suppressed anger, bottled up just beneath the surface, ready to explode at the merest perceived slight.

Based on Conlee's record, which was provided to me by his law-yer, it looked like his anger had a tendency to burst forth more of-ten than not. He had so many charges of simple assault against him that following his trial for attempted murder—that convic-tion was the reason he was now in jail—the Crown tried to have him declared a dangerous offender, a uniquely Canadian legal term that allowed courts to imprison him for life. The attempt failed but no doubt the Crown would try again, even though Conlee would get life without the possibility of parole for twenty-five years if he was convicted of the two murders he was charged with.

I spent ninety minutes with Conlee, and from the first moment I was in the generic interview room with its white walls and metal furniture bolted to the floor, I felt the urge to get up and walk out. His story, which he laid out in a distracted tone, punctuated every few sentences with a nervous laugh, paralleled Grace's story. Like her, he was a child of the foster care system. His mother was a young teenager who, instead of giving her child up for adoption, had been forced by her parents to raise the child on her own, as some sort of punishment for getting pregnant. He lasted almost three years un-der her care until Children Services took him away, and he never saw or heard anything about her again.

Like Grace, Conlee was bounced from foster home to foster home, some not so good but most of them decent. Despite anyone's good efforts, they just couldn't handle him. He grew up not angry or violent but unconcerned. Unconcerned about anyone else, un-concerned about himself, unconcerned about what would happen whenever he did something stupid or criminal.

Since his mother smoked and drank every day of her pregnancy, he probably suffered from fetal alcohol syndrome (FAS). When I asked him about it, he offhandedly noted that some doctor of some type at the prison had diagnosed him with FAS and had told him that it was important to keep a routine.

For the only time in our interview, Conlee laughed freely at that, not the nervous one that disrupted his speech every few minutes. "I'm in fucking prison pretty much for the rest of my fucking life, they tell me when to sleep, when to eat, who I should talk to, and what the fuck I should be doing every minute of my fucking day, including when I can take a shit and smoke a smoke, and he tells me it's important that I keep a routine. What the fuck they paying him for?"

That was the only thing, word for word, that I remembered him saying.

I didn't care what he said, how he felt, what annoyed him. I didn't care if he thought he didn't deserve prison, if he thought he had been set up, misunderstood, and fucked up by the system. Sure, that was probably partly true, but since he seemed so unconcerned about everyone, even himself, I was completely unconcerned about him.

Most reporters would kill to have an interview like this, even though the story couldn't be written till after the trial. But I really couldn't have cared less. My desire for a great story was fading, because I felt that someone like Conlee did not deserve the same coverage of his life as had Grace. It seemed that every time there was a horrendous murder or violent act, everyone, not just the media but the readers and consumers of the media, was keen to get as much information as they could about the murderer.

It was the name of the perpetrator that would get the biggest play, that would get filed in the memory of the event, when in truth it was the victims that deserved to be remembered. It was sad that most everyone can remember the name of the Son of Sam or the guy who shot the twelve women at the Polytechnique in Montreal, but hardly anyone, save for the families, remembers the names of the people who were killed. The perpetrator was the one that should be forgotten, not the act they carried out. Because if we remember the act, then we could perhaps prevent it from happening again.

A number of times during my meeting with Conlee, I thought about erasing my interview. In fact, I almost erased it as soon as I stood up from the table at the end of the interview. Both Conlee and his lawyer offered hands to shake but I just turned and left the room, my finger poised on the delete button. But I pulled my hand away, the journalist in me aware that even though I could write nothing prior to the trial, I had another story.

Canadian law is extremely strict about prohibiting the release of any information in any way related to a trial, save for the basics like the charges and the names of the victim and the accused. Judges even regularly issued publication bans on information prior to the information being heard in front of a jury, and any reporter or person who violated those bans could face huge fines or even jail time. These laws were considered so serious that if you violated them, a judge could hold you in jail for an indefinite period the same way they could hold someone deemed a dangerous offender.

Only sometime in the future, sometime after Conlee was found either guilty or innocent of the two murders, would there be a major feature that could run for at least two pages, probably more. Instinct made me hold out for the story.

Detective Whitford had been watching the interview through the one-way glass and was waiting for me outside the room. His face was a mixture of disgust and relief as I walked out. "Get what you wanted?" he asked, with a slight bit of sarcasm. "All set to write your 'Inside the Mind of a Killer' story?"

I looked at Whitford for several seconds, then I held up my recorder to Whitford and pointed at the erase button. "Push that," I said. He froze, so surprised I was making such an offer that he probably thought I was joking. I shook my head to show him I wasn't. "Go ahead, push it. You took a chance on me by taking me into the orange tent to see Grace. You put your job on the line because you thought it was the right thing to do, so now I'm returning the favor." I kept holding up the recorder, and after a second or two, he reached out and pushed the button. It beeped once, indicating that the information included in file number twenty-eight was now erased.

"Now there will be no story," I said with a nod.

"There's no way you can get the information, no backup button that you can push to renew the file?" he asked.

I wasn't insulted by his questions because it was something I would have asked. "No chance. These recorders are pretty flimsy that way. One wrong push of the button and the interview is gone. That's why the first thing we do when we get back to the office after an interview is to download the file into the computer. Because we don't really trust these things."

"What about your notes, didn't you take notes?"

"Only to mark down times on the recorder at which I thought he said something interesting. As a rule, most of us reporters are pretty lazy and if we're conducting an interview using a tape machine, we rarely take notes."

Whitford shook his head at me. "You never cease to surprise me, Leo. Usually it's for the bad, but this time . . . wow, I don't know what to say."

"You could just tell me how you managed to find out about this dipshit in the first place?"

"Geez, Leo, don't hold back. Tell me how you really feel about him."

"Come on, I'm curious."

"That's because you're a journalist who likes a good story."

"That's a load of bullshit and you know it. You know that I can't write anything about that."

"That's true, but you could later."

"Yeah, but by then all the information would have come out in the trial and every journalist and their dog will have the same information, the TV guys hours before our paper gets out. I'm just curious, that's all."

"All right, that's true, but it's no big deal, though. Just basic police stuff dealing with luck and a stupid criminal and another one looking out for his own interests," he said with a shrug. "Conlee, as you could probably tell, isn't the smartest person in the world, so for the last few years in the Max he's been quietly bragging about how he killed someone. Mostly, everyone's been ignoring him because almost everyone in the Max says the same thing. Makes them look tough and dangerous so no one will mess with them.

"But one day he mentioned a name and an astute fellow inmate overheard him and offered the information in return for a move to a less strict facility. Once we got the info, we plucked a hair from Conlee and matched his DNA to some we found at two of the sites."

"Any way to connect him with any other of the murders?" I asked, Grace's name being the one at the back of my mind.

Whitford shook his head, reading my mind. "Sorry, Leo, but Conlee was inside when Grace got murdered so there was no way he killed her. And there are a few others that are the same. As for some of those that occurred when he was out, we just didn't collect that kind of DNA evidence at the time to make a conclusive link."

"So he might have been involved?"

"Maybe, but my gut feeling is that he wasn't."

"Why do you say that?"

"Well, after we used DNA evidence to link Conlee to two of these murders, we found that he had some personal connections to those women. He was, for a time, their pimp. As for the others killed when he was not in prison, we found no connection between him and them. My experience tells me that in most cases, someone like Conlee kills on an impulse. Usually at first he just wants to do harm and isn't intending to kill them, but he does anyway. He's not the kind of guy to randomly pick someone up and kill them."

"But what about a serial killer? They usually don't know the people they are killing."

"That's not entirely true. Even with serial killers, especially their first victim, there is some sort of a connection, directly or indirectly. Something about that first victim made them go through with the act of murder for the first time, and from that they progressed to more random killings. But the first one, there is always a reason and connection, always." He paused and clapped his hands together twice, bringing his index fingers together and pointing them at me.

"Although I don't want you to get the wrong idea, that I am conceding that there is a serial killer at work. In fact, our arrest of Conlee in these two murders proves to me that we're not dealing with just one murderer, but a bunch like Conlee. The fact that there are similarities about the murders, how they were killed and where they were found, just makes sense. Strangulation is a pretty personal and impulsive crime, and a farmer's field on a quiet rural road is a perfect place to drop off a body of someone you've killed, especially those a few kilometers from the city limits and especially at night. And if you look around in any area just outside the city, you'll find many quiet fields."

My ears heard what Whitford said, but my mind barely registered.

When he told me that even a serial killer has some sort of connection with the first victim, two disparate details that had been floating around in my brain finally connected. And disappointment filled me.

39

I found him at a car repair shop near the Westmount Mall located in the west-central part of the city, one of the spots where the blending of older neighborhoods and suburban sprawl begins. I stormed into the shop, my anger barely contained. But once I saw him at the desk, talking to a customer, I held back.

How does one take on a person they believe to be a serial killer? Do you confront him with your suspicions face-to-face, accuse him of the crimes in front of everyone to ensure that even if he isn't charged with anything, those witnesses to your accusations will spread the word? But what would that accomplish besides the ruination of his reputation, or more likely, provide further proof that I had a tendency to become so overwhelmed with an obsession that I'd accuse someone of being a serial killer with little or no real evidence. But would it be wise to meet the person in private? If my suspicions were correct, would I become his next victim in an attempt to keep from being exposed?

I should have brought the police, I thought. But then again, the official police stance was that there wasn't a serial killer on the loose, a contention bolstered by the fact that they had just arrested someone in connection with two of the murders. I had an inkling that Detective Whitford suspected there was a serial killer even though officially he said there wasn't. It was one way to explain why he had let me into the tent and why he had been so helpful when he was officially ordered not to give me information. But I knew there was no way he would accept my new theory on who the killer was.

Even though instinct and hunches play a key role in a police investigation, he would need more real evidence before he would agree to come along with me to confront the person I now thought was responsible for the death of a good number of native women.

In fact, he would have tried to convince me not to take that step, that it was better if I left things alone. He would have heard me out, though. He was that kind of guy. But in the end he would have sadly shaken his head, urged me to drop this obsession and seek professional help. He would have been right, of course—throughout the drive to the auto shop, I kept telling myself that I was wrong, that it was the chemical imbalance in my brain sending me on a false path.

At the same time there was another voice in my head, and it was louder and stronger, telling me that I couldn't ignore the connection between his name and that of the first victim. I couldn't ignore it, and even if I came out of this looking like an idiot, that would be better than not pursuing the lead. If I let this one slide, it would hang over me forever, forcing me to second-guess myself.

I was spotted a few seconds after entering the auto shop and he smiled a great smile at me. "Hey, Leo," he said brightly. "What a surprise. What the heck are you doing here?"

That smile and the bright tone of his voice made me cringe—did he use that smile and voice to lure his victims? Did he use his position of authority to convince them that climbing into his truck was safe?—and I hoped he didn't see it. By this time I realized that confronting him publicly would not be wise. I would do it privately, and maybe the element of surprise would minimize any physical reaction. Even so, I figured I could handle him, considering that he was more comfortable killing people who were weaker than him. "I need to talk to you," I said, as calmly as I could. "And in private 'cause it's important, Francis."

He blinked twice. I don't know if that meant he was surprised by the request and he should be suspicious or that he was pleased I was coming to him in a time of need.

"Yeah, yeah. Sure. No problem. Can you give me a sec, I got to finish with Brian here and then we can talk." He pointed to an office across from the entrance area of the shop. "Grab a seat in my office and I'll be there in a jif."

I paused, wondering if that was his way of putting me aside, because he knew that I knew, and the first chance he got, he would run. But I dismissed those thoughts because there was no way he could know I was there to accuse him of being a serial murderer. He probably thought I was there to interview him for a story or because I needed his advice as a native elder on something related to my Aboriginal background.

"Sure, no problem," I said, trying to put an easygoing tone in my voice. "Take your time." I turned and went to his office and stood by the door. I figured that sitting down would only give him more power when he came into the room. I wanted him to find me standing and hoped that would throw off his equilibrium.

I ignored his office, ignored the native paintings, the dreamcatchers, the certificates and photos of him with various native dignitaries and politicians, and I simply waited. I had no plan, no real idea what to say, except to ask a single question, and if the answer was the one I wanted, then I would take it from there.

In an interview between a journalist and a subject, there are usually only one or two questions that the journalist really wants an answer to. Of course, there will be a lot of Q and A in the interview, but the fate of the interview and the story usually rest on one or two questions. And it was not considered proper or smart to ask those important questions at the start. The key was to ask a good number of background questions first, establish a rapport with your subject. Then you built a momentum with the questions, each subsequent one bringing you closer to what you wanted to know, keeping in mind that you had to listen for anything that could lead to follow-up questions. When you believed the time was right, you asked the question that was key to the entire story.

But when Francis came into the room and asked me, in all sincerity, if everything was okay, I didn't wait for the right time. I had only one question to ask him.

"Who is Lydia Alexandra?"

"Who? What?" he stammered. At first he was confused, probably because I didn't begin with polite niceties such as, Hey, how ya doing? Weird weather, isn't it? Or, Man, can you believe the Oilers this year? And he probably wasn't expecting someone to confront him with the name of the person who in all probability had been his first victim. He may have even forgotten the name since he had first killed her. "What the hell are you talking about, Leo?"

"Lydia Alexandra. She was a native woman, more like a girl 'cause she was barely nineteen years old when police found her body in a field in 1988." I slapped down an eight-and-a-half-by-eleven copy of the news story, one that I had downloaded from Infomart and printed off. "She was strangled and then dumped off, like a bag of garbage. But it didn't end there. There were many others, but Lydia just happened to be the first one."

I slapped down another story, the one that Brent Anderson wrote, the side piece to my story that broke the idea that a serial killer might be on the loose in Edmonton, the story listing all the women who may have been victims. Lydia Alexandra's photo was the first one, at the top of the page. "She had the same last name as you, and even though I'm not that knowledgeable about native culture, I know that Alexandra isn't that common a name."

Francis gingerly picked up that copy, holding it like it was the most valuable thing in the world and stared at it. He muttered something I couldn't make out, blinked tears from his eyes, and slumped back into his chair like a boxer collapsing onto his stool after the round in which he knows he had lost the fight.

A wave of triumph surged through me—I was right, goddamn it, I was right!—but it lasted only a second. A rush of disappointment and dismay roared through after that, so I fell into a chair, also defeated and destroyed, almost physically sick, by the knowledge that this man, this Aboriginal elder, had killed a good number of women, many of them members of his own community. Talk about sacred wound.

"Lydia," he muttered. "Damn you, Lydia."

I had the answer to one question; he knew Lydia. But the first question still hung in the air. "Who is Lydia Alexandria?"

It was like he had forgotten that I was there. He heard my voice and looked at me, a gaze of blank confusion for several seconds as he came back from wherever he had gone—the farmer's field in which he'd dumped her body, or the yellow pickup truck in which he'd squeezed the life out of her—and returned to the present, only to be confronted by this strange and obviously crazy journalist that he had thought he had befriended but in the end turned out to be the Wendigo, a Cree monster that was once a normal human being but now ate human flesh, either literally or metaphorically.

"Ly—" He started to say something but the words got caught in his throat. He eyes appealed to me for help, to ground him so he could get the words out, but he got no help from me. I remained silent; if he wanted to fill that silence and tell me the story, then he would have to do it on his own. If he didn't, I would go to Detective

Whitford and tell him what I knew. I would go to Whitford even if he did tell me.

"Lydia," he started again, this time completing the name, but the effort seemed to drain him. Several seconds passed before he finished the thought. "Was my niece."

Whitford was right about the connection between a serial killer and his first victim. But the knowledge that my hunch had turned out to be correct wasn't gratifying. This was even worse than I had thought; she was not only a vulnerable member of his native community, she was a member of his family. The power of that information did not give me any pleasure. "So,"—I stumbled over the words—"you killed her."

"Yes," he croaked, followed by a short nod. I wanted nothing more than to jump across the desk, bash the back of his head against the wall behind him, and strangle this piece of shit until every bit of his bodily fluids came pouring out of him in the agony of his death throes.

A second later he shook his head, reading the anger in my expression. "But not in the way you are thinking," he said. "I wasn't the one who actually killed Lydia, but I was the one who put her in that person's path. I was the one who could have helped her, who had the chance to help her but in the end didn't. I dismissed her as a stupid native girl who was throwing her life, her family, and her culture away with drinking, drugs, prostitution. I condemned her as someone who was giving natives a bad name with her actions, and I thought that if she had a sense of what a good native person was, she could rise above it all. I could have helped her but instead I judged her, and because of that, she was killed."

I didn't know which feeling was the strongest; the relief that Francis wasn't the killer I was looking for, or the disappointment that Francis wasn't the killer, and I had to keep on looking. But first I needed more information from Francis, I wasn't sure why. Maybe I could turn this into a story about Lydia, about how a member of her family, an elder in her community, dismissed her as just another drunk native who needed to be judged and put away, dismissed and ignored, the way all of us in this country did. "So did she come to you for help and you told her to fuck off, or what?"

He looked at me again, a long, vacant look that said that while all Aboriginal people may have that sacred wound he had talked about, for some this wound was deeper and fresher. He shook his head. "No, she didn't come to me, per se. Her mother, my sister, God rest her soul, asked me to talk to her. Lydia had been on the streets for a few months, hooked on drugs, boozing it up, and the only way she could keep up with her addiction was to sell her body to the lowest bidder.

"One day she ended up in the hospital and they talked about getting her clean, and since I was the wise uncle who was connected to the old Aboriginal ways, it was decided that I should talk to her and appeal to her as someone from her family but without the baggage that her mother, father, and other siblings carried. So in keeping with my image of the wise and helpful elder, I said yes and visited her at the hospital."

"Why was she in the hospital? Had she overdosed or something like that?"

"If she had overdosed, then we could have done something to help her, we would have had evidence of a serious drug problem and could have had her committed in some way so she could have gotten the help she needed," he said with a sigh. "But such was not the case. She had been in a traffic accident, hurt pretty bad with some broken bones and some internal injuries. Some john who had picked her up was drunk and ran his truck into a pole. Despite her injuries, she had been lucky because he had been killed.

"She was in the hospital for about six weeks, and every few days I went to see her, tried to convince her to get the help she needed, but she refused. She had friends from the street smuggle in booze and drinks for her, and one day I came to see her, she had been vomiting up blood, and while it wasn't life threatening the doctors and the nurses were still concerned. But when I talked to her about it, she laughed and said she was sick because she had had too much to drink. Even then she was laughing about it because she was drunk.

"So I went off on her and told her she was just another drunk Indian who was ruining everything for the rest of us, and if she wasn't going to listen to her family and her people, she didn't deserve us. I told my sister that Lydia was too far gone, and the best thing for them to do was to cut their losses and focus on the children they had left." He paused as the guilt settled onto him, loading him down with the weight of what he had done.

He whispered the rest of the story. "Just over a month after she got out of the hospital, Lydia was dead, her body found in a field near Leduc. After her family buried her, I actually drove to that field, stared out at the openness of the space and the brightness of the night sky, the millions of stars blazing, something we never see in the city, and I thought it was a beautiful place to see when one was alive, but it was probably a very lonely place to die."

As I thought about the circumstances of how Lydia died and how she had gotten into the hospital in the first place, the chill that had appeared when I first found out about the number of dead women from the streets of Edmonton came back and clung to my bones.

40

✻

I had to go into the hard copy section of the morgue but I found what I was looking for. I made two copies of the story, wrote a short note on each of them, explaining the connection between the story and some names involved in the story, and dropped it on my desk. If I didn't come back, if they found me somewhere, they would find this on top of my desk and might make the same connection.

Once I finished that piece of business, I signed out another car from the lot, gave a time a half hour later than the actual time, and drove out of downtown.

I did a short drive by the house, checking to see if anybody was home, and on the off chance that I might spy a yellow pickup parked nearby. There was no pickup: I couldn't expect such luck. But the house looked empty, the windows dark as the sun faded to the west. I made another tour, trying to pass myself off as someone lost.

I parked around the corner half a block down, and pulled a piece of paper out of my pocket and looked at it, but that was only for show. There was nothing on the paper but I was hoping to fool the neighbors. I slowly walked around the block until I got to the front of the house, saw there were no lights on so I was pretty sure that nobody was home.

Should I get back into my car, go back to the paper, and leave things be? Or should I search the house for evidence that was probably not even there? Going back seemed to be the smart move, the one that made more sense, careerwise, lifewise. Walking away from this case and letting it die quietly would allow me to keep my job, allow me to continue in this life that I had created.

But I couldn't go back, and yet couldn't walk away, either, even if doing so would have resulted in getting my family back and removing all the bad things that had happened in my life so far. I owed Grace that much. Her death had given me so much. Standing over her body in that field had put me on the path that resulted in some of the best stories I'd ever written, helping rebuild my career. And if I walked away from her and put that field behind me, she would never leave. She would sit at the back of my mind, calling to me, nagging at me, her face rising every time I wrote another story about a dead person. In fact, every time I wrote any kind of article, she would be there, reminding me that there was an unfinished piece back there, a story that I could have brought to an end but hadn't. If I wanted to live my life in peace, I had to find some kind of peace for her.

But the real reason I couldn't go back to my new life was that the whole thing was a lie. I had not created anything new for myself. Sure, the places were different, I had a job, success, and money, but not much had truly changed. I had congratulated myself for beating the temptations of the casino, the cards, and the horses, but that didn't mean I was no longer gambling. Every time I walked into a bank with my ball cap pulled low to hide my face, every time I scribbled the note on the back of a slip and politely handed it over to the teller, I was no different from when I sat down at a blackjack table or disappeared into the empty time of a VLT.

I had gambled with money and lost my family and my career in the past, but I was still gambling. And I had played enough games to realize that the odds always favored the house. I had been on a winning streak for a while with the banks, but soon, today, tomorrow, next year, I would lose, and every incident that I thought was a win would actually become a loss as the authorities put two and two together and connected me with all the other similar robberies. And before that happened, I had to do something that meant something. If not to the world at large, then at least to me.

There was no way I could turn my back on Grace, or Lydia, or any of the women who'd ended up in a farmer's field.

First, the garage. If there was an actual yellow pickup, if such a vehicle truly existed, then there was a good chance it was there. There was no window in the door so I entered the side yard, not checking to see if anybody was watching because that would look like I was worried about being seen. Instead I just walked in like I belonged, and if anybody saw, they would think that.

Once inside the fenced area, I had plenty of cover from the thick pine trees surrounding the yard. The lawn, even at this time of year, was cleanly cut, no leaves or debris, just the brown grass ready and waiting for the first major snowfall of the year. There was also a deck that further wrapped around the house and it, too, was bare, the outdoor furniture probably stowed for the winter. I gave the house one quick look, waiting to see if I could spot any signs of life, but there was nothing. So I stepped up to the back garage door.

I reached for the handle but then stopped. If it's locked, I told myself, I will turn around and walk away. So far I was okay, no laws had been broken, but once I stepped into the garage of a private citizen, then all bets were off. Even if the door was unlocked, it was trespassing, more like breaking and entering, both criminal offenses.

It was then that I realized that I had no plan of action, no idea what to do if I did find any evidence. Nothing I could find, save for a corpse or blood from the same, could be used in a court to convict anyone. Not even in something as simple as a newspaper article.

There were laws, serious laws with serious consequences, that prevented newspapers from publishing articles based on stolen evidence or illegal sources without a solid basis in truth, or at the very least, truth that could be proven in court. Freedom of the press was an important statute in Canada's constitution and its Charter of Rights and Freedoms, but that didn't give us the right to be able to print just anything. The legal system and Canadian society as a whole took a dim view of such antics.

So I could do nothing if I found any evidence, could not write a front-page article on the discovery of Edmonton's serial killer. Nothing. My only possibility, and it was a slim one at that, was to hand off whatever I found to someone like Detective Whitford and see if the police could do something with it. But even if they couldn't, at the very least I would know the truth and Whitford would know it, and maybe, just maybe, that little fact would deter the killer from killing anyone else. I could live with that and hoped that Grace would accept that, as well.

The door wasn't locked and I really shouldn't have been surprised. It was a relatively respectable neighborhood and there was also a good chance that many people here left their front doors unlocked while they were home. So I opened the door, and after a few seconds of adjusting to the lower light, I saw it standing there in plain sight: a yellow pickup truck.

I actually gasped with shock and took a couple steps back at the sight of the thing. I was not only surprised that it actually existed, I was jolted by the brazenness of this vehicle, the one that had struck fear in the entire community of Edmonton's street prostitutes, being kept in an unlocked garage. It just showed how unconcerned he was about being caught and how much faith he put in the system to protect him. And he was correct to have that faith because it had protected him for two decades and, in a sense, was still providing that protection.

I walked around the truck, noting any irregular features, spots of rust, type of tires, shape of the cab, debris in the box, anything that I could use to build a solid description to take to Grace's roommate Jackie and her fellow streetwalkers in order to get enough evidence to maybe start something. I knew that no cop in his right mind would take on the case on his own, but maybe I could scrape together enough evidence to write something that would spark enough public concern to force the EPS to act. The key question was whether the public was concerned enough about dead prostitutes. I hoped so.

One thing I did know was that I would not rest until I could write something, and even then I wouldn't stop until someone in the justice system, a cop or a prosecutor, decided to do something like investigate and press charges. There was no longer any indecision or concerns at all in my head and heart.

I would pursue this case, make noise about it, until someone listened, or until someone stopped me. I would stay on it, chase it down to the very end, even if people thought I was chasing another ghost and needed to up my medication. Even if it meant the loss of my job and reputation. Those things didn't matter. I had lost them before so another time would make no difference. Only death would stop me. And I was okay with that.

For the first time in years, I felt comfortable. There was no confusion, no muddled brain questioning every move I made and being watchful of falling into the abyss. It no longer scared me, because even if I did fall into it, I would have Grace pushing me on, nagging at me to pursue her killer to the very end.

The cab of the truck was locked, but for a pickup of this age, it was oddly clean. The dash was clear of dust, the seats were the original vinyl with no rips, tears, or patches of duct tape. There was no debris, no garbage, nothing to show that this truck had been driven in months. Even the windows were spotless, with no cracks, chips, or even fingerprints. The box of the truck was the same, perfectly clean, no dead leaves, no sand, no bits of wood, the paint free of rust spots or chips, nothing to show that this pickup had been used the way the typical Edmontonian uses an old pickup, for moving, hauling, and/or discarding old furniture and garbage.

There were two stacks of sandbags piled on the opposite sides of the box right behind the cab. That was not unusual because they added weight to an empty truck box to help with traction in snow and ice. Every single pickup or rear-wheel-drive vehicle in the city had sandbags either in the trunk or the box.

I stood on my toes and peered through the driver's side window to see if I could see the odometer. The dim light and the placement of the steering wheel made that difficult so I jumped up, rested my butt on the side of the box to see if looking through the back window offered a better view. It did. The odometer read about 45,000. Based on the age of the truck, that was probably in miles, not kilometers.

Canada had switched from the old-style imperial system to the metric in the later seventies and the early eighties, and it took manufacturers a few years to make the adjustment, so that meant this truck was almost thirty years old. Still, the mileage was nothing for a vehicle of this age, and when you added its almost pristine state to the equation, then it proved that someone used the truck very sparingly, although the sandbags showed that the vehicle was driven from time to time.

I jumped off the truck, looking around the garage for anything that might give me a clue, but it was just a garage with the typical garage things: lawn equipment, tools, and the like. The truck rocked a bit on its shocks as my weight left it and a couple of the sandbags from the driver's side rolled over. A decaying cardboard box had been underneath the bags and I peeked over to look inside.

At first glance, the contents of the box seemed typical and not unexpected, a set of booster cables twisted and tangled like a psychotic Möbius strip, a bottle of windshield washer fluid with just an inch of blue liquid at the bottom, a set of frayed and worn work gloves, several crumpled rags, bits of string and wire, and tiny bits of debris and metal, things you expect to find in a cardboard box in the back of a prairie pickup. But the rags seemed a little unusual. One of them was pink and the other was purple. So I took off my glove, reached in, pulled one out, and untangled it from its folds.

It turned out to be a baby doll T-shirt, something worn by small kids or teenaged girls trying to look sexy. The shirt intrigued me, so I dug deeper, pulling out the bits and pieces that weren't obviously related to vehicle maintenance. A long bit of broken plastic could have been the length of a stiletto heel. Another rag could have been a piece of torn scarf or a section from a pair of panties. A tiny piece of metal that could be a piece of a paper clip or the end of an earring.

I grabbed these pieces and shoved them into my jacket pockets. They could be nothing, or they could mean everything. What was the owner of a truck like this doing with a broken stiletto heel or a piece of silk unless all these pieces had belonged to his wife, were meant to be thrown away, but had been casually tossed into the box instead and forgotten.

But there was something else in the box, and that couldn't be included in a list of harmlessly discarded female clothing. It was a cell phone, spattered with mud and dirt. The size and brand showed that it was a recent model. I pulled it out and flipped the handset open. I pushed the red button and it beeped, showing a bar and a half of battery power. I thought about making a call on it, to see if it worked, but I stopped. I pulled out my notebook, found the page with the number Grace's roommate had given me, and punched the series on my own cell. An eternity passed, so long that I breathed a sigh of relief that I had dialed the wrong number.

But the phone began to vibrate, buzzing like a disturbed fly, and then gave a tiny ring, barely audible. In the shock of the moment I dropped both phones and my notebook into the back of the truck. A female voice, impossibly young but incredibly mature, came through my earpiece, the sound of the phone at the bottom of the truck box producing a tiny echo.

"Hi. You've reached Grace and I don't really have time for this kind of shit. I'm a busy, busy working girl and if you need any important services, wink, wink, leave me a name and number that you can be reached at, and if you're worthy, I'll call you back. Till then, fuck off."

My head spun, my heart stopped, and I was no longer breathing. I froze, even though I knew that I had to leave this place this instant and spread the word.

But I was still so shocked by the realization of my discovery that I felt like someone who has gone to church all his life, someone who has faith and says he believes what he is supposed to believe, even if there are nagging doubts that he can't explain away and really can't tell anyone because that would brand him as an unbeliever. But then, out of nowhere, out of the fabric of the strange universe, this person finds actual proof, tangible evidence that he can hold in his hands and possibly show to others, of the existence of God. Or in this case, the Devil.

However, the only problem is that he knows he cannot tell anyone, because in fact, no one will believe him. Everyone, even those in his own church, his family and his friends, will regard him as some sort of crackpot if he dares to bring this evidence to light. And even if he does so, or at least threaten to, there will be those who will try to convince him not to do it. "For the sake of the public good, you cannot reveal this evidence," they will argue. "If you do you will erode the public's faith. And then where will the people turn?"

And they would be right. For the past number of years, Edmontonians' faith in their police had suffered much. And while people still called the police when they were in need of protection, they were no longer surprised or shocked when a local police officer was involved in something not entirely criminal but not entirely ethical. They were disappointed but no longer surprised.

But if news of this evidence and the truth behind the death of these women came to light, the public's faith in the local police would be completely eroded. Especially since the police had done nothing for years, had no ongoing investigation even though there was evidence that at the very least, women—mostly native women—were being killed. Trust was implicit in law enforcement; the public must trust their police to do the right thing, especially in a social democratic society like Canada.

But faith built on lies, faith built on murder and death, isn't true faith and is destined to fail. Whether it happened now or later, it was not a question of if it might happen but when. And despite the pain and anger and sickness, it was always better to deal with a cancerous tumor as early as possible. The treatment would be painful, perhaps fatal, but the body always had a better chance of coming through in the end, alive and kicking, if you took care of the disease as soon as you found it.

I was jerked out of these thoughts when a man-shaped shadow

stepped into the doorway. "Couldn't let it rest, could you?" a voice asked, curious but flat. No fear, no threats, just speculation. I jumped and Grace's voice on her cell seemed like the loudest thing in the world. After a quick catch of my breath, I reached into the truck, grabbed the phones, and shoved them into my jacket pocket.

41

Even though my heart was pounding, I calmly walked around the truck to the front, tucking the notebook into my front pocket, slipping on my gloves, making the gestures bigger than necessary so he could clearly see me.

"No. I couldn't," I responded in a similar tone, but adding a bit more weight in my voice. "But I like your truck. It's old as heck but it's in incredible shape. It's a shame you don't take it out much."

"Are you sure you want to do this?"

"Do what, Detective Gardiner?" I asked as calmly and with as much good humor as I could manage. Inside I was seething, angry that this fuck had fooled me with his helpful attitude. "I'm just interested in your truck. I've heard a lot about it, didn't think it was yours, but there you go, sometimes you get disappointed. And I'll admit that it's a big understatement when I say I'm disappointed to find this particular vehicle in your garage."

"Disappointed," he said with a laugh. "I find you in my garage without permission, looking over my pickup, illegally going through my possessions, and you say you're disappointed. You're lucky I don't call the police."

"Knock yourself out, Detective Gardiner," I said, leaning against the truck as nonchalantly as I could. "I'll wait right here for the police to come. I'm sure they'd be really interested in your truck. I'm guessing it belonged to your son, although I'll admit it's in damn good shape considering the accident. Or did I say that already?"

I was pushing him, pushing hard, but this bastard had to be pushed hard enough so that he would fall to the ground, and then I could kick him around the yard and step on him and smear him across the grass like the piece of shit he was.

His eyes narrowed and he made a tight fist. "You have no idea what the fuck you are talking about." His voice had lost all of its calm. It was now full of menace.

But that's exactly what I wanted; I wanted him to break, confess, threaten me, attack me, I didn't care, I just kept pushing, hoping to break him.

"Yeah, I'm sorry he died, really I am. I have a son of my own and I have no idea what would happen if he died. I mean, Jesus Christ, I'm a mess now as it is, but if something happened to my boy, God knows what I'd turn into. Is that what happened to you, after losing your son?"

"Keep talking like that and the shitstorm that I will bring on you will break you in fucking half, you worthless piece of shit. I may be a retired cop but I still have plenty of friends on the force that can fuck you deep and hard up the ass."

"Yeah, I think I met some of those guys already. But go ahead, call them up again, 'cause you know one thing, Gardiner, I don't really care what kind of shitstorm you can bring, because the one I've got for you is ten times worse," I said, taking a step forward.

"You don't have shit and you know it."

"I have plenty of shit and it all comes down to your son. The son that apparently died in a single MVA. And you know what, I assumed that since it was a single MVA, he was the only one in the fucking truck. But you know what? He wasn't. There was someone in the car with him, wasn't there. A woman by the name of Lydia Alexandra."

Either the name of the girl surprised him or it was the fact that I knew the name of the girl, because the anger in his face dropped for a second and he looked like he was going to stumble. He stuck out a hand and grabbed the bench against the back wall to steady himself.

"Piece of shit, piece of shit," he muttered several times, and I had no idea whether he was talking about me, his son, or Lydia.

But considering what happened to the girl, I assumed he was mostly talking about her. It was typical of this type always to blame some woman for the problems of his son and of the world, when all Lydia did was get into the wrong truck on the night that Jason Gardiner was driving so drunk he didn't notice the telephone pole until he wrapped his truck around it. And since Jason's father's shame was so deep, he couldn't accept the fact that his boy had fucked up, so he had to find blame somewhere else: Lydia.

"And you know what's really a coincidence? Not long after Lydia was discharged from the hospital because of the injuries your son caused, she was found dead in a farmer's field not far from Leduc. And fortunately for you, the case was handled by the Leduc detachment, so nobody made the connection between that dead girl and your son. And as the years went on, because it took a while for the various types of law enforcement in the area to communicate with each other, nobody made a connection between all the other girls that were killed in the same way.

"Even now they still haven't, and that's why Robert Picton and other shits like you got away with their crap for so long, because the various police types decided not to talk to each other. And of course since so many of the victims, like Lydia, Grace, and the others, just happened to be native women, nobody really gave a shit. I mean, who gives a shit about another dead Indian, happens all the time, so for upstanding citizens it's nothing to worry about."

He laughed, turning the whole thing into a joke. "You're crazy, you know that. Completely crazy."

I nodded. "A lot of people have told me that and I'm even on medication because of it. And there are plenty of times when I have no idea what I'm doing, when I tell myself that the whole world is all fucked up and there is nothing to do but to let it all go. But unlike you, I keep trying; even when I hit rock bottom, I see hope somewhere and keep at it, no matter how hard it is.

"Still, there is one thing that I know for sure: You killed those girls and if there is any decency left in you, if there is a remnant left of good cop that you used to be, you would turn yourself in."

He laughed again, waving an arm in dismissal. "Nobody's going to believe you. All the evidence you have is shit."

"Well, the thing about shit is that it smells, and if you throw enough around, it eventually sticks," I said. "I think I have enough to throw around to get people annoyed and talking. Especially that bit about your son and what turned out to be the first victim in a series of other victims."

"Not this shit. It hasn't stuck for years and not even you can make it stick. You can try writing about it in your fucking paper but no one will believe you. I'm a decorated police officer, not some jerkwad loser like yourself. And soon you'll be out on the streets like one of those disgusting hookers. A big fat loser who deserves to die, and that's exactly what they got. All of them. Death."

I took several quick steps forward, went right up to him, not afraid of him because even though he was a killer, he only killed those he believed were weaker than he was. And since he thought that his words had sunk in, and I was trying to escape, he stood up straight to block the door.

"You sure the hell aren't going anywhere, you piece of shit. You're staying here while I call some old friends, and we'll take care of you the way we used to. I know your type and your type won't be able to handle even something as simple as the remand center. You're in deep shit now."

"You know nothing about nothing," I said, and to show him that he didn't I placed a hand on his chest, and shoved him against the door frame. The back of his head banged against the wood, and for several seconds, he was stunned. I kept my hand against his chest, and though he struggled to break free, he couldn't.

I leaned close, my breath harshly hissing into his face as I whispered. "You keep telling me I don't know shit but you have no idea what you are talking about. You think I'm just some white-collar journalist who lives in a nice house and drinks a nice red wine with my takeout sushi, but you're wrong. I'm not afraid of your remand center because I've been there. On the inside. Other places, too. I know what they are like, I know it all. If you don't believe me, get one of your old buddies to run my name through your system and you'll see where it takes you."

Gardiner's eyes darted back and forth and his lips twitched as he processed the information I had just given him.

Is he lying? I could see him thinking. He must be lying because nobody is that fucked up. I knew his thoughts because I had seen the same reaction from many other people when they learned about my past. On the outside I looked so normal, and was able to function reasonably. Most of the time, that's what my world was like, but there were times when inside, things were all messed up. Medication helped but modern pharmacology could only do so much.

He struggled to break free, so I shoved him back, this time harder than the first so that there was an actual sound as his head hit the frame, and his body wilted and he slid to the floor. I knew I'd hurt him that time, maybe given him a sight concussion, but I wanted to do more damage.

"And you know what, Mr. Gardiner? I won't honor you with the title of detective because you're retired and you don't deserve it," I said, hissing. He moved to get up, but I put my hand on his chest and easily pushed him back down. "You're the one who's fucking dead, you know that? You have no idea how dead you are. Because even though this might not get to court because your buddies in the higher-ups will do whatever it takes to save your sorry piece-of-shit ass, you're still dead. Because I don't need court for this. I have everything I need. I don't even have to write a story, I can just pass the information on to some of my friends. Thank God there are enough good cops in this fucked police department who aren't afraid.

"But even if they are afraid, they'll know that this is something they can't turn away from. They'll know this isn't some idiot cops calling Indians like me morons or greedy traffic cops getting season tickets from a photo radar company for giving them a contract. This is fucking murder. It's something they know they can't walk away from.

"Even your friends will know that, and they'll learn pretty quick that they'll have to cut you loose. You know that they aren't the kind of people to take a bullet in their career for someone like you. Am I right?" His vision cleared and he looked into my eyes.

Seeing Gardiner on the floor of his garage reminded me of how ordinary a killer actually looked. How the skin wrinkled with age just like everyone else's, how the hair turned white, how the eyes were flat and gray, yet tired. Killers like Gardiner, or any of those others like Picton, Bernardo, or Olsen, weren't necessarily monsters. They weren't agents of the devil or the result of mutated DNA. They were human, just like the rest of us, with the same fears, the same ability to rationalize their actions, and sometimes, the same hopes to do the right thing.

But I still wanted to kill him. I wanted to wrap my hands around his neck and squeeze the life out of him the same way he'd squeezed life out of all of the women. I wanted to feel him struggle against me, kick and flail, squirm and struggle, see the life drain out of him and smell the shit and urine as his bodily functions collapsed at the point of death.

That's what I wanted to do and could have done, because we are all capable of murder, we have all perhaps thought about killing someone. We are all capable of great evil because many times we believe that what we are doing is right. We can all be monsters. But at the same time, we are all capable of greatness, all capable of doing wondrous and incredibly good things in this world. And maybe if people will figure that out, they'll stop killing each other for no good reason.

"You're right," he croaked, waving a hand. "I am dead. Cancer got me in the fucking prostate. They did all they could but nothing worked so I've got six month, tops."

I hadn't expected that. My hand dropped, and in that moment Gardiner surged to life, shifting his weight to his side, jerking his hand to his hip and pulling up his service revolver. He pressed it against my chin. He laughed.

"Does this gun look familiar? Remember when you were down in my office and you saw it in my desk?" he said, pressing me back with the barrel.

He stood up, and since he kept the gun pressed against my chin, I had to move and stand up with him.

"And you're probably thinking that I have the cartridges somewhere else, and you'd be right. You can't turn off twenty-seven years of police training just because you've retired. But don't fool yourself into thinking that I didn't have time to load my gun, because I did.

"I saw you drive around the block twice, watched you park your car to the side and walk around as if you were lost. You were good, I'll give you that, so good that I actually thought you were lost. I was going to come out and see what you wanted, but then you went into the garage and I asked myself, What the hell does he want in there, all that's there is my truck?

"And that's when I realized that the truck was what you were looking for and that it might be a good idea to get my service revolver. And you were in there long enough for me to lock and load. Even after a decade of retirement, some things your body doesn't forget.

"Barely took me fifteen seconds, a little slower than when I was younger but enough time to get ready for you."

He smiled, set his finger on the hammer and pulled it back. Either the action was so deliberate or time slowed so much from my point of view that I could see the tendons flexing in his thumb. And each time the hammer clicked as it was pulled back, I could see each of its miniscule jumps as it passed each of the cocking mechanisms. When it reached the final cocking position, I could see the revolver turn so that a bullet slid into the chamber.

All Gardiner needed to do was lightly squeeze the trigger and my chin would be blasted through the back of my head. He jabbed the gun once against my chin and I imagined it was all over, in a split second I would be dead and there was absolutely nothing that would save me. A thin stream of urine trickled down my leg.

"That's the one thing that I always remember and relish about all those other times," he said, smiling again. "You hold someone's life in your hands and there is nothing they can do except maybe piss their pants. Nothing beats that. But in your case, I'm going to make an exception. You get a choice whether to live or die, but first you have to convince me why I shouldn't just blow your fucking head off. Sure, you could try something like 'You'll never get away with it' but that would be stupid.

"You trespassed on my property, you assaulted me twice, and in order to protect myself from someone who has a history of mental illness, I was forced to shoot you. You don't have to worry about any of the evidence you claim to have found because I can take care of that.

"Besides, most of the cops here will be more concerned about your body and how it got that way than a few bits of circumstantial evidence that may or may not be related to another case. So that's it. If you give me one good reason why I shouldn't shoot you right now, then I'll let you go and we can both decide to let this matter drop. That sound all right with you?"

It did sound good to me, but I knew there was nothing I could tell Gardiner to convince him not to shoot me. Because when he'd faced the greatest challenge in his life, he'd called it quits. He hadn't died, but his choice, blaming all those women for the loss of his son, was like just like choosing death. He was only messing with me. My only hope was to act as if I didn't care. To play him the same way I played all those tellers and the same way I played Jackie's neighbor.

"Sorry, I got nothing. You might as well pull the trigger," I said with a shrug. I felt my face and body relax, and I leaned some weight into the gun, pushing him back a step. There was a moment of confusion, when he realized that the power he had had over those girls didn't translate to me, and he faltered.

In that second, I slapped the gun hand away and hit him hard in the chest with the open heel of my hand. He fell back against the door frame and I pushed him to the ground. He tried to raise the gun again, but I pinned his wrist to the ground with my foot. With the other foot, I stepped on his other shoulder, bent forward and placed my hands around his neck and jerked his head up so I could stare in his face. "Told you, you son of a bitch," I growled at him, my spit splattering his face, "you're dead. You just haven't figured it out yet. But you will."

As my hands grew tighter around his neck, I witnessed complete helplessness in Gardiner, saw his total fear, saw the pleading and praying in his eyes, and I felt power. A surge rushed through my system, a mix of excitement, of strength, of control, and yes, a tingle of joy. This was how he had felt when he killed Grace; I knew it. This was how he had felt when he killed for the first time, when he killed Lydia, when he felt that dominion over somebody's life, someone he saw as lower than him, weaker than him, and how that powered the endorphins into his pleasure center to create an ecstasy he had never before experienced.

When he realized that he would get away with it, that no one would suspect him, that no one would even think about him, when he realized that he could do it over and over again. It was powerful, and intoxicating, better than any game of chance or any visit to the bank.

And then I saw Grace, saw her face as she lay under the orange tint of a crime scene tent. Saw her as the forensic cops buzzed around her body, saw her graduation picture on the front page of the Insight section, and then saw her, probably less than six months after graduation, walking the streets for the first time, a scared little girl forced to give herself up because everyone else had given up on her.

She spoke to me, the same way she spoke to me that cold night in the middle of nowhere. She spoke to me in the voice from her voice mail message.

Stop, she said. *Stop. Leo.*

"No, Grace," I said out loud. Gardiner's eyes widened at the sound of my voice, and he pushed against me. I pushed back and squeezed harder. He jerked and twitched.

Stop, Leo, Grace said. *Please stop. You don't have to do this.*

"Yes, Grace. I do."

No you don't. You've done enough. Please stop.

"Sorry, Grace, but it's not enough. It ends here whether you like it or not."

Gardiner was right about his rules: Bad things happen and you can't change it, even if you try. But like many cops, reporters, and others, Gardiner forgot an important and equal part of the equation: No matter how bad it can get, good things can and do happen. Despite her death, Grace was one of those good things. All those women who were killed were. Larry Maurizo was another and so was Mandy Whittaker. My wife, Joan, and how she protected our children, even from their father, was another. But in order to protect that good, I had to do this. I knew there were possible consequences: arrest, conviction, and prison; endless nightmares and guilt; and the knowledge that I could and possibly would do it again, but I was fine with that. It was a part of me, a part that hoped this story would end in this way.

42

✳

"Okay, we have another body in a field," Whittaker said, holding up a piece of paper, which probably had the location written on it. "Who wants it?"

I looked up from my desk. I had been reading that day's issue of the paper, circling ads in the Suites for Rent section.

"You take it, Leo," Anderson said. "You're the 'body in the field' expert."

I turned to look at Mandy. "What about Franke?" I said to the reporter who had the desk opposite mine. "He doesn't look busy."

Franke looked up, annoyed. Mandy looked in his direction and waved the suggestion away. "Sorry, this one needs someone who can drive and Franke is on month three for an impaired conviction. So it's between you two."

"Like I said, you take it, Leo," Anderson said with a shrug.

I really didn't want to take it because I knew what I would find out there: an old retired cop, shot dead, apparently by his own service weapon. That had been the hardest part, getting the shot off. Everything else had been relatively easy. Closing the garage door on his body and leaving it behind so I could return the car to the newspaper. Fudging the paperwork again, so it looked as if I had returned a half hour earlier. Going back by bus after work, loading the body onto the back of the truck, and driving it past the city limits to find a quiet farmer's field. All that had been easy.

Whitford was right, there were so many quiet farmer's fields that I had trouble deciding which one was best. Even leaving the truck behind and walking back into the city was relatively easy compared to getting his gun to go off.

Every time I tried to squeeze the trigger with his thumb in it, I pulled my hand away, like I did during that biology experiment in school when you had to prick your own finger to test your blood type. The second time, my prereaction knocked the barrel, and I had to reposition it in his mouth. And when I finally succeeded, the noise and violence of the event was greater than I expected. The shot exploded into the night, echoing across the fields like thunder from a bolt of lightning striking right next to you.

Gardiner's head jerked and exploded out the back, and the recoil of the gun yanked on my hand so hard that my glove was ripped off and fluttered away into the dark. I danced about in pain, frantically searching for my glove as Gardiner's body flopped back onto grass, looking, I hoped, like a suicide.

I expected every distant farmhouse to light up in surprise as the residents were jerked awake. But the sound and the surprise faded seamlessly in the distance. In less than a couple of seconds, the quiet and dark of a prairie night was back. I found my glove about ten feet away, and instead of putting it on, I tucked it into my pocket. Like the tarp that I had used to wrap his body, I couldn't leave the glove there. I stuffed the tarp into a culvert a couple klicks away.

The truck, though, I had to leave behind. It had to remain near him to shore up the story of his suicide. It also held evidence that could tie him to the deaths of a number of women, at the very least to one of them, Grace. And if they tied him to just that one, that was okay with me. Even if they didn't, even if they didn't find any evidence, I doubted they would investigate his death any further. Despite what Whitford said about looking at every homicide with equal vigor, this one would not receive much effort. To many in the EPS, Gardiner was a rat, and it would only be suitable for such a rat to take his own life.

But even if they discovered he had been strangled before he was shot, there was little chance they would tie it to me. My gloves had been on when I strangled him and throughout all my actions afterward. However, I was ready just in case they somehow tied me to his death; I would plead self-defense. Gardiner had been a serial killer pointing a gun to my head, I would say. Fighting back and killing him was my only means of protecting myself.

As for taking his body to a field and trying make it look like a suicide, I would say I panicked because I was worried that some police officers had a vendetta against me. It also wouldn't look good for the police to pursue too deeply the person who had not only discovered an ex-cop was a serial killer, but who was also threatened at gunpoint by that same serial killer. In the end, I would probably be charged with committing an indignity to a dead body and, based on the circumstances and my sometimes mental state, be given a complete discharge. That is, if they did connect me to his death.

Despite this, I didn't think I had the strength to stand there like a nice quiet reporter and get the information about the situation without confessing that I was the one responsible.

"You take it, Brent," I said with a sigh. "I don't think I got the strength to deal with another body in the field. At least for a while."

He nodded, understanding. "All right, all right. For you, Leo, I'll take this one," he said, pulling on his jacket and taking the piece of paper from Mandy. "But you owe me one," he added as he stood up with his notebook.

"Who knows," Mandy said, "maybe they'll let you in the tent."

He gave her the finger. "Yeah, right. Thanks to Leo, that's never going to happen again."

"Who knows, it still might be something," Mandy said.

"Whatever," Brent said, and he left.

As I watched his back, I knew that it would be something more than he expected. At the very least, he had the death of a retired police officer, the possible suicide of a cop who had recently broken the news of bad doings by bad police in the past. If Anderson played that one right, and he probably would because he was a decent reporter, he could run this for a few days, even turn it into something deeper: the culture of protecting bad cops by the police, and the animosity about rats even if they were exposing wrongdoing.

And if he got really lucky and the police discovered the significance of the stuff I left in the box, he would have a much, much bigger story and I would be relegated to helping him by writing a sidebar or two.

But I was okay with that. Even though I had no control over what stories came my way, I was hoping that things would stay calm in the newsroom, at least for a little while.

Whittaker tapped me on the shoulder, waking me up from my thoughts. "Now that's settled, I got another story for you. Nothing big, but the police want a little bit of help from us." She held out a press release.

"Right, boss," I said, picking up my notebook and pen. "What you got?"

She read from the release. "It seems that there's some guy out there robbing banks, nothing major, no violence, but the police are getting annoyed and want him to stop. Or at least they'd like to catch him. They've asked if we could run a short piece along with a photo from the security cameras. The photo sucks, you can barely see the guy, but heck, we might as well do it as a public service. Besides, it's a good story 'cause all the tellers who have been robbed say the guy is nothing but really polite. If you got nothing better to do,

I'd like you to handle it, otherwise I'll give it to Franke here because he doesn't need to drive for this one."

Franke looked up expectantly, and I first thought about giving the story to him. He looked like he could use a break. Instead I looked at Mandy and gave the only answer I could give:

"How many words do you want?"

-30-

ABOUT THE AUTHOR

WAYNE ARTHURSON, like his protagonist Leo Desroches, is the son of Cree and French-Canadian parents. He has worked as a newspaper reporter, a drummer in a rock band, and as a freelance journalist. He was born in and lives in Edmonton, Alberta, Canada, with his wife and child. *Fall from Grace* is his first mystery novel.

ABOUT THE AUTHOR

WAYNE ARTHURSON, like his protagonist Leo Desroches, is the son of Cree and French-Canadian parents. He has worked as a newspaper reporter, a drummer in a rock band, and as a freelance journalist. He was born in and lives in Edmonton, Alberta, Canada, with his wife and child. *Fall from Grace* is his first mystery novel.